Also by Mark Beauregard

Blood & Chocolate

The Scarlet Dove

The French Art of Stealing

The French Art of Revenge

The Whale: A Love Story

GIVE THE DRUMMER SOME

Give the Drummer Some

a novel by

Mark Beauregard

A GIANT BOOK

Second Giant Publishing Edition February 2019

© 2010 by Beauregard Mark Zero

Bibliographical Note: This novel is an unabridged reprint of the same novel published in 2010 under the name Mark Zero. Mark Zero and Mark Beauregard are both pen names of Beauregard Mark Zero. First Giant Publishing Edition June 2010.

Library of Congress Control Number: 2019932909

ISBN: 9781933975115

10 9 8 7 6 5 4 3 2

cover photograph © Brand X Pictures/age fotostock.

www.giantpublishing.com

Funkiness for our purposes is an aesthetic of deliberate confusion, of uninhibited, soulful behavior that remains viable because of a faith in instinct, a joy of self, and a joy of life, particularly unassimilated black American life.

—Rickey Vincent

The historical significance of Brooklyn, Illinois, lies mainly in its being the oldest Black town in the United States. Nonetheless, outside the St. Louis metropolitan area, Brooklyn is largely unknown. Very few Americans, Black or white, have heard of it.

—Sundiata Keita Cha-Jua

But you can see the triumphant monument to progress on the other side of the river, St. Louis's great steel arch, "The Gateway to the West," from any place in Brooklyn. . .

—Elin Schoen

One Bad Apple

"You tell Mr. Grant how much you appreciate this. He don't have to do this, you know." Mrs. Watkins sat at her kitchen table stirring Metamucil into a glass of orange juice.

"I know how to act, ma." Thirty-nine years old, Mouse thought, and my moms still tellin me what to do.

"Wait a minute. You not going dressed like that? You'll freeze. Besides, you wanna look nice for your interview."

"He already said he'd give me the job."

"Put on a coat, at least."

"Gateway took my coat."

Mrs. Watkins frowned. "Take one of my coats, then. You caint walk around like that on a cold winter day."

"I gotta go." Mouse banged open the door and soldiered into the street.

Brooklyn felt like a ghost town, shrouded in dense fog rolling off the Mississippi River. The noxious tang of chemicals clung to the mist—industrial morning breath. Mouse walked past the remains of a burned-out duplex, past a shabby aluminum-sided house with fallen gutters, a boarded-up corner store tagged with generations of graffiti. He crossed Second Street toward the railroad tracks.

A slow train was drawling south. The clack-clack of the wheels and the exhausted chuff of the engine sounded like the death rattle of a giant animal. Its whistle groaned plaintive and close, but the engine remained invisible in the dense morning fog. Mouse hurried to cross ahead of it.

Beyond the tracks, a quarter-mile strip of flaxen, winter-killed grass edged the eastern bank of the river. Mouse heard car traffic on the Martin Luther King Bridge, the whirr and thump of tires crossing, the hard lap and splash of the Mississippi against its banks, the slow clacking of the train: a secret percussive language Mouse recognized but couldn't understand.

Thump-thump-lap-thump-splash-whirr-clack
thump-splash-thump-clack-thump-lap-whirr-clack

The train played its throaty whistle again, and Mouse huddled into his hooded sweatshirt, walking in syncopation against the staggered rhythms of the morning.

The hulk of the abandoned Westex Glass factory loomed out of the mist at the river's edge. Mouse picked his way between rusting metal shopping carts and discarded pasteboard boxes toward the factory's concrete pilings. It was cold even for November, and Mouse had lost his best winter coat four days before, on Halloween night, after the Bad Apples' final gig. Gateway had "loaned" it to a groupie dressed as Catwoman and then disappeared with her behind the club. He had returned an hour later, without the coat or the girl, and Mouse could only stare in disgust. Gateway had glibly promised to find Catwoman again and get the coat back, and that was the last time Mouse had seen him.

In the last three days, Mouse had gone to Gateway's girlfriend's apartment in Shaw, to his mom's place in East St. Louis, to Tammy's house in Compton Heights—he had been all over St. Louis—but nobody had seen Gate since that night. Mouse feared that he'd already squandered their last royalty check on drugs and booze.

Gateway and Mouse were the only original members of the Bad Apples left. They had spent their entire adult lives in one smoky club after another, and after twenty years of striving they had ended up exactly where they had started: Brooklyn. It seemed fitting to Mouse that their last gig had been on Halloween, the day the restless dead walk the earth.

Thump-thump-lap-thump-splash-whirr-clack
thump-splash-thump-clack-thump-lap-whirr-clack

He kicked a piece of loose concrete from the Westex pier into the Mississippi. The disintegrating pilings ended at a low steel gate guarding a private access road. Mouse jumped the gate and followed the road to a chain link fence, then ducked through a ragged hole in the fence and jogged up a ramp to Collinsville Avenue: the edge of downtown East St. Louis.

Steam from his breath evaporating in front of him, the slap of his footsteps against the sidewalks, cold numbness creeping over his ears: Mouse concentrated on small things, real things he could see and feel. He arrived at the MetroLink stop, purchased a ticket and took his place with a dozen other people on the platform who were smoking cigarettes and sipping coffee from styrofoam cups.

When the train glided up with a shrill electric whine, a bell rang and the sliding doors opened. A mechanized voice announced the train's direction.

The car was crowded, and Mouse found a spot to stand, in front of some white college students near the back. They read their books or peered uneasily at their own reflections in the windows. He imagined catching this train every morning, seeing these same people every day on his way to work, no need to juggle the set list or audition new players or worry if Gateway would show up on time. His new job would last only till January, but it would be money in the bank till he knew what to do next. Get up, go to the brewery, go home.

A white kid stared directly at him and continued staring even when Mouse glared back. Mouse watched the courage grow in the kid's eyes.

"Aren't you in the Bad Apples?"

Mouse stood silent for a moment before giving in. "Yeah."

"I saw you on Laclede's Landing three weeks ago. That was a great show, man."

"Thanks."

"Seriously. I danced my ass off."

"Alright, thanks, I appreciate it."

Mouse remembered that gig as disjointed and ragged. He pointedly gazed out the window as the train crossed the river: he had been through this dance of recognition a thousand times before. There had been a time when he would have preened before the kid's enthusiasm, but this morning such smalltime fame seemed more like notoriety. He saw the muddy Mississippi below Eads Bridge as an echo of brown against the white fog smothering its surface.

"When's your next show?"

"I aint sure."

"Do you have a mailing list? I could give you my email."

"Sorry."

Mouse knew that people went to clubs just for escape, that his music was the rhythm of horny guys picking up drunk girls in the dark corners of bars, nothing more. As his enthusiasm for the music scene had waned, bookings for the band had slipped; the pay had been sliding anyway, and the tastes of the times had long passed them by—it was all hip-hop and smooth soul these days, or nostalgia radio playing the same twenty Motown songs over and over. The Bad Apples had become parodies of themselves, trying to extend a minor musical sub-genre whose day had passed even before the band had started, playing dead funk songs to hawk beer in second-rate bars. It had become a mystery to Mouse why the world needed another musician; it was clearer why the world needed another beer warehouser.

Mouse's mother had arranged his interview at Anheuser-Busch this morning, with an old family friend named Bobby Grant. Grant had assured Mrs. Watkins that Mouse could get a temporary job in the warehouse, loading palettes of beer cases into long-haul trucks for the holiday season, making sure the beer got from the brewery to stores and clubs all over America.

The train sloped gently down to the other bank, into St. Louis, "the Gateway to the West." The mechanized voice announced the Arch stop and passengers jostled on and off. The Arch was America in a shimmering steel rainbow, the symbol of a country so triumphant it didn't have to wait for rains and floodwaters to renew its covenants with God—it built permanent reminders of those covenants to keep God in line.

The train started again, and they rolled past the Arch through downtown. In a few moments, they arrived at the Convention Center and Mouse shuffled toward the exit. He hesitated in the doorway and hung his head while people slithered past. He turned back to his white fan and said, "Hey, man, thanks for comin to the show."

He left the train platform and headed down Broadway. Gargantuan, abandoned brick buildings that had once held business centers and department stores occupied entire blocks, their empty windows looking down at the street like the eyes of hungry giants. Mouse felt like these old commercial monuments, once dynamic and industrious, now derelict and useless—downtown St. Louis, downtown East St. Louis, downtown anywhere in America, boarded-up dreams forgotten by the dead.

Mouse had discovered his love of drumming from his grandmother's jazz records. When he'd first heard Sonny Payne, he'd whirled around the house like a dervish, beating on the chairs and lamps and tables in a fit of rapture—then he demanded to hear the records over and over again, day and night, and when he wasn't listening to them, he was pounding and cuffing every object his little arms could reach, until his mother bought the child-sized snare drum that gave his life shape and meaning. From then on, his nickname no longer applied: "quiet as a mouse," his mother had always said, he'd seemed so docile and introspective, always with his nose in a book; but the drums gave a noisier part of his soul its voice, and he soon lived for the rhythms he could make.

For Mouse, drumming wasn't just time control, though that was part of it, breaking the earth's natural rhythms into tight grooves, shaping life into a four-bar pattern, making the collective heart beat loud in everybody's ears. It was metered propulsion toward ecstasy, toward the joy hidden beneath everyday life: drumming was measuring time in order to elude its effects. Feeling the band laying back in the groove, horns gliding over heavy bass kicks, the club pulsing, bodies on the dance floor jumping and slinking, the whole world coming together on the downbeats. At least, it had been, once, but Mouse couldn't remember the last time he'd been transfixed by a new sound, the last time autumn leaves had swirled through the air like the percolating sixteenth notes in his imagination. He had once heard music everywhere, in every sound, every moment—music was what being alive had meant—but now music resided only in his drums and in his head, and the rest of the world was separate and dull. The swirling patterns of autumn leaves represented nothing now but the coming winter. Time would now be simplified to train schedules and shift schedules and digital clocks. He would no longer be time's sly accomplice. Time would carry him along with everybody else, everyone a prisoner of time.

Mouse played with this phrase: A Prisoner of Time. He thought it a good idea for a song, but then he felt heavy and defeated, lacking the willpower to shape it into anything meaningful. He tried to blot this internal reverie, this knee-jerk habit of making songs, by concentrating on the noises of the morning around him, the combusting mechanical whorl of car engines, a jackhammer at the very edge of hearing, his own footsteps, one after another, carrying him to Soulard and Anheuser-Busch.

The Apples had played Soulard hundreds of times over the years, the little clubs and restaurants tucked into the ground floors of nineteenth-century walk-ups. Soulard reminded Mouse of the French Quarter in New Orleans: concrete fan steps, carved wooden doors, second-story balconies, curling black iron railings, vines climbing the walls to dormer windows with flowerboxes and candles on the sills. South of Chouteau Avenue on Seventh Street, the ornately styled houses looked bedraggled and tired, showing the grime of centuries of smokestack fumes and river winds laden with half-alive muck; but as Mouse approached the Soulard Farmer's Market, the bricks beamed with the sheen of restoration.

A few farmers were already sitting in stalls in front of the Market with their produce laid out on tables, their scales waiting for customers; but most were milling in a Monday morning hangover haze, dressed in overalls and weather-fretted coats, drinking coffee and chatting on the platforms, their heavily laden flatbeds and pickup trucks parked haphazardly on the street. These outside stalls would soon close for the winter and local produce would become a hazy dream of hibernation.

Mouse entered the Market's enclosed center arcade, where the butcher shops, dairy cases and snack carts were located.

He bought a cup of coffee and took it outside to the playground: a strip of grass adjoining Lafayette Street, with a swing set and monkey bars to keep children occupied while their mothers shopped at the Market. The playground was empty now, and he sat down on the cold center pole of a teeter-totter.

The fog was loosening as the sun climbed. The green spire of Saints Peter and Paul Catholic Church rose out of the mist three blocks away, as if it were rising from the distant past. Mouse felt like a character in someone else's movie. "I'll be the hero of your movie," he thought, trying the phrase out with a melody, as he always did. Too clunky, too long, too square. The Movie of Your Love? Most ideas were bad, as a rule, but these phrases only emphasized Mouse's defeat this morning. He stood up and walked down Lafayette Street, drifting and shiftless.

Whatever else had happened, Mouse had always known there would be another Bad Apples gig, another recording session, another tour—he had known because he had been the one to organize the shows, send demo tapes to record companies, call clubs for bookings, hustle studio time. There had been nothing else, no life outside the flow of the songs, the next set list, the next gig, and as long as he'd measured time carefully in his head, the whole world had glimmered and glowed between the beats. It was difficult for him to be in the world, to hear its industrial clamor, without reorganizing it through his hi-hat and ride cymbal, adding snare drum breaks to the MetroLink rhythm, retooling the squealing of the train wheels into horn lines with rim-clicks; abstracting the time in a nightclub through the rhythms he brought with him from his morning walk, changing the way the dancers on the floor moved by doubling up or laying back, altering the oscillation of the whole world with his tom-tom and bass kick.

Half a block from the Market, he heard a hard click above him, a loud rubbing of metal against wood, the squeaking of hinges. The French doors of a second story balcony opened and a woman stepped out: straight blonde hair, olive-green army jacket. She leaned on the balcony's florid black railing, lit a cigarette and stared down at him.

The blonde jutted out her chin, defiant bleary eyes set on Mouse's voluminous, bushy afro. She was tousled with sleep. She pushed her hair away from her face and blew smoke, and Mouse felt like a stray. He nodded up to her. She did not even blink. He cast his eyes down and walked on.

Mouse felt his loneliness as a thick dressing of gauze around his heart—the idealized blonde on the idealized balcony and him down below, real. The cold damp of the morning chiseled into his bones. He turned to take a last look at the woman, but she had gone back inside.

His coffee tasted acrid now, and he threw it into a trash can, trudged back to Broadway and let its looping curve take him toward One Busch Place. A red brick wall topped by black iron *fleurs de lis* protected the hundred-acre compound of the world's largest brewery. Mouse followed the wall until it opened at an asphalt drive, where a guardhouse with mechanized red-and-blue gates stood vigil.

A rotund, completely bald guard with mocha skin and wraparound mirrored glasses stepped out, thumbs in his black leather gun belt. He said "hello" more as a warning than a greeting.

"I have an appointment with Bobby Grant."

"Alright. Name?"

"Mouse Watkins."

"Mouse?"

"Joseph Watkins."

"Alright."

The guard stepped into his guardhouse, picked up a gleaming red phone and dialed. He spoke into the phone and then waved Mouse over and handed him a red-and-blue visitor's pass with a metal clip attached to it. "Clip this to your shirt and wear it at all times when you're on the premises." He handed Mouse a photocopied map of the grounds and drew a path from the guardhouse to Bobby Grant's office. "You get lost, just ask somebody and they'll help you out."

Mouse walked through the pedestrian gate. The road called One Busch Place was landscaped with equine-shaped topiary bushes, and he walked past them toward a sprawling brick building that looked more like a German castle than a brewhouse. Inside that building, they were turning water into gold.

He and Gateway had taken the tour once, on the afternoon of the Bad Apples' first gig in Soulard, the day after Mouse had turned twenty-one. He remembered the clydesdales, Anheuser-Busch's giant horse mascots, which were stabled on the premises. Nothing about Anheuser-Busch looked welcoming or amusing now, the way it had back then, and the giddiness he'd felt with Gateway as they'd sniggered and clowned through the tour and stood in awe next to the huge horses was now a mazy skein of bitter memory.

Mouse wondered whether this period of bad blood between him and Gateway would prove to be just another phase in their long friendship, or if this was really the end. Maybe, he thought, without something to organize them, he and Gateway would cease to be friends altogether. They didn't need a partnership if they didn't have a band, and maybe all these years their act had been their friendship, and Mouse had mistaken one for the other.

He walked around the German castle brewhouse to a more modern steel and glass structure on its flank. He opened a heavy glass door into an airy reception area tiled with gray faux marble. Viciously manicured trees in polished silver pots stood in the corners. A receptionist, sitting behind a fat curving lip of steel desk, greeted him.

"Bobby Grant?" Mouse said.

The receptionist pointed to her right. "Take the elevator to the fourth floor. Turn left when you get out. Suite 435."

Mouse turned the word 'suite' over in his mind. Anybody who came from Brooklyn, Illinois, and got a *suite* at Anheuser-Busch was considered a success: Bobby Grant had worked long hours, long years in menial jobs at Busch, clawing his way up, and he was extending the credibility he'd earned through a lifetime of hard work to Mouse, to get him a job—yet, as Mouse rode up in the elevator, he felt only contempt. When he stepped out, he found Bobby Grant waiting for him.

"Hey, Mouse, how you doin today?" He smiled and shook Mouse's hand warmly, patting him on the shoulder, guiding him down the hall and into his suite. "Long time no see." Grant's hair was gray, and there were deep, grandfatherly wrinkles around his eyes. "You not wearin a jacket today? I about froze just walkin from my car, and I had a big thermal coat on."

Mouse shrugged. "I'm alright. You know."

"Go ahead and sit down."

Grant's suite included a meeting room, where Mouse now sat at a round glass table; an inner office, which Mouse could see had wide, double-plated windows looking out over the grounds; and two other doors, painted blue and red, which were closed. On the table in front of Mouse was a thick red-and-blue folder emblazoned with the Anheuser-Busch logo. Grant sat down across from him.

"You remember the last time we saw each other?"

Mouse searched the dim corridors of his mind for signs of Grant. "Down at Lovejoy Academy?"

"Naw, not even close. Just a couple years back, over at Flinty's on Twelfth. Here in Soulard! Edwina was in Chicago, and I decided to paint the town a little. I talked to you between sets, pretty early. I asked if you'd play some Joe Tex."

"Yeah," Mouse shrugged. The gigs from the last few years blurred together into a single, static, out-of-focus snapshot of a dance floor hazed with cigarette smoke. "Sorry I don't remember."

"Your mind was probably somewhere else," Grant said. He bobbed his head gently forward so that Mouse had to look him directly in the eye, insinuating that Mouse's mind was somewhere else right now.

"You know your suite number's a Pythagorean triad?" Mouse asked.

Grant sat back in his seat. "What's that?"

"It's a ratio of a right triangle. The measurement of the sides. Four, three, five makes a right triangle."

"Yeah?"

"Yeah. They use geometry and physics rules like that for tuning instruments."

"How so?"

"Well, if you pluck a string, it makes a sound, right? And if you pluck it again with your finger on it halfway up, it makes a sound an octave higher. If you stop the string two-thirds up, it's a perfect fifth, and three-quarters up, it's a perfect fourth. The sounds have the same ratios of pitch as the ratios of distance of a right triangle. Actually, I learned that stuff from Jackie, from her piano tuner." Mouse's sister Jackie was a classical pianist.

"That's real interesting, Mouse."

"Anyway," he said, "that aint really why we here, I guess."

"We can talk about whatever you wanna talk about, but it's true we really here to get you a job." Grant's demeanor was a study in avuncular, responsible, example-setting accomplishment. Mouse was a failure, sitting in the suite of a company man who wanted to make him a company man, too: a success.

But didn't he come to my shows? Mouse thought. He didn't have to come to my shows, but he came because he wanted to hear my music. Mouse looked from the company folder on the table to the actual company outside the office windows. He wished he were somewhere far away.

"Can I ask you somethin?" Mouse said. "My moms said you be a good person to talk to, you know."

"That's what we here for."

"How do you handle doin the same thing day after day? Don't it all jus look the same after a while?"

Grant brought his palms together in front of him, almost in a gesture of prayer. He touched the tips of his index fingers to his lips. "Don't the audiences in the clubs all start to look the same? Don't the shows kinda run together? Thing is, Mouse, no matter what you do in life, you gotta do some things over and over. That's jus life. Nobody get out of it. What's gonna get you through, though, is you believe in the bigger picture."

Mouse waved his hand at the little conference room. "You believe in this?"

"Yes I do. I believe in what it *does* for me. And I think beer's a good thing. You know what Benjamin Franklin said about beer?"

"What?"

"He said it's evidence that God loves us and wants us to be happy." Grant smiled. "And I think that's true, I really do." He leaned forward and lowered his voice confidentially. "Look, Mouse, I know you not sold on this—we both talkin here today to please your mama—but it's only a seasonal position. And, you know, I started out here seasonal myself and liked it a lot, and here I am forty years later, so you never know. And I'll give you some more advice, since you seem to want it."

"Yeah?"

"These jobs, they aint so easy to come by. Good steady factory job, union job, you know, with benefits. You think it's dull? People should be so lucky. Companies outsourcing, gettin they workers from China and Malaysia, firing people quick as they hire'em, chasing cheap labor off in Timbuktu. All the good jobs around St. Louis now are in computers, internet, technology what-have-you, stuff you need college degrees, advanced degrees for, and even that kinda job aint secure. And forget about East St. Louis, or Brooklyn. What you got here at Anheuser-Busch is a specific, highly desirable product—beer—somethin people always gonna want. Now, if you aint got college, a steady union job with a steady company that makes a product that everybody likes—that's about as good as you can get. I aint tellin you what to do with your life, but it's hard out there, tryin to find a decent wage, a job you can count on, so don't sabotage it before you even fill out the papers. You can start out seasonal, join the union, work your way in. Keep your mind open, try it out. I know your thing fell through with the band, but that don't end the world. Lotta people gotta try lotta different things to survive—you know that."

Grant was right about one thing, at least: the Bad Apples were over and somehow the world hadn't come crashing to a halt. "Alright," Mouse said. "I appreciate it."

"Now let's get some forms filled out."

Mouse filled out what seemed like a ream of forms, writing the same information over again in different places, while Grant told him about the job. It was simple warehousing work: Mouse would help load cases of beer bottles onto wooden palettes; drive a forklift that moved the palettes from warehouse platforms into long-haul trucks; and feed packaging materials into a machine, which would automatically put beer bottles into their cardboard carrying cases. Grant explained that the forklift job required the most concentration and the least physical labor, but that all of the jobs were exhausting in one way or another and that Mouse would feel good about working for Anheuser-Busch, because at the end of the day his hard work would be compensated by a fair wage—twelve dollars and fifty cents an hour—which he said was nearly twice the amount most service jobs were paying. When the paperwork was completed, Grant suggested they go down to the warehouse so Mouse could meet some of his coworkers.

"You'll wanna bring a coat to work," Grant said, "cause they keep the loading docks cold, and you'll want some good gloves, too. I'll show you what kind to get. Here, I thought of something. Wait a minute." He went into his office and came back with a lined red parka, which carried the blue Bud Light beer logo on its left breast. He handed the parka to Mouse. "Whyn't you wear this for right now, so your teeth don't chatter while we walkin around." He smiled, as if this were a joke, but Mouse found nothing funny about it. "You have a heavy jacket you can bring?"

Mouse wavered between his pride and the truth, but Grant knew his family and his circumstances, so there was nothing to be gained by vanity. "Not really."

"Well, keep that one, then. Plenty more where that came from."

"Really?"

"Yeah, don't worry about it."

"Thanks." Mouse put the jacket on and looked down at the Bud Light logo on his chest. He felt like he'd just sold his soul to Budweiser and the brand on his coat showed everyone who owned him. It was, however, a warm coat and it fit him well.

"Now let me show you where you gonna work, and then I'll take you down to the administrative offices, where you'll pick up your i.d. badge on your first day."

Mouse was scheduled to start on Monday of the following week, six days away, and as he toured the facility with Grant, he wondered if he might come up with a better idea before then, a hustle or an unemployment dodge, a big win at craps.

In six days, he could probably find Gateway and get his royalty money, provided Gate hadn't already wasted it; but even then, his share of the royalties would buy Mouse little more than a few weeks' worth of potato chips and beer. He needed a new idea, but Anheuser-Busch was all he could muster.

Grant introduced Mouse to the workers on the loading docks with unqualified enthusiasm. One of the guys had heard the Bad Apples play and complimented Mouse on his music, though Mouse barely kept the sneer out of his voice when he accepted the praise. Mouse spoke as little as possible; when he did speak, he self-consciously made upbeat comments about the facilities and the prospects for his employment, but the unmistakable sullenness of his tone poisoned his words, and every optimistic thing he said broiled in the rancid fat of failure and scorn. He could not remember the names of the people he met, and he was sure that he seemed as unsuitable to them as he seemed to himself: he was worn-out clothes and an unkempt afro, and they were clean bald muscular brothers and crewcut Aryans with Marine Corps tattoos. They were all working hard, manly men doing manly things, and he clearly did not belong among them.

After Grant had introduced Mouse to the administrative secretary who would process his paperwork, they walked back to the sleek lobby of the steel and glass building where Mouse had come in. Grant shook Mouse's hand.

"I hope you like it here as much as I do," he said. "I know the fellas'll like you."

"Thanks, Mr. Grant."

"You can call me Bobby. We practically family, right?"

"Alright."

"You tell your mama hello for me, okay? See you Monday morning."

Grant turned back to the elevators. The receptionist who

had greeted Mouse earlier told him to have a nice day, in such a way that Mouse was certain she was laughing at him, laughing at his little temporary job. He saw no way to point out to the woman that he was a great drummer, the leader of the baddest, nastiest, funkiest band in St. Louis. He told her to have a nice day, too.

It was after eleven o'clock when he turned in his visitor's badge at the brewery gates. The morning fog had burned off, replaced now by sheets of translucid white clouds, through which the sun shone watery and thin. A sharp, icy breeze was blowing, and Mouse thought the air felt like snow. He was glad for his new jacket, even if it did mark him as a tool of Budweiser.

He now had no plans and no appointments until he showed up at work the following week. He thought of visiting his sister in Tower Grove, making some calls to track down Gateway, going back home and telling his mother how his interview had gone. Nothing seemed right, and as he walked aimlessly back the way he had come, he decided to find the first likely grill and stop in for some food. The restaurants in Soulard tended to be expensive, but there were a few bars that served the same cheap, greasy food in the middle of the day that they served to drunks at night, and Mouse thought he could find a bartender he knew, who might front him a beer.

Nowhere to Go

Mouse walked into Sweeney's Blues Bar and shivered. Even inside, he could see the faintest fog of his own breath.

Sweeney's had once been a high-toned dinner club, but it had been deteriorating for decades under thicker and thicker coats of paint and ever-changing management. Now it featured greasy food, cheap drinks and nightly gutbucket blues shows. Fifteen cafe tables with ancient clumps of gum stuck underneath were scattered around a permanently sticky black-tiled dance floor, and a bulky walnut veneer bar on one wall lorded over the space. Mouse caught his reflection in the frosted mirror behind the bar. His boyish face and bright eyes surprised him: he was thirty-nine years old but felt like a haggard old man.

Dishes clattered violently in the kitchen, followed by garbled shouting. Mouse stared at the dance floor and shoebox stage. He had seen Mad Jim Clayton play harmonica here with his band the Claytones: the show went three straight hours without a break, the whole band sweating through their matching plaid sports coats, the club shimmering and viscous like melting metal. It was not the best show Mouse had ever seen, musically—the time was sloppy and the band wasn't tight—but Mad Jim had willed the songs into shape, and two dozen gleeful dancers had quaked all night. Every object in the room had been transformed, superheated, refined, distilled into a groove and poured back into the bar, back into its old

place with a new coating of molten brass and blues. The Claytones had more soul than skill, more faith than knowledge:
they were all passion and no foresight, and they made the kind
of magic the Bad Apples had once made, magic that became
magical because you believed it was magic. There was barely
enough room for four people to stand together on that stage,
even without their instruments, yet a touring blues band in
plaid sports coats had turned that seedy, dirty, scrubby little
space into a palace. For one night at a time, a dive like Sweeney's could become Beulah Land, and all you had to do was
believe.

The kitchen door swung open and a scruffy white guy
with curly brown hair and a drooping mustache stepped into
the bar. He wore a button-down shirt that had once been
white but was now nicotine-yellow, and a black leather vest.
He headed behind the bar without really looking at Mouse.
"Sorry, I didn't hear you come in," he said in a graveled tenor.

"No worries, Sidney, I know you jus rolled out."

"Mouse! What the hell you doin up at this hour?"

Mouse shook the bartender's hand and sat down on a
stool. "Interview. Guess I had to get me a regular job."

"You're kiddin! You never worked a day in your life!"

"Neither did you. But I guess somebody gotta keep business in business, right?"

"You serious? You lookin for a job?"

"Got a job. Over at Busch."

Sidney widened his eyes theatrically and threw up his
hands. "Why *on earth* would you want to do a thing like that?
They actually work over there."

"Aw, you know, Sidney." Mouse suddenly reached his ca-
pacity for banter and hunched his shoulders toward the bar.
"The Apples broke up, man."

"No way."

"Me and Gate had enough."

"Damn, Mouse." Sidney put his hands on the bar and shook his head dramatically. He was used to making broad physical gestures to accompany his remarks, to make himself understood over the noisy clamor of the bar, and it had become such a habit that he did it all the time now, even when the place was quiet. "And now you got a straight job? Don't leave much hope for the rest of us, I guess."

"It's temporary, though. I mean the job: the Apples are over for good."

Sidney reached below the bar for a pack of cigarettes. He took one out and pushed the pack toward Mouse. "You gettin a new band together, or what?"

"No. I dunno. I dunno if I'll ever play again, the way I feel now. You ever have them days where you jus had enough, you had it with the drunks and the owners and noise and all that? It's hard to keep strugglin when it look like you never gonna make it, you gettin nickel and dimed all the time, the whole thing's a grind."

"But what about 'Afrobatics?' They got that song on the jukebox over at Obie's. I hear people playin it all the time, heard it on the radio, even."

"That aint 'Afrobatics.'"

"Well, 'Jawbreaker,' whatever, it's still your groove."

"No it aint. I been askin Obie to put our records on his jukebox for years, and it was always, 'not if it aint a hit.' And now this—it's a hit and it aint even our song."

A local hip-hop group called Catfish Crunk had recently had a minor club hit with a rap single that included a sample from a Bad Apples song. "Jawbreaker" had been high-profile for a while on local college radio, had even made it onto the playlist of one of the AM urban stations, took off on iTunes. It had generated modest royalties for Mouse and Gateway, who were credited as two of the song's many writers, and it represented the only time Mouse's music had ever been played on commercial radio; but it was not even technically his song. The rappers had distorted the riff from "Afrobatics" so thoroughly when they'd sampled it that, unless you already knew its source, you would never have recognized the Bad Apples' original music in it. For Mouse, it was worse than anonymity: it was obscurity spiked with insult, especially since he considered the rap asinine.

"Still," Sidney said, "you know how many bands come through here that never did anything on record?" Mouse felt like punching Sidney in the mouth—the Bad Apples had produced eight full-length original albums, but that apparently wasn't "doing anything on record." Having a song sampled and turned into a booty-call rap was doing something, though, because somebody had played it on the radio, and you could download it from iTunes. "You want a drink?"

"Bud Light." Mouse pointed to the logo on his jacket. "Gotta be a good company man. And you can turn the heat up in here, too—it's like Iceland or some shit."

"Yeah, the boss likes to keep it cold till we open." Sidney pulled a Bud Light from the ice box below the bar, twisted the cap off and set the bottle in front of Mouse. "I keep tellin him it's cheaper to leave the heat on, but who knows why people do anything?" He snapped a black-and-white checkered rag against the bar and sauntered back toward the kitchen.

Mouse sipped his beer. He preferred stouts and dark ales—Bud Light tasted like cold liquid nothing cut with seltzer. Nothing, he thought, tastes like the King of Beers, and he raised his bottle in a toast to his new bosses.

He heard the heat kick on. Warm air tickled his face and neck. A delivery truck rumbled by on the street. Mouse had nowhere to go, nowhere to be.

As the Bad Apples' de facto manager, Mouse had always had something grand, or at least grandiose, to work on, and an inner pressure had governed every move he made. He had taken all the responsibility: to write and arrange new music, to sell the band to clubs, to produce and distribute compact discs, contact the major labels, collect and budget money and pay the players. The joyfully absurd aesthetic of the Funk had kept him sane, but he'd found it harder and harder to maintain joy and absurdity in the face of limited rewards. Even the bounce of a joyous groove could not make financial failure merry. He thought his whole life had depended on writing songs, producing records, arranging the next tour that might break the Apples into the bigtime; but in reality, if he had never done anything, if the Bad Apples had never existed, no one would have known the difference. There was nothing necessary about the Apples to the world at large: only Mouse's sanity had been at stake, and now that he could no longer exert the will to make the band mean something, the world lacked sense.

He sipped his beer. The high that he got when a show really came together, that euphoric buzzing in his ears and nervous lightness in his chest—did the beer warehouser or copier salesman get that when he did his job? Could any straight job be fulfilling the way performing was?

Sidney returned and sat on a stool behind the bar. He opened a bottle of mineral water. "I used to have a band, you know?" he said. "We used to play out a little. We were called Dot Dash Dot—that's the Morse Code signal for 'understand,' like we were tryin to bring people *understanding* with our music. Get it? Dot Dash Dot. *Understand*?" Sidney laughed. "We broke up after a while, too."

Mouse hid his disgust by taking a long pull on his beer. He hated being compared to weekend guitar heros. He had dedicated his whole life to the drums, to the business of music, to the dance grooves of the Funk: the Bad Apples had toured almost nonstop for more than a decade. Mouse had forgotten more about rhythm than most people ever knew, and now he would forever be lumped into the same category as Sidney, who could barely hack his way through a three-chord folk song.

"Can I get a menu, man?" Mouse said. "Y'all serve lunch, right?"

"Sure thing."

Outside, on the sidewalk in front of Sweeney's plate glass window, a man stopped to ask a woman something, and Mouse watched them, wondering where they were going, what they were doing. Snowflakes were beginning to drift against the window, where they turned to water and slid toward the street. Sidney handed him a laminated menu.

"You want another beer?"

"I got nowhere to go."

Sidney opened another bottle and set it on the bar. "I gotta check on something." He disappeared into the kitchen again.

Mouse stared at the menu —it was dog-eared and stained under its lamination, as if someone had tried to rescue it too late, and its layout showed no attention to detail. Mouse's imagination had always imposed symmetrical forms on things and searched for balance, and he thought this menu deranged. In his mind, he reorganized the layout of the beverage list and side orders, so the titles and descriptions created a harmonious pattern. He still had not actually read the words by the time Sidney returned, so he just ordered a burger and fries. Sidney again excused himself.

Sweeney's front door swung open. A woman with pale white skin and long, straight, strawberry hair walked in. She wore a threadbare black peacoat over a green turtleneck, and black corduroy pants. She was five-feet-one and slender and she shifted her handbag from one shoulder to the other. When she saw Mouse, her bearing changed—she strode resolutely to the bar and took a seat. She had deep black circles under her eyes, and she stifled a yawn as she slung her purse over the back of her stool.

Sweeney's sound system crackled to life with a burst of feedback, then static, then a slow-moaning torch song. Sidney emerged from the kitchen and greeted the woman.

"What'll you have?"

"Whatever Mouse is having."

Mouse started. As far as he knew, he had never seen the woman before, but today of all days the Fates were torturing him with the ironies of smalltime celebrity.

"Bud Light," Sidney said. "With a burger and fries."

"That," the woman agreed, "and a shot of top-shelf tequila." She still had not taken her eyes off of Mouse.

"*Patron* all right?"

"Fine," she said.

Sidney went to work filling her order, while she fluttered her eyelashes at Mouse, a mocking coquette. She looked as exhausted as Mouse felt: her eyes were opaque and red-rimmed, but they smiled at Mouse's confusion.

"Sorry," Mouse said. "I dunno who you are." He was now certain that he should go lie down on his mother's couch in Brooklyn and not get up again for six days.

"I guess a big star like you must throw girls away every day."

Mouse could not conjure a memory of her, much less an episode in which he had "thrown her away." He drank his beer and looked to Sidney for help. Sidney set a bottle and a shot down in front of the woman, raised one eyebrow at Mouse and gave the slightest shrug.

"How do you want that burger?"

"Rare." She downed her tequila and banged the glass on the bar.

A young couple walked through Sweeney's front door, and Sidney told them to have a seat anywhere. He hurried back into the kitchen, leaving Mouse to deal with the redhead alone.

She continued to stare at him mischievously—it was not an unfriendly look, but there was something unsettling behind it that prevented both conversation and evasion. Mouse imagined she was a scorned groupie from his more reckless days.

"I don't throw people away," he said. The proclamation echoed sullen and self-important in his ears.

The woman slid down the bar and took the stool next to Mouse's. "No need for drama. I'm just having fun." She held out her hand, and Mouse shook it. "I'm Shauna. I'm a friend of Tammy's." Tammy was Gateway's sister.

"Oh," he said. "Sorry. I aint thinkin too straight today."

"Don't knock yourself out."

"I saw Tammy a couple days ago, actually."

"I mean, we *did* sleep together, kind of a lot, and you left town and never called me again, but mostly I was a friend of Tammy's."

Mouse felt steamrolled. Shauna was toying with him, as he had probably toyed with her. No matter how he tried, though, he couldn't remember sleeping with her or speaking to her or ever seeing her, but it was possible that he'd had sex with her in some altered state a decade before. Those distant times had been powdered under the rubble of bigger collapses since.

"Strange days, I guess," Mouse said, looking at the bar. "I mean, I dunno when we, when I knew you. I mean, when did we. . . ?" This fumbling for words made him despondent.

Shauna smiled. "It doesn't matter now, does it?"

"Let's drop it, then."

"But what should we talk about?"

"I don't wanna talk at all."

Shauna recoiled, but the wry glint never left her eye. "That's not very friendly, Mouse. I remembered you as a kind soul."

"You said I threw you away!"

Sidney reappeared and set a plate of food in front of him. The smell of the greasy burger made his mouth water, and Mouse picked up a french fry, dipped it in ketchup and ate.

"Look, Shauna," he said, still chewing. "I'm sorry for whatever I did. I'm sorry I don't remember you. I aint nothin *but* sorry. But whatever you need to do, go ahead and do it, cause my memory aint gonna get any better and I caint apologize for what I don't know." He ate another french fry. When Shauna didn't respond, he pursed his lips and shook his head and started angrily dressing his hamburger with lettuce and onions, muttering ostentatiously under his breath.

Shauna stood up and slipped her handbag over her shoulder. She grabbed her beer bottle and then snatched Mouse's plate right out from under his nose. "Hey!" She walked to a table, set Mouse's plate on one side and then sat down on the other side, facing him.

"We never had sex," she shouted over the music. The young couple across the bar looked from Shauna to Mouse. Mouse was still holding a tomato slice suspended over the bar where his hamburger had been. "Come on, let's have lunch," Shauna said.

She's pretty enough, next to most deranged women, Mouse thought. Why she look so strung out at eleven-thirty in the morning? He took his beer and his tomato slice to the table and draped the tomato over his burger.

"Why you wanna play me like that? Whatchyou want?"

"You seemed down, that's all, like maybe you could use some cheering up."

"Jus cause I'm down don't mean I want cheered up. What's it to you, anyway?"

"Tammy told me about the Apples," Shauna said. "It's too bad."

Mouse took a big bite of his hamburger. "So you are a friend of Tammy's," he said with his mouth full.

"C'mon, Joseph. I *am* a friend of Tammy's, and we *did* used to sleep together."

"You and Tammy?"

"Mouse, you're gonna piss me off." She took a swig of beer.

"Piss *you* off?! You pissin me off. We slept together, we didn't sleep together, we know each other, we don't know each other. I didn't ask to sit next to you."

Four workmen in denim coveralls walked in and shouted a greeting to Sidney, who went behind the bar and poured drafts.

"All right, fuck you, Mouse. I was just having fun. Obviously you're not in the mood for fun."

Mouse felt like an idiot—as if *he* were doing something wrong. He wondered if this woman had that effect on everyone.

"Buy me a drink," she said.

"What?"

"It's the least you can do."

"I'm already doin way more than the least."

A waitress came from the kitchen with Shauna's food, and Shauna ordered another shot of *Patron*. "And bring Mouse another Bud Light."

"I hate Bud Light," Mouse said. The waitress hovered next to their table.

"Why are you drinking it then?" Shauna said. "Why are you wearing a Bud Light jacket?" Mouse slumped into his seat and rubbed his forehead with his fingertips. "Another Bud

Light, please," Shauna said. The waitress left.

"Did we sleep together or not?"

"There are good reasons to hate you, Joseph Watkins."

"Good reasons to hate everybody. Did we?"

"Think about it." Shauna squirted mustard onto her hamburger. "I roomed with Tammy when we were in nursing school. We had an apartment off Cherokee, near antique row? You were there all the time."

He did remember that apartment, and he and Gateway had spent a lot of time there, it must have been twenty years before. "Oh my God," he said.

"So, did we sleep together or not?"

The all-male choir chanting from a scratchy vinyl record, the tapering white candle in the antique sconce above the bed, the hand-dyed orange sheets. He had slept with Tammy's roommate for more than six months. Homemade spikenard incense burning, the sweet smell of dung and cherries. The musky funk of the woman's sweat. Black lipstick, blue-black hair, henna body paint swirling crimson circles around her tiny button nipples. Still, except for her stature, he couldn't make the woman sitting in front of him match his memories of Tammy's roommate in that little apartment. Even her name seemed wrong.

"Shauna. . . I never knew no Shauna. Your name was Cheetah or some shit like that, right?"

"Vita. DuPlease."

"Right! Oh my God! Vita DuPlease. You had inky black hair and pancake make-up and big-ass false eyelashes! And you was always mixin up, like, witchcraft and Kama Sutra and shit, and makin your own clothes!"

"And dancing!"

"You'd dance around that apartment naked!" Mouse felt something he hadn't felt in a long time: surprise. "Stark naked!

And you had all them biohazard stickers all over everything!"

"At least you remember."

"How could I forget *that*? You even had Tammy goin all Goth, like Cruella de Ville." The waitress returned with fresh drinks. "Man, you sure don't look the same now."

"But you still do."

"Yeah, this 'fro's original, 1982, never been nothin but."

They grinned at each other like prison guards. It was the first time Mouse had smiled in days, thinking about Vita Du-Please and the distant epoch when the Apples were just starting out, when he was still on a mission to shake the whole world with his grooves. Vita would go to nursing school by day and then party in the clubs half the night dressed in leather dominatrix gear or flowing vampire gowns. She would often be the only white girl in the clubs where the Bad Apples played, and she looked so freaky that the sisters stayed clear. Despite her small stature, she was usually the one up in somebody else's face, and she mostly got her way.

"I never even knew you had red hair."

"And I'm left-handed, too. I'm a rare, rare gem, Mouse Watkins."

"So you still friends with Tammy, huh? How come I never see you around?"

"I don't get out the way I used to, you know, clubbing. I see Tammy from time to time, though. She still works up at SLU Hospital, and I work for a hospice company, so we have the same patients sometimes."

"But you said you knew about the Apples, so you must've talked to her in the last week. Our last gig was jus Friday night, and it all happen kinda sudden."

"Yeah, she called me Sunday. She was worried about Gateway, thought I might've heard something. I guess Gate's on a bender. I haven't actually seen Tammy in person for months, though."

"How did you know where to find me, then?" Mouse asked. "I didn't even know I was comin here till half an hour ago."

"I wasn't looking for you."

"You were lookin for Gateway?"

"I was looking for lunch and a few drinks. It's just a coincidence that Tammy called me and I know about the Apples and then I met you here." She gulped her second tequila, made a face and washed it down with beer. "Coincidence. I've got a home-hospice patient around the corner. I just pulled a twenty-four hour shift and wanted to blow off some steam before I went home."

"So this is completely random?"

"Maybe not random, just coincidental." She sat back in her chair. "I mean, Tammy calls me out of the blue two days ago, and then I come in here—I haven't been in Sweeney's in ten years—and I find you. Is that random? It would have been smarter for me to stop at a bar closer to home, or just go home and collapse with my own bottle of tequila, I don't know. But I wanted to come here today for some reason. I actually thought of it like that, I wanted to come to this exact bar, and then here you are, so maybe I needed to see you. Maybe I drew you in here today, too, so I could clear the old Bad Apples vibrations out of my chakras."

Despite her name and image change, Shauna was still the same Vita DuPlease—she had always talked about energy and wavelengths, witchcraft and hindu astrology, had always found hoodoo connections between things. Mouse had always thought she was too self-consciously eccentric, praying to weird saints, celebrating Winter Solstice instead of Christmas; but meeting her now was a strange chance, and maybe she was right: maybe she had a deep soulful connection to the band. As a hospice nurse, maybe she was tuned into death, and she was drawn here because of the death of the Bad Apples. That idea, at least, was more interesting than the dreary things Mouse had been thinking, and he was glad for Shauna's company. The fact that she had been present at the beginning of the Bad Apples' career, and here she was at the end, was comforting in a way he didn't fully understand.

"What did Tammy say about Gateway?"

"He showed up at her apartment Sunday morning, wasted and talking crazy, and they got into a fight. She was afraid he was gonna do something foolish. She must've been really, really worried, because I'm pretty far down the list of people to call if you're looking for Gateway. Last time I saw him was probably the last time I saw you."

A few more people had wandered into Sweeney's, and Sidney and the waitress were steaming around the dining room, taking and filling orders. Mouse took a long drink and stared out the window, where snow was now falling in flurries.

"I been lookin for Gateway, too," Mouse said. "Lookin for a couple days now. Gate and I kinda had a falling out."

"Is that why you broke up the band?"

"Part of it. Lotta things. Mostly I'm burnt-fried, jus caint do it no more."

Shauna reached her hand across the table and left it there, palm up. She closed her eyes and wiggled her fingers. Mouse looked at them, at her tired face. She kept wiggling her fingers. "Would you give me your hand, god damn it?" She opend her eyes and then rolled them. "What do you think it means when someone wiggles their fingers at you?"

Mouse placed his hand in Shauna's. She closed her eyes again and breathed deeply a few times. "Breathe with me." Another thing Mouse remembered about Vita: her commands came with the tidal force of her oversized personality, and when she told people to do things, they did them. She and Mouse breathed deeply in unison, while the juke box played Bo Diddley's "Bo Diddley." Finally, she released his hand and opened her eyes again.

"I feel that way a lot, lately," she said, as if Mouse had confessed something. "I mean, with nursing, especially this hospice company. Like, where is this going, what am I doing this for? Right? I've been a nurse my whole life, same as you and the Apples."

Mouse felt that she really did understand how he was feeling: something in her tone, the look in her eyes. It wasn't exactly the same, he thought, but the vibe was close enough.

Shauna signaled the waitress. "You want anything else, Mouse?"

He looked at his third beer, three-quarters gone, and didn't know what he wanted. He told himself he should look for Gateway and get his money, but more than anything right then he wanted to stay with Shauna.

Perhaps because of their long exhalation of relief together, perhaps because of his loneliness and the beer, Mouse wanted to sleep with Shauna again. He remembered the crazy nights when she was Vita DuPlease, earth-mother dominatrix, the exotic sexual adventures trying to duplicate illustrations in tantric love guides, when they were both young and flushed with the novelty of ambition, their energy pouring out in every direction. He looked into her eyes and felt that she genuinely knew what he was thinking, and he remembered that you didn't have to spend much time with Vita before you believed in her extrasensory theories—all her talk about energetic vibrations and chakra alignments soon seemed like common sense.

"You headin home?" he said.

"I'm gonna have another shot and then walk it off. I'm a

little spacey. I need to burn myself down from work so I can sleep when I get home."

The waitress came to their table and Shauna asked for a shot of Patron and the bill, and Mouse said he'd have a shot, too. "Same tab?" the waitress asked.

"Yeah, one check," Shauna said. "My friend here owes me." The waitress left.

Shauna grinned impishly at Mouse, and he took stock of his wallet. There was no way he could afford both their bills. He was counting on Sidney to cover his first two beers, otherwise he probably couldn't afford his own meal.

However she had changed, Shauna was still unpredictable, and Mouse thought she might make an unpleasant scene about the bill for her own amusement. Flapping papers of emotion blew across Mouse's face. He hated games. He longed to be in the distant past with Shauna for one moment more, to forget about Anheuser-Busch and Gateway's meltdown and the world of jobs and money and just be with Vita again. He wanted to feel the certain prospect of success with the Bad Apples one more time. One Moment More, he thought. How many songs had been written around this tired cliché? One more time, one last time, one moment more with you. He wondered how long it would take before he broke himself of the habit of looking at the world through song titles, melodies, chord progressions and drum breaks. No more songs ever. He saw the bottomless abyss of his failure yawning before him again.

The waitress returned with two shots of tequila and the check. Shauna raised her glass. "To misspent youth."

She drank the liquor all in one go and slammed the glass down, and Mouse followed suit. The tequila flushed warmth through his chest and arms, and he chased it down with the rest of his beer. He wanted to be very drunk, but then he thought of Gateway and remembered that he still had to be the responsible one, he still had to take care of Gate, to the bitter end.

Shauna examined the bill. "You lucked out—they comped your beers. So we're in for two burgers and fries, four shots of *Patron* and my one Bud Light. I'm a cheap date." She flicked the check across the table.

"I don't remember leavin town and never callin you," Mouse said, staring at the check. "I mean, all those years ago. You said I left and never called, but I thought we fell out over—"

"For Christ's sake, Mouse, I was busting your balls." She snatched the check back from him and stood up. "You don't *owe* me anything, you cheap bastard." She took a credit card from her purse, marched to the bar and waited for Sidney to charge her account. Mouse joined her.

"You takin off, Mouse?" Sidney said. While the credit card terminal connected to the bank, Sidney poured drafts for other customers.

"Yeah, Sid, thanks for the beers."

"You oughta come around more often."

"I'm gonna be workin around the corner, so I'll be seein you some nights. I'll buy *you* drinks next time."

The electronic terminal spat out Shauna's receipt, and Sidney tore it off. She signed it, and Sidney gave Mouse a jokey 1970s soul brother handshake.

Shauna and Mouse walked out of Sweeney's into the swirling snow of an early winter storm. "Wanna walk with me?" she said. A snowflake settled on the high arch of her right eyebrow and glistened icy gray before melting.

"You not cold?"

Mouse now felt plush and warm in his Bud Light jacket, but Shauna's small frame seemed to shrink into her tattered pea coat. The snow was sticking to the ground.

"I'm wearing silk thermals," she said. "Let's head for Gravois and make a loop past the Market."

Shauna set off down Barton Avenue so suddenly and quickly that Mouse had to lope to catch up with her. At the corner of Tenth, he grabbed her arm.

"I thought you said walk."

"That's what I was doing."

"You live your whole life in a hurry? Talk fast, walk fast—"

"You want me to stutter and limp?"

"No, jus walk."

"Just keep up."

"Why don't we *stroll*?"

Shauna shrugged. "I'll follow you, then. I don't care."

Mouse put his arm through Shauna's, and they strolled to the corner and turned toward the Soulard Farmer's Market. The heavy thock-clock of Shauna's hard-heeled boots fell a millisecond before the rubbery thwat-thap of Mouse's sneakers, hinting at a mambo rhythm, and Mouse felt almost as if they were dancing. Snow had already dusted the front porches and low brick walls of the walk-ups, and if he soft-focused the cars along the avenue into indistinct blobs of color, he could imagine they were walking along this street a hundred years before, that they were living harder, less complicated lives. The alcohol seeping through his liver and the silence shrouding his brain, the snow rubbing the edges off the corners of buildings, the icy points and nubs of tree branches, the warmth of Shauna's body rubbing against his arm made the walk seem dreamy and impossible. The etching of their footfalls into the delicate veneer of snow on the sidewalk made the earth itself seem like a brittle shell of ice curving eerily around a cosmic pocket of nothing, slinging through dark space at a speed that made Mouse shrink in terror.

"Did you start a new band?"

"Naw."

"Then what did you mean when you told that bartender you were working around the corner?"

"I got a job at Anheuser-Busch."

"Yeah?"

"Temporary. My moms called in a favor—she's worried, and I figure I gotta do somethin till I find where my head's at, you know."

"I know where your head's at."

"That makes one of us. Anyway, it's a lay-down job. Movin boxes, puttin labels on bottles, settin up six-packs. Be helluva lot easier than bookin tours and giggin and dealin with all that bullshit."

"Maybe. But I bet you'll find it's easier doing what you really love, no matter how hard it seems, than doing something supposedly easy that somebody else wants you to do. Something you don't care about."

"I dunno what I really love no more. I dunno what I care about. The Apples is over, so things gotta change, and this here's a change. That's all I know."

Mouse stopped in front of a house on the north side of Menard Street—a French-style brick row house, three stories tall, that had been sectioned into apartments. A placard advertised a vacancy. He imagined living there in Soulard, walking around the corner to work, going to the Market every day, the way everyone had done in the 1800s—everything strictly local. Mouse had become so used to staying with his mother or his sister when he wasn't on the road that anything else seemed like a fantasy, but he figured it was only natural to have a real home of his own, if he were going to have a real job. That's what people do, he thought, they don't live vagabond lives, they get jobs and apartments, so why shouldn't I have a nice place in a good neighborhood? Why should I always be sleepin on somebody else's couch or in Jackie's basement? My job's real. Whyn't I have a real life? A real place and a real life.

Shauna was shivering. They had been standing in front of the "For Rent" sign for a long time. Her eyes were trained on Mouse's face, scrutinizing him.

"Where do you live now, Mouse?"

"I'm stayin with my moms out in Brooklyn—you know, East St. Louis."

"I know where Brooklyn is. You wanna move out? This looks like a nice place."

He took a step down the avenue and pulled on her arm, but Shauna refused to budge. "I aint even started at Busch yet," Mouse said, "and it's only for two months, that job. It aint even a real job. I aint got no money."

"You have no money whatsoever?"

"Got some comin. You ever hear that song 'Jawbreaker?'" Shauna shook her head no. "Well, this hip-hop group sampled one of the Bad Apples' beats, so we get a little royalty off it, but I sure caint afford one of these rich-ass places offa that. Gateway's drinkin through the money right now anyway, so I dunno if I got anything left, to be truthful."

Shauna opened her purse and pulled out a cell phone. She dialed the number on the rental sign.

"Whatchyou doin?"

"Let's see if we can look at it."

"What for?"

"For fun. You got anywhere else to go?"

The fact that Mouse had nowhere to go did not make looking at this apartment seem like a good idea. He thought he would rather go back to Brooklyn, would rather let the wrecked structures of his mind crumble into disorder than prop them up with rented fantasies, but Shauna was already speaking with someone, learning details about the apartment and asking the terms of the lease. Mouse wandered a few steps away and stared diffidently down the street.

He didn't know if it made any difference at all whether he showed up for work at Anheuser-Busch or not, whether he saw this apartment with Shauna or not, whether he ever did anything again or not, and this pervasive feeling of meaninglessness ate at his mind. He suddenly wished he had never run into Shauna, and the good will they had built up over drinks vanished into the soft gray sky.

Shauna was thanking the person on the phone. "He'll be here in twenty minutes."

"Who?"

"The landlord. He's running errands downtown, and he said if we wanted to wait, he'd be here in twenty minutes."

"Now I remember why I never called you again. You caint stay outta other people's business."

Shauna seemed genuinely taken aback by his reaction. "Jesus, Mouse, if this is how you are, I'm *glad* I broke up with you."

She whirled on her heels and stomped off, back toward Sweeney's. Mouse watched her for half a block, unsure exactly what was happening, but he was so lonely and this reversal was so sudden that he couldn't stand it. Each step that Shauna took seemed like a body blow, and he realized that she was not only a link to his past but a clue to the shadowy depths of the present—something about the memory of Vita and the presence of Shauna was helping keep him sane.

"Wait! Don't go." Shauna did not stop. "Come back." She walked even faster.

By the time she crossed Shenandoah, Mouse knew he had to run after her or let her go. So he ran.

Daydreams of Home

"How come so many nurses smoke? I see'em all the time outside the emergency room at SLU, just suckin'em down."

"Why shouldn't we smoke?"

"Uh, let's see. . . oh yeah, it kills you."

They paced in front of the walkup on Menard, waiting for the landlord. Shauna flicked ash into the street.

"I mean, your whole mission is helpin people be healthy."

"That's not the mission of a hospice nurse."

"You know what I'm sayin."

"You mean nurses should know better than to smoke."

"Right."

"We should set an example."

"No, but you see how it's gonna come out if you do it. You know better'n anybody."

"How do you want to die, Mouse?"

He stopped pacing. He had thought a lot about death—he always imagined he'd die in some nightclub brawl, or by being in the wrong place at the wrong time in East St. Louis—but he'd never thought much about how he *wanted* to die. "I guess I wanna die in my sleep."

"Of what?"

"Failure to wake up."

Shauna blew a stream of gray smoke into his face. "Unless you die instantly, by trauma, you're gonna die a painful death. That's the rule, you can take it from me. Doesn't matter how healthy you've been, what your habits are. If you live to a hundred, your body will fall apart and your senses will fail and you'll get some dread disease and you'll be in pain and misery at the end, probably for years. If you have healthy habits now, your painful end will come later and last longer. That's what nurses know." She took a deep drag on her cigarette. "That's the example I'm setting."

"But don't it make you feel bad now, while you doin it?"

"Sometimes it's really satisfying." She blew smoke again. "Sometimes it's so nasty it makes you sick. But I feel the same way about cauliflower. Anyway, Mouse, you've inhaled enough secondhand smoke in the clubs to be a cancer risk, at least as much as I am. These are the choices we make."

Snow fell in faster flurries now. Mouse's ears had gone completely numb and his face felt drum-tight. For all her dismissive stoicism, Shauna was wiping her nose with the back of her hand every time she took a drag on her cigarette.

"How long's it been?" Mouse asked.

"The guy's not here yet. That's how long it's been."

"What's your problem? I thought this was sposed to be fun, right? We havin fun?"

"It is fun."

"Then why you gotta jump down my throat like that?"

"Watching the clock won't make the guy get here any faster, that's all."

"I aint watchin the clock. It's watchin me."

Shauna shook her head. Mouse looked straight up into the sky. He loved the patterns snow formed on its way to the earth, the way objects overhead seemed to shimmer behind a veil of sky, the way sudden breezes swirled the air into chaos. Snow mocked the static forms of cars and signs, molding them into milky emblems of calm. He wished the snow would bury him so he could lie dormant until a warm idea brought him back to life.

A rusted yellow Volkswagen pickup turned onto Menard. Its engine missed and chugged, coughing its way up the street. Shauna dropped her cigarette and ground it out with her boot heel.

An older white man sat behind the truck's wheel, talking on a cell phone, trying to write something on a piece of paper on the dashboard while driving. The man accidentally leaned on his horn, jumped back, then said something into the phone and tossed it onto the passenger's seat. He parked right in front of them and got out.

"Shauna Duprey?" He approached Shauna and shook her hand, without looking at Mouse.

"This is my friend Joseph," Shauna said.

He turned to Mouse, scanned him quickly up and down and hesitated an instant before holding out his hand, which was calloused and strong.

"I'm Nick Hoffman. I own the place."

Hoffman walked briskly past them, opened the knee-high iron gate at the edge of the property and marched up the concrete walk. Shauna ushered Mouse in and made a bright happy face at him, coaxing his enthusiasm, which made Mouse feel angry, like a child.

A blast of warm air greeted them as they entered a narrow hallway. On their right was a heavy wooden door painted buttery yellow, with a brass number 1 nailed into it. On their left, a staircase lead to the second floor. Posters from art exhibits at the St. Louis Museum hung in wooden frames in the stairwell. Someone in the building was cooking curry.

"This landing used to be the entry hall to the whole house," Hoffman said, "when it was all one residence." He spoke with a phlegmy, nasally voice that Mouse found unpleasant. "When it was divided up, the front door here became the main entrance for the first two floors, and the back door became a separate entrance for the third floor apartment. You have to go around to the alley to get to the back yard, but it's a common space shared by all the residents."

They followed Hoffman up the stairs. "The vacant apartment covers the whole second floor," he said. "You'd have one neighbor above you and two below you." The staircase ended at a heavy wooden door, identical to the one below except for the brass number 3. Hoffman unlocked the deadbolt and stepped aside.

The first thing Mouse saw when he walked into the living room was a fireplace bracketed by built-in bookcases. Too rich, too much, he thought.

"The last guy who lived here kept a Hibachi on the balcony and grilled out all the time, even though the back yard has a charcoal grill everybody shares. There's also a clothes line back there, and a hammock I put up in summer."

Shauna made a beeline to the master bedroom in the back, leaving Mouse and the landlord in the living room. Mouse walked slowly around it, aware of Hoffman's eyes on the back of his neck.

The hardwood floors were gleaming. The crown moldings were carved with ornate, symmetrical botanical patterns that massaged Mouse's brain from the inside. He wandered over to the French windows and looked out at the houses and taverns across the street; the balcony was bordered by a wrought iron balustrade shaped into even more pleasingly symmetrical floral patterns. He fingered one of the braided gold velvet ropes drawing back crenelated yellow curtains, which seemed to have emerged from the 1850s.

He stared at the peaceful scene outside. He thought it cruel of Shauna to suggest seeing this place: if he'd had any money at all, he would have rented it on the spot, just for the moldings in the living room and the view of the neighborhood. The order and harmony here resonated through his spine like pedal notes through a pipe organ. He imagined the life he could have—how it would change him to have his own place in a funky neighborhood in St. Louis. He could forget about the Apples and all those nights on the road and the struggles to keep his mind and body together while everything else perpetually fell apart around him.

He turned back into the living room. Hoffman was still standing by the front door, staring at him. He wore a mask of indifference that Mouse knew all too well, a mask that could not hide the fear and mistrust in the landlord's eyes.

"How much this place cost?"

"Eight-fifty a month, plus last month in advance and a deposit."

Mouse's heart sank. If the Bad Apples had made it, he thought for the millionth time. . . he wouldn't be fantasizing about renting an apartment, he'd own his own apartment building. He wouldn't be begging for a job at Busch, he'd start his own brewery. Vain daydreams of success. And the daydream of living a working class life in Soulard seemed just as distant and painful as the dream of musical stardom. i should go back to Brooklyn where I belong, he thought.

"There's a beaded chandelier in the dining room!" Shauna called. "And you won't believe how big the kitchen is!" Mouse didn't understand her excitement, as if she had just found her own dream apartment. "And the view from the smaller bedroom is divine!"

Mouse walked into the kitchen. Shauna stood admiring the flames from the gas stovetop, all of whose burners were on.

"The layout is a little unusual," the landlord said, addressing Shauna. "There was only one kitchen in the house when it was built, so when they modified it, they had to put kitchens where there used to be bedrooms or bathrooms. That's why the smaller bedroom in this apartment opens off the kitchen." He pointed to a door. "Also, you have to go through the master bedroom to get to the bathroom, which some people find awkward. But some people find it charming. It lets you be more creative with how you use the space than you might be in a more conventional apartment." Hoffman cleared his throat and looked at his watch.

"I think it's just beautiful," Shauna said. "Did you see the detail on the chandelier? Those roses are hand-painted!"

Mouse stepped into the dining room and looked at the chandelier. The glass beads hanging from the metal frame dripped golden light. Between each small, flame-shaped light bulb were yellow and scarlet ceramic roses, and they were not only hand-painted but hand-formed, each rose slightly different from the others. They made him feel lonely. He loved this place, one more thing he couldn't have, one more thing he wasn't good enough for.

"Are you two married?"

"No."

"Just living together?"

"What makes you think we're a couple?" Mouse snapped.

"Well. . ." Hoffman shrugged. "It wouldn't be any of my business, except I need to know who may be living on my property, who's going to sign the lease. Whether you'll both be living here or just one of you, who's going to pay the rent. I'm gonna ask where you work, too, so don't let it ruffle your feathers."

"We're not living together," Shauna said. "The apartment's for Joseph—he just got a job at Anheuser-Busch and wants to live in the neighborhood."

"Ah, that's a good company." Hoffman glanced at Mouse's afro. "If you'll excuse me, I need to make a phone call. You'll want to walk around the place a little. Feel free to look at the laundry room in the basement, the back yard. If you have any questions, we can talk about them when I come back." He walked through the living room and shut the front door behind him.

"What's wrong with you?" Mouse said. "Why you drag me up here?"

"It's a beautiful apartment, isn't it? You haven't even seen the master bedroom—it has French doors leading to a balcony. And the second bedroom has a bay window you can sit in. And that view! You half-expect Victorian women with parasols to come waltzing up the street."

"Let's get outta here."

Shauna put her hand on Mouse's chest. "Are you breathing?"

"I'm standin here, aint I? Let's go."

"Would you *relax*, Mouse?" She unzipped his Bud Light jacket and put both palms against his chest. "Now watch me, look deeply into my eyes and *breathe* with me."

"Goddamn it!"

"I'm trying to help you, Mouse. You seem like you're in hermit crab mode, like you want to draw back into your shell. But you can't say no to everything. You have to say yes sometimes." She fluttered her eyelashes. "Accepting one positive thing into your life can open the way for a whole series of others."

"You the one told me I shouldn'ta took that job at Busch, that I aint gonna be happy there. I already said yes to that today! But I guess that was the wrong thing to say yes to, and this here's the right thing? If I say no to Busch, I caint say yes to this, so what you say don't really make sense."

"What I mean is, you need to be receptive to the organic opportunities that present themselves, not the ones that your brain tells you are right, but the ones that your heart gives you."

"How is draggin me up here an organic opportunity?"

"Our meeting, Mouse, after all this time, is the opportunity. Don't make me spell every little thing out."

Shauna massaged Mouse's chest, leaned into him to apply pressure, so that he had to push back in order to hold his ground. Her fingers were surprisingly strong, and he could feel himself tensing against her and then releasing as her fingers kneaded deep into his muscles. It was like a magic trick: his breathing began to grow deeper.

"There you go," she cooed. She exhaled flamboyantly, like an acting coach in front of a class. Mouse felt himself drawn into her eyes. "Just relax with me, breathe with me. Focus. Follow my breathing and breathe with me."

He felt as if she were hypnotizing him. He thought back to his time with Vita DuPlease. She had always gotten her way, and not just with Mouse: she had gotten her way with everyone. "Focus," she said. Mouse felt himself on the precipice of a long spiraling fall. "In. Out. Breathe in through your nose and out through your mouth. Now close your eyes. In. Out." He closed his eyes and followed Shauna's breathing. When he had breathed deeply for just a little while, he did indeed feel better. Her massaging changed in tone as he relaxed, until she was rubbing his chest and stomach gently, more a lover's caress. He opened his eyes and discovered Shauna staring at him with an old, familiar look: the bedroom eyes of Vita DuPlease.

"Why don't we look at the rest of the apartment?" she said.

She seemed dangerous and vulnerable at the same time, exhausted, floating on a thin film of tequila, and Mouse finally understood the organic opportunity she was offering him. This was her way of seducing him, and he wanted to be seduced. She led him into the empty master bedroom, took him by the hand and walked him through the French doors, onto the back balcony.

The balcony was partially shielded from the elements by the third-floor landing above it, but a delicate layer of snow had gathered around its edges, and their shoes crunched it. They leaned on the cold iron railing together and stared into the back yard at an empty stone birdbath, the skeletal winter branches of a mulberry tree, a bare trellis and a garage opening onto the alley.

"Wouldn't it be great to live here?" Shauna said.

"You got an extra eight-fifty a month?"

"How much will you make at Busch?"

"Not enough. Cause you got electric, gas, all that shit, probably cost you a grand a month minimum."

"How much will you make?"

"Twelve-fifty."

"Twelve hundred fifty a month?" Shauna recoiled.

"Twelve-fifty an hour."

"Oh. Well. Forty hours?" She calculated in her head. "That's still two thousand a month."

"Minus tax and shit."

"How much does Gateway owe you? What about those royalties?"

"He owe me two thousand, but I gotta give some of that to my sister, if I ever get it. And that aint money you can count on for income, that royalty money—that's record sales, and they only pay every three months. That song'll be over soon— it's practically over now—club DJs stopped playin it already, which mean nobody's gonna buy it in a month."

Shauna held her hand out over the railing to catch snow-flakes. "At least you've got enough to get started," she said. "You could move in, have a beautiful, energetically clean space to get your head right in, see how it goes."

Mouse walked back into the bedroom. He didn't know

which was worse, his own depression or Shauna's delusions.

"In the first place," he said, "I aint got no furniture, so I'd be sleepin in this 'energetically clean place' on the floor. In the second place, I aint really got a job, so come February, when I couldn't pay the rent, I'd get evicted out to the energetically clean street. In the third place, this cracker ain't gonna rent nothin to a brother like me."

"Bullshit, Mouse, you don't even know him."

"I know how he was lookin at me. What is that—'are you two married?' You know what he was askin."

"Yeah, he was asking if we're married."

"No, he was askin if you done gone and married that nigger."

Shauna rolled her eyes. "If you don't like the place, Mouse, just say so. There's no reason to project your hateful feelings onto everybody else."

"What?!"

"You didn't even see the bathroom. It has an antique claw-foot tub and a seashell sink. And did you see the radiators in here? You'd be snug as a bug in a rug."

"Except I ain't got no rug to be snug in. I'm out." Mouse strode resolutely through the dining room. Before he reached the front door, he heard the latch click and the landlord stepped in.

"Sorry about that," Hoffman said. He was holding a clipboard and a pen. "I had to finish up some business from earlier."

"That's all right," Shauna said, catching up to Mouse and putting her arm through his.

"I brought an application, in case you're interested. You have any questions?"

Shauna held out her hand and took the clipboard and pen. "Could you give us another minute please, to talk it over?"

"Sure thing. I'll wait for you in the kitchen. We can fill out the forms at the breakfast bar." Hoffman left them alone.

"I'll bet you didn't even notice the breakfast bar," Shauna said.

"Whatchyour game anyway?"

"I'm just trying to help you."

"You run into me after twenty years and all of a sudden you tryin to *help* me? Who asked you to help me?"

"Nobody's twisting your arm, Mouse," she said, holding his arm. "You can leave any time you want, but you chased after me on the street and then you came up here and looked at this apartment with me, and I know you're glad to see me again. I see it in your eyes. I feel it in your breath. You can't hide from me—I see what's going on."

"What's goin on?"

"Wake up, Mouse. Things are changing fast. The Apples break up, you fall out with your best friend, you get a new job. You can't see the pattern in it that I see right now, and I'm telling you, this apartment is part of the pattern. I'm part of the pattern, and you're part of my pattern—all these patterns interlock, and that's how you can tell they're productive. One thing leads to another leads to another to another, instead of conflicting with each other. Think about it. We're just walking along—we can pick any street to walk down, and we pick the street with this beautiful apartment. We call the landlord and he comes right over, immediately, and here he is with the paperwork, ready to rent you the place. Nothing is a total coincidence, Mouse, you have a role in bringing these things about, and I can see that you love this place, so now—look at me— now you have to be an agent of your own fate. Now! Come on. You're looking for the next thing that's gonna happen to you, and the next thing is happening all around you! Your head is back there with the Apples, with everything that means, and you can stay in that space as long as you like, or you can do the next thing. That's the only reason you came to Soulard today, right? You said it yourself, something new has to happen."

"Doin any old thing that come along don't sound like the next plan to me."

"Even if you apply for the apartment and get it, that doesn't mean you have to take it. You're not making any commitments today. I mean, what happens if you don't show up for your job next week? Nothing. But you took the job, right? You said you'd show up, but you don't know if you really will or not. It's the same here. If you don't apply for this apartment, then this amazing sequence of events ends right now, and you'll go back to your mother's place in Brooklyn, with what? But what would happen if you trusted the events that you yourself set in motion and just filled out the application?"

"He still aint gonna rent to me."

"Not if you don't apply. Don't you love it? Imagine sitting on the balcony in the summer. And that little bedroom off the kitchen would be perfect for your drums—you could be play-ing and then wander into the kitchen for a snack and then go right back to playing."

"Neighbors'd love that." Mouse's drums were packed up in his mother's garage, and he was not convinced he would ever set them up again. He wondered how much a pawn shop would give for the whole set.

"It'll take five minutes, all right? And then we can do something else, something special you've always wanted to do but never let yourself—anything, just for fun!"

"I thought you wanted to go home and go to bed."

"We can do that—if that's what you want." She smiled.

It had been months since Mouse had slept with a woman, and he thought writing his name on a form a small price to pay for Shauna's companionship. "Alright, let's fill in some boxes."

They went into the kitchen, where Hoffman was doodling on scrap paper. "You folks have any questions?"

"Naw. I'd like to fill out the application."

They all sat down at the breakfast bar, on rotating cushioned seats atop metal pillars bolted to the floor. Mouse took up a pen.

"I should tell you," Hoffman said, "that there's a forty-nine dollar non-refundable application fee. That covers the credit check and my time while I call your references."

Mouse looked at Shauna, who put one hand up reassuringly. She slung her purse off her shoulder, set it on the breakfast bar and nodded that Mouse should go ahead and fill out the application. Mouse knew that the landlord was going to take the money and reject his application, probably without even checking the references, but if Shauna wanted to lose her money, it was her choice.

He imagined kissing her and taking her clothes off. He wondered if she had any children, any tattoos, how her body would feel twenty years later. Through her body, he could travel backward in time.

Even the first lines of the application were challenging: current address and length of residence. Mouse knew that his mother's address in Brooklyn would count against him, so he put his sister's in Tower Grove. He wrote that he had lived there for five years, which was in fact how long his sister and brother-in-law had owned the house, though whether or not Jackie would back up the lie of his personal residence there remained to be seen. He wrote down Anheuser-Busch as his employer; he entered Bobby Grant's name as his supervisor, though he was pretty sure that was technically incorrect.

His personal references were sketchy. The only non-family members he could think of to testify on his behalf were club owners and other musicians, most of whom were wildcard personalities he didn't entirely trust. He finally wrote down his sister's husband Marvin, who worked for a high-profile law firm, and his high school music teacher, Kevin Werner. Though Mouse had never graduated from Lovejoy Academy, he remembered Mr. Werner fondly and had occasionally seen him around town; and then he wrote down Gateway's mother, Mrs. Leona Collins, who had known him all his life, though what she might say about him at this moment was an open question.

Mouse's biographical information was a patchwork of lies and fronts, shaded versions of events, and the fact that Shauna was paying his application fee was an unmistakable clue to Hoffman that Mouse was a bad risk. But then, he thought, he was not filling out the application so he could live here, he was filling it out so he could sleep with Shauna; and his sketchy references would not surprise or disappoint this landlord.

As Shauna wrote a check for the fee, he felt distinctly patronized, a boy who had to have someone take care of him because he couldn't take care of himself. It was humiliating, the whole world of jobs and apartments and respectable people, and yet he sat and let it happen and even made small talk while the landlord brazenly stole Shauna's money. He wondered if he could actually have sex with Shauna, now that she had paid for the privilege.

He fingered the Bud Light logo on his jacket. After twenty years of standing up and being his own man, making his own choices, being the leader of the best soul band on the circuit, going against everyone's safe counsel to follow his dreams, he had taken exactly four hours to sell his soul not once but twice. He told himself that this was just the world that everyone had to live in, the world of jobs and rents and compromises, that he shouldn't be dramatic about it, but he felt the walls of the apartment closing in on him.

"Okay," Hoffman said. "I'll process this and give you a call, probably tomorrow." He shook both Shauna's and Mouse's hands. It must be easier to shake my hand when you jus took my money. My sugar mama's money. "If you have any questions about anything, you can call me." He took out a business card and held it between Shauna and Mouse before swinging it more in Mouse's direction. Mouse slipped it into his back pocket, along with his Busch paperwork.

The landlord escorted them down the stairs. "I don't know if you're familiar with the neighborhood," he said. "There's a great spot for lunch around the corner here called Mack's Crab Shack. And there's a new coffee shop just up Lami near Seventh called The Daily Grind."

"Alright, thanks."

They watched Hoffman get into his truck and drive off.

"See there?" Shauna said.

"See what?"

"He's not some Klansman. He's telling us about the neighborhood."

"Right. We just paid him forty-nine dollars to tell us where to eat lunch."

"Where's your faith in human nature?"

"I guess faith is what you gotta have, cause you sure caint go by evidence."

She put her arm through his and they walked down Menard Street, back toward Sweeney's. Mouse looked over his shoulder at the outside of the apartment they had just seen. It was idyllic, the balcony partially obscured by the bare branches of a healthy old elm tree, snow falling fat and wet as the storm settled in, giving the whole street a composed, intentional quality. Mouse thought of the blonde woman he had seen earlier in the morning, standing on the balcony of an apartment near the Market, smoking a cigarette. He could be her neighbor. No one like that lived in Brooklyn, no place like the Soulard Market existed in East St. Louis. Even Sweeney's, which was undeniably a dive, at least lacked the whiff of violence and corruption of the clubs in East St. Louis.

He put his arm around Shauna's waist, and she took his hand and slid it down to her hip. He didn't care about her theories of fate and coincidence. He suspected that everything that happened today would matter exactly not at all in the long run: he would not get the apartment, he already knew his job was temporary, and he could guess that Shauna was as flighty, freaky and erratic as Vita DuPlease had always been, no matter what her name or hair color. None of it mattered. He would remember the day as a minor episode, just another of the unpredictable consequences of breaking up the band, but for the moment he was glad not to be alone, glad to be doing anything besides simmering in his own juices or arguing with his mother.

They reached Shauna's silver Mazda Miata parked at the corner of Lami and Ninth. In an affected show of reverse chivalry, Shauna opened the passenger door and waited for Mouse to climb in.

"Where you livin now?" he said, as she climbed into the driver's side.

"I've got a house in Rock Hill."

"Hah. No shit? Vita DuPlease in the suburbs! I never woulda guessed."

"Well, it's not Clayton or Ladue, for Christ's sake. Rock Hill is a lot more like Kirkwood than Webster Groves."

"I always thought you'd be a city girl."

"It's basically South City."

"No it aint, and you know it—it's South County. That's alright, you know, things change for everybody."

"I'm not apologizing for it."

"Why should you?"

"Things change, Mouse, sometimes for the better. I don't have to live up to your ideas of Vita DuPlease."

"Nobody said you did."

She started the car and let it warm up before shifting into gear and pulling gingerly away from the curb. The snow was still mostly slush on the street, but this kind of storm was dangerous because it first slicked up the oil patches in the road and then coated them with black ice when the temperature dropped. Shauna switched the defroster on, and the initial blast of frigid outside air made Mouse shiver violently. He blew on his hands and wrapped his jacket tight around him.

"Hey, can I borrow your cell?" he said. "I should tell my sister that landlord might call her. She'll be pissed if she get a call outta the blue."

Shauna handed her cell phone to Mouse. Jackie answered on the first ring, and as soon as she recognized Mouse's voice, she told him Gateway had been there.

"He came about an hour ago," Jackie said. "He left a package for you."

"What's in it?"

"I don't know. It's a big manila envelope, and there's a flier taped to the outside."

"A flier?"

"A handbill. You know, for a show. At Boxcars, it says. Today's date."

"Did Gate say anything about it?"

"He said a lot of stuff about a lot of stuff, but he was drop-dead drunk, and most of it didn't make sense."

"Well, what's in the package?"

"I said I don't know."

"Open it."

"All right, hang on." The line went silent while Jackie

opened the envelope Gateway had left. "It's money," Jackie finally said. "A lot of money."

"Cash?"

"Cash money. And there's a note in here for you."

"Read it."

"I'm not going to read your private business over the phone, Mouse. Just come and get it. Where are you?"

"Soulard."

"Well? Come up and get it."

"Yeah, alright. I'm comin." He clicked off Shauna's phone and gave it back to her.

"I take it there's a change of plans," Shauna said.

"Gateway left some money at my sister's."

"Hey! See? That's great news! It's all working together now. That's what I'm talking about. It's serendipity."

"I aint sure. Somethin sounds real off about this."

"Like what?"

"Why he go to Jackie's house? Why not my mom's, where I'm stayin?"

"Maybe he didn't know."

"He know. And she said there's a flier for a show tonight at Boxcars. What's that? He know where to find me, if he wanna see me. Why he tellin me about some show?"

"Maybe he wants you to see it. Maybe it's his new band."

Mouse shook his head.

They rode along in silence, until Mouse realized they were still headed for Rock Hill. "Can you take me to my sister's?"

"Where's she live?"

"Tower Grove. Utah and Grand."

Shauna took the next right and the car fishtailed. Mouse thought she should probably not be driving. Her eyes had already been bloodshot and puffy when she and Mouse had met at Sweeney's, and now, as she strained to concentrate on the road, her crow's feet seemed to multiply like the spindly creases in a pressed flower.

"Seriously, you think he's got a new band together?" Shauna said. "It might be the best thing for both of you."

"I dunno. My sister said he was drunk."

"If I remember right, you don't have to be sober to start a band."

They exchanged a glance and Mouse smiled in spite of himself. "I dunno," he said. "Tammy said he was wasted on Sunday and he was drunk just now at my sister's, and the Apples only broke up on Friday. You caint get a band together in three days if you fallin down drunk. You don't know Gateway like you used to. He's fixin to do somethin stupid—I jus caint tell what it is."

"You don't know that, Mouse. I have a good feeling about all of this. Maybe it's exactly what it looks like, and now you have one less thing to worry about. I mean, whether or not Gateway gets drunk is hardly your problem, you know. I think you're just depressed right now or you'd see this for what it is: pure good fortune. A lot of money, the money he *owes* you, with no more strings attached. This whole day has gone entirely in your favor, one thing after another falling right in line, and you just can't see it because you're so down."

Mouse thought about the day. He had gotten a job, been treated to lunch, met an old girlfriend who wanted to sleep with him, applied for an apartment he couldn't afford in a nice old neighborhood, and now Gateway had given over the money he owed him voluntarily, without a fight. His day might, in fact, have been going well.

"You ever meet my sister?" he said.

"I don't remember."

"You'd remember if you had. She lucked up and married this lawyer, and they got this big plush house. He made her take all these speech classes to learn to talk right, so she didn't embarrass him at all his lawyer parties, and she loved it. She was always waitin for somebody to come along and raise her up where she thought she should be, get her designer shoes and dresses, all that fancy shit, garden parties and whatnot, all the work you gotta do to make your life look easy."

"Is that what she does, then? Perfect housewife?"

"Piano teacher. And perfect housewide. And she's on all these boards and committees, for the symphony and chamber music and the opera. She got a degree in piano from Wash U, and she gives lessons."

"So your whole family's musical, huh?"

"Yeah, my moms play some piano, and my granpa played a little everything, saxophone, accordion, banjo, you name it. My granma too. Plus, that was the one thing in school they always had enough money for, music, so we got it at school. That and sports. Toilets be overflowin right into the hall, books all outta date, hundred degrees and no air conditioning, but they's always instruments and sheet music to go around, you know, and that's what we did at school, seem like all day, was play music."

"That's weird. At my school, music and art were always the first programs cut."

"Where'd you go?"

"SLU High."

"There you have it, then. Private school. White school."

"What's white got to do with it?"

"People got different priorities for white schools. They love to keep the Negros singin and dancin and playin basketball, but white kids gotta go to college, gotta learn chemistry and English and shit."

"Weren't the teachers and administrators at your high school black, too? I mean, why would black teachers want to keep black kids down?"

"But where's the money come from? Not from black folk. Who you gotta ask if you want new textbooks?"

"I don't know, Mouse."

"I'm tellin you how it was at Lovejoy, at East St. Louis High, that's all. I dunno what the Catholics do, to be honest. I didn't even know you *was* Catholic. Vita DuPlease never said nothin 'bout Jesus."

"I'm Cafeteria Catholic. I don't go in for the pope or the virgin birth or any of that. And SLU High was my parents' idea. I still feel closer to the Hindus, but I like the saint icons and all the flummery of the Mass."

Traffic was moving slowly, windshield wipers slapping violently at the delicate coconut shavings of snow as they drifted peacefully down. Mouse fogged a little patch of the passenger side window with his breath and drew a cross in the condensation.

They turned onto Utah Street and rolled through a neighborhood of Victorian two-story houses, built from typical St. Louis red bricks. The houses were dilapidated and ramshackle, though not all of them had gone completely to seed, and children's toys lay under a patina of snow in the tiny patches of earth that passed for front yards. The street was so narrow here that Shauna had to slow down and maneuver around parked cars to avoid oncoming traffic, and the sidewalks and front stoops of the houses crowded close to the curb, giving the neighborhood an unpleasant, claustrophobic feeling.

"Tammy and I lived a couple blocks from here, remember?"

"Yeah. Right down Grand from the nursing school."

"It seems like another lifetime now."

They stopped for a red light at Grand Boulevard. West of Grand, where Mouse's sister lived, the neighborhood became decidedly fancier and better-maintained—Utah Street even changed its name west of Grand Boulevard, opening up into Utah Place, a wide avenue with a lavishly landscaped median. The area had been gentrifying over the last ten years, and Mouse expected that the people who now lived east of Grand, in the section that was still run-down and claustrophobic, would be the next ones replaced, their homes renovated by a higher income class. When they say urban renewal, Mouse thought, everybody know what they mean.

The light turned green, and Mouse directed Shauna to a parking spot in front of Jackie's house. Though the houses were of the same vintage and construction on both sides of Grand, here they looked regal and imposing, with freshly painted trim in designer colors. Two life-sized stone lions guarded Jackie's front walk.

"Maybe I'll wait for you," she said. "I feel a little ragged to be meeting your sister."

"Naw, come on in," Mouse said. Shauna hesitated. "You look fine, you look good."

"All right. She's your sister."

Family and Friends

The front door opened and Jackie waved them inside. She had fine brown blow hair, a pretty oval face and dazzling, perfectly straight white teeth. "I've got hot chocolate on the stove," she said. She wore satiny green slacks and a white angora sweater woven with green and gold flecks. "Come on in and get warm." Shauna introduced herself, and Jackie and Shauna shook hands. "Let me take your coats."

Jackie's living room was brimming with rigorously premeditated charm: heavy maroon drapes echoed the patterns of the matching Persian rugs. The bulky white sofa and armchairs held colorful throw pillows meticulously arranged to appear haphazard, and the floor lamps were carefully chosen to harmonize, their cream-colored necks swooping in curlicues over the chairs. Thick clusters of family photographs, knickknacks and decorative candles crowded built-in shelves and end tables. The color of the walls—a rich, warm cinnamon—made the room feel close and comfortable despite its grand dimensions, and the cozy fire burning in the fireplace gave it the welcoming, sweet smell of home.

"I'll have to get an extra mug," Jackie said. "I'm sorry, Shauna, Mouse didn't mention he was bringing a guest. Actually, why don't I just serve us in the kitchen, it'll be cozier in there. Unless you'd rather sit by the fire? Why don't we sit by the fire? Sorry, I'm a little bit scattered today. I'll bring the chocolate out and, Mouse, why don't you get the package Gateway left you, it's in the office, and you can be sorting this business out while I get the drinks. On second thought, why don't you come in the kitchen and help me, Shauna, and we can get to know each other a little, and Mouse, you can arrange some chairs around the fire."

Shauna looked at Mouse, and Mouse shrugged. His sister always spoke too fast and too much, with an odd patrician accent that revealed no trace of her upbringing in Brooklyn.

Jackie led them through the drawing room, where a black parlor-grand Kawai held court, and shelf after shelf of sheet music and compact discs lined the walls. Classical string music lilted softly from stereo speakers bracketed to the upper corners of the room. Shauna ran her finger along the body of the piano as she passed.

The dining room was as lavishly and carefully decorated as the living room, with a cherry-wood sideboard and grand buffet, an antique china hutch filled with real china and a drop-leaf serving table, all surrounding a Versailles dining table. Mouse watched Shauna as she took in the opulence of his sister's house, as she drew a new map in her mind of Mouse's emotional topography.

Jackie and Shauna continued into the kitchen, Jackie yammering away about the strange early snowfall and the prospects for the winter ahead. Mouse went into Marvin's office.

Gateway's manila envelope sat by itself in the center of Marvin's heavy oak desk. Mouse sat down in the high-backed leather chair and took the package in his hands.

Taped to the outside of the envelope, as his sister had reported, was a handbill photocopied on orange paper advertising a show that evening at Boxcars, a hole-in-the-wall club in a nearly deserted area of the old garment district downtown. The headliner, Beanie Rice and the Chickens, was a campy joke band composed of local musicians who got together to play shows when their regular bands weren't working. The handbill's artwork, a childish drawing of an anthropomorphic pumpkin waving a butcher knife, clearly betrayed Gateway's hand.

Mouse opened the envelope. In addition to several handfuls of cash rubber-banded together in untidy stacks, there was a tissue-fine sheet of stationery. "Mouse," Gateway's unsteady printing read, "Here's your money. I tried to close the Apples account at the bank but they won't do it without both of us signing. Come down to Boxcars tonight. I'm playing a set with Oscar. We need to settle some things." The note was not signed.

Mouse made a quick count of the money: several hundred dollars more than Gateway owed him. He returned the money and the note to the envelope, and took the package into the living room.

Two armchairs already faced the fireplace. Mouse scooted another around to the fire as Shauna and Jackie came in. Shauna carried a serving tray laden with three matching white mugs, several little porcelain pots and a steaming pitcher of hot chocolate.

"That's fine, Mouse," Jackie said. "You can sit in the middle between us two ladies, and would you clear the pedestal and bring it over so Shauna can set the tray down? We'll have a little pick-me-up right by the fire."

A low pedestal, designed to look like a miniature Doric column, stood near the front door. Mouse lugged it over to the hearth. Shauna set the tray on it, and Mouse's sister hovered over it.

"Sit down, sit down," Jackie said. "Now, this is pretty strong chocolate and I like it on the dark side, so there's cream in this bowl if you want to cut it and sugar if it's not sweet enough, and there's cinnamon if you want, and this little jar has toasted almonds, in case you'd like a little something to munch on."

Jackie had whipped the chocolate together from scratch, as usual. How she had managed it in the short time since Mouse's phone call from Soulard was a mystery to him, but Jackie was always planning ahead, preparing shortcuts for such an occasion. What if Marvin brought one of the law partners over on short notice? What if someone from the neighborhood association called from around the corner and needed to talk? Her entire life was designed to make the extraordinary things she did appear admirably offhanded. "Now, tell me what Gateway wrote in his note. Oh, I've forgotten the napkins. Go ahead and help yourself to the cocoa and I'll be right back." Jackie rushed back into the kitchen.

Mouse poured three cups of chocolate from the fat-bellied pitcher, then stirred a demitasse of sugar into his. Shauna sampled hers and her eyes widened.

"Oh my God, this is the most delicious hot chocolate I've ever tasted. What's in here?"

Mouse shrugged. "That's how my sister is. It's probably from some internet subscription club."

Jackie hurried back into the living room and handed out white cloth napkins. "So what about Gateway?" she said. She sat down next to Mouse. "What's gotten into him? He had a wild look in his eye."

"I dunno. He don't say nothin in his note really, jus to meet him tonight. He and Oscar gonna play a one-off at Boxcars."

"And the money?"

"He owed me. It's from 'Jawbreaker.' I didn't count it all real close, but I think they's too much."

"Well, that's a change for the better."

"He was probably too drunk to get it right. He tried to close the Apples' bank account, too. Can you imagine him all drunk, up in somebody's face at the bank?"

"He was in sad shape when he was here."

While Jackie and Mouse were speaking, Shauna was sipping her chocolate and staring at the fire, her hands wrapped tightly around the mug, the mug close to her face so she could smell the steam as it rose. She daintily plucked a single almond from the dish and put it in her mouth, then sipped chocolate and swirled it around the almond.

"How'd your interview go?"

"Got the job, but he was gonna give me the job already."

"You should call mom and let her know."

"Alright, but listen, I wanna talk to you about somethin else, cause a guy name Hoffman might be callin you. I listed you as a reference for this apartment I applied for down in Soulard. I told him I been livin up here with you for five years, and I gave him Marvin's name, too, at his law firm. I figure that impress him, if he call Sanders and Finch for a reference."

"Mouse," Jackie said indignantly. She glanced at Shauna. "Why didn't you check with me and Marvin first? It would be nice to be informed when you make decisions that affect us! You can't just tell people anything that suits your purposes about us any time you like."

"I know, I know, but it kinda came up sudden. And I'm tellin you now! That's why I called, that's why we here. Anyway, what the hell difference it make if I live here or not, or how long? Who'd ever know one way or the other? Why caint you jus cover me once without makin a federal case?"

"Mouse, it's obvious that the truth will get you further than lying, especially if your lie puts *our* reputation on the line. What if this man has already called Marvin? What do you think Marvin would say? Do you think either one of them will be happy with that conversation, and do you think you'll get what you want? Putting Marvin on the spot! If you're honest with people, they'll give you the benefit of the doubt."

"Like now?" Mouse said. "Anyway, he probably won't call, but I thought you should know in case he did. That's all. You can tell him whatever you want, and you can tell Marvin or not and Marvin's gonna do what he want anyway. I don't see no harm, don't know why you caint take my side sometimes."

Mouse looked at the extravagance of Jackie's living room. Marvin made over two hundred thousand dollars a year and Jackie made another fifteen thousand teaching piano lessons, and Jackie sat in this den of luxury and had the nerve to tell him that people would give him the benefit of the doubt if he were honest. Jackie had always cared more about money, status and officially sanctioned kinds of achievement than Mouse had. She had earned a scholarship to Washington University and had put herself through graduate school in music on her own, before she ever met Marvin. She believed that people got what they deserved. Marvin had grown up poor in Oakland but had earned a full scholarship to Washington University Law School. He touted himself as living proof that hard work always paid. They were an open-up-the-door-and-I'll-get-it-myself couple, and their lives provided evidence at every turn of the success of that philosophy. Mouse's method of scraping by and getting over had always rubbed Marvin the wrong way, and Jackie had become less tolerant of Mouse the longer she was married to Marvin.

"The apartment is really beautiful," Shauna chimed in. "The one Mouse applied for." She described it enthusiastically, two bedrooms, balconies, close to the Market and the brewery. "It was lucky Mouse happened to see it."

"I didn't even know you were looking for an apartment," Jackie said. "I thought you were going to stay with mom."

"Yeah. I dunno. I was. I'm sick of that whole Brooklyn scene, though."

"But mom said your job was supposed to be temporary.

Isn't that right? You've never had your own apartment in your life, and now all of a sudden you get a temporary job and it's time to set up house? Do you think that's wise?"

Jackie's disapproval washed over Mouse like spilled crude over a sea otter. He could see the words 'reckless' and 'irresponsible' in her eyes. Despite the fact that he had raised these same objections to Shauna when they were looking at the apartment, he now felt defiant.

"Mr. Grant at the brewery said he start out temporary forty years ago, and you jus gotta work your way in at Busch, and then you find the regular jobs and move up. So maybe it aint temporary. Besides, you always harpin on me when I stay at mom's, tellin me to grow up and be responsible, and now I'm tryin to be responsible and that's all wrong too."

"How much is the rent?"

"Five-fifty," Mouse lied.

"For a two-bedroom in Soulard? You're kidding!"

"Anyway, it don't matter. The landlord aint gonna call." Mouse looked to Shauna for support.

"I thought he liked Mouse a lot," Shauna said. "He was a nice older man, not a real estate type at all, if you know what I mean. He owns the property and manages it, too, just a small operation. I think Mouse would be really happy there."

"I still don't see why it would hurt you to stay with mom for a few months and save a little money," Jackie said. "Have you been looking at other apartments? Why do you always act so impulsively? I'm sure Marvin knows someone who could find you a real bargain, better than Soulard, and it's always better to deal with friends. You know that. Why don't you use the resources available to you?"

Jackie believed that Marvin knew people who could solve any problem, no matter what the problem was, and he usually did. Marvin could find a better rate, get better service, make just the right introduction: he was so well-connected that his solutions usually took no more than a single phone call. It was Marvin who had introduced Mouse to the lawyer who had overseen the royalty negotiations between the Bad Apples and Catfish Crunk, when Crunk had sampled "Afrobatics," and Marvin's friend had negotiated for a lot more money than they would ever have thought to ask for on their own. Marvin had then lectured Mouse and Gateway for an hour about the proper way to do business, and they had been forced to sit there and take it. Marvin's generosity always took the form of morality plays for Mouse's edification.

"Shit," Mouse said. "I'm *tryin* to let you help me, but you won't do it. I'm askin for help and you sittin there bustin me. I mean, you right, I should probably jus lay up in Brooklyn till I figure this shit out, but. . . why caint you help me get this apartment?"

Jackie stared at him. The fire popped and hissed. Shauna looked at Mouse, a look pleading with him to make nice with his sister. Whatchyou care 'bout my sister, Mouse thought. You don't know nothin 'bout it anyway. He longed to be alone.

"This is the most luscious hot chocolate I've ever tasted," Shauna said.

Jackie turned a winning smile on her. "Thank you so much."

"There's a taste in here I can't quite place, like vanilla, only smoother, more like custard or something."

"There's vanilla, but I also use condensed milk, which is probably the special creaminess you're tasting."

"Really? I'll have to make this myself. It's wonderful."

"I'm glad you like it. I'll give you the recipe."

Shauna and Jackie ran out of small talk, and the dire mood settled back in. Mouse stood up and opened Gateway's envelope.

He counted out two hundred dollars and handed the money to Jackie. "We don't wanna take up your time," he said. He retrieved his and Shauna's coats from the coat rack. Shauna stood up and put her coat on, looking an apology at Jackie. "I know you probably got students comin," Mouse said. He put his own jacket on and moved toward the door.

"Thanks for the cocoa," Shauna said. "It was really nice meeting you."

Jackie took both of Shauna's hands and squeezed them warmly. "It was nice meeting you, too. I hope you'll come again sometime." She turned and looked daggers at Mouse.

Mouse hesitated with his hand on the doorknob. His shoulders dropped, and he turned back into the room. "I'm sorry you had to deal with Gateway," he said.

Jackie's posture softened, too. "He has his own problems. Thanks for paying me back the money."

Mouse opened the door for Shauna, and they stepped out into the snow. Jackie closed the door behind them before they had even reached the porch steps.

"Whole city gonna be snowed in, this keeps up," Mouse said, to squelch conversation about the scene Shauna had just witnessed. He walked Shauna to her car. "I think I'm gonna go up to Cafe Nine, try to sort this mess out."

"By yourself?"

"I guess."

"You don't want to come to my place for a while?"

"I gotta lot to think about. I'll take a rain check."

"I don't give rain checks. Come on, you can't walk around with an envelope full of cash like that. At least let me drive you to the bank."

"Naw, thanks jus the same. There's a branch of the credit union up by SLU."

"You're gonna walk all the way to SLU in this weather?"

"It aint that far." They stood facing each other on the sidewalk. "You oughta give me your number, though," Mouse said. An unintentional sneer crept into his voice. "So I can call you from my new apartment."

"You are an ungrateful fuck, Joseph Watkins." She marched into the street and unlocked her car. "Don't you have any feelings at all?" She flung her door open so hard that it rebounded and slammed shut again.

"I got more feelings than I know what to do with."

"How about sparing one for me, then? Why do you have to be such a prick about everything?" Her eyes brimmed with tears.

"You kiddin me."

"Would you think about how I feel for one moment?"

"I got no idea how you feel. What the hell you care what I do, anyway?"

She enunciated slowly. "I am trying to help you."

"No, you tryin to help yourself. How you doin it through me I aint sure, but I aint your project and I aint your trip down memory lane. I got some serious shit goin down here."

"Fuck you, Mouse."

"Why don't you jus tell me what you want?"

"I *wanted* you to come home with me."

"Why?"

"Up until now, I wanted to sleep with you."

"Is that all?"

Shauna gasped as if Mouse had hit her. "You just don't get it, do you?" She opened her car door again and stood poised to get in.

Snowflakes floated gently down, sticking in their hair, clinging to their coats. For all her talk about breathing, Mouse could tell that Shauna had now stopped doing it. Finally, she let out a long breath that wreathed her face in disappointment.

"Give me my money," she said. She slammed her car door and stalked back to the sidewalk.

Mouse was sure that Jackie was watching from her living room, embarrassed about the impression this drama would make on her neighbors. Shauna was confirming all of Jackie's worst misgivings about Mouse. "What money?" Mouse said.

"For the apartment. The application."

"Alright." Mouse opened his envelope and found a hundred-dollar bill. "This'll cover lunch, too."

Shauna snatched the bill out of his hand, ripped it into pieces and threw the scraps in his face. The breeze caught the little bits of money and swirled them along the sidewalk like drifting snow.

Shauna stormed back to her car. This time, she got in and slammed the door and the engine roared to life. She gunned it into the street and fishtailed halfway down the block. Mouse was sure she was going to crash, but just when she seemed completely out of control, she eased up and slowed down, righted herself, and coasted to a stop in the middle of the street. Mouse waited for her to reverse direction or get out and yell at him; then he thought she was waiting for him to chase after her once again and apologize, as he had done in Soulard. He did nothing. The car's exhaust pipe spewed so much steam and fumes into the frigid air that Mouse couldn't see Shauna through the rear window. Finally, her taillights dimmed and she rolled slowly down the block. She turned left on Gustine Avenue and disappeared behind the houses.

Mouse rearranged the cash in his manila envelope so he could fold the whole thing double, and then he slipped the awkwardly crumpled package into his Bud Light jacket. He turned on his heels, carefully avoiding looking up at his sister's house.

He headed toward Tower Grove Park. It was nearly four

miles from Mouse's sister's house to the credit union, and he did not relish the long walk in the cold, but staying with either Shauna or Jackie had simply seemed out of the question. He was in no mood to go home to Brooklyn and have his mother congratulate him on his new job. He felt unfit for human company, and the hush that now calmed the city suited him.

He crossed Arsenal into the park, scuffling a track into the fresh powder of the open meadow. Snow fell heavier and thicker with each passing minute, and he wondered if there were any safe haven nearby. He couldn't go back to his sister's house now. He imagined sleeping in Shauna's bed, and then, the next morning, sitting in her warm kitchen while she fixed him breakfast.

Mouse blamed Gateway for everything: for making him get a job, for the disagreement with his sister, for what had happened with Shauna. It was because of Gateway that he was trudging across Tower Grove Park in the snow. Mouse's hatred of Gateway grew until it felt like a spinning metal disk in his chest. Once he had named the feeling, his contempt expanded and hardened and replaced all his other confusion.

Gateway was a counterfeit, he thought. He didn't care about anything any more but standing up there on stage, preening for the drunks, laying as many women as he could. For Gateway, the "Afrobatics" royalties justified his life, validated every crazy choice he'd ever made. Every time "Jawbreaker" had come on the radio, he'd crowed and strutted, telling everyone which part of the song he'd written, augmenting his contribution with each telling. Through "Jawbreaker," Gateway dreamed of slipping in the back door of the big time, and his delusions of grandeur had exploded like steam from a long-dormant geyser. He had no mixed feelings about this so-called success; on the contrary, he saw it as the golden road to happiness, and he wanted to hire Marvin's friend, the copyright attorney, to help the Bad Apples get more deals like this one, to publicize their songs on the internet as a treasure trove of rare, undiscovered hip-hop sampling material.

The prospect of having any more of their songs sampled disgusted Mouse, and he regretted every second that "Jawbreaker" boomed out of St. Louis car stereos. Mouse thought hip-hop little more than highway robbery, imitators and pretenders stealing music from talented artists to create bastard simulations of songs. Even when he got paid for the use of his song, he thought it cheap and degrading: any fool could take somebody else's beat and yap over it. It required almost no musical skill or knowledge, and Catfish Crunk's rhymes were nothing more than boasting and ranking, crude catcalls over a tiny snippet of a beat Mouse had laid down five years before. Mouse felt embarrassed to be associated with it. When he'd said as much, Gateway had called him an old lady and told him to go back to church, but it wasn't just the juvenile sentiments of the rap that bothered him, but the fact that the soul of the original song had been anesthetized. He had felt the same way when the Temptations' anti-greed anthem "For the Love of Money" had been used as the theme song for a television show that celebrated greed, and when Parliament's "Give Up the Funk" had been used in commercials to sell fast-food chicken strips. Having a bunch of trifling, talentless brothers use his beats to get glory offended Mouse to the core. He was a purist, and the fact that his culture wanted rappers more than funkateers alienated and enraged him. He thought rap was a failure of imagination and will, that if you had something to say in music, you should at least know how to make music, and most rappers couldn't tell the difference between a bass clef and a snare drum. He had refused to allow any more of his songs to be sampled, and that had been the irreconcilable difference that had finally broken up the band.

Mouse's feet were turning to blocks of ice as he wended through the trees and trudged across the wide fields of Tower Grove Park. The regular crunch of his shoes against the snow, his loud, heavy breathing in the stillness of the park, the shush of his wet pantlegs against each other, and the audible tick of his hood's drawstrings against his jacket created a complex calypso rhythm. The sway of the beat of his own body as he marched and the Caribbean warmth it conjured up jarred in Mouse's mind against the actual frigidness around him, and he consciously chose to lose himself in the sunny rhythm. Even when he was most vexed by day-to-day problems or philosophical questions, the pattern of a distinct rhythm could mesmerize Mouse, soothe him and focus his mind. He toyed with the rhythm of his gait, walking a little faster, dragging his feet a little more, bending his legs to create more swing and bounce for the drawstrings of his hood against his chest. It was an old, satisfying game, but by the time he reached the playground at the corner of the park, he had tired of it, and he returned to worrying about Gateway.

He secretly relished the idea of punishing Gateway with the breakup of the Bad Apples. He knew that Gate didn't have the discipline or savvy to lead a band or book gigs and that he could never handle himself in a businesslike way with club owners. Gateway had a smooth voice and an oversized magnetism, a charisma that drew people to him when he sang, but he had stopped improving on the guitar, and the songs he wrote were formulaic and simple, relying more on attitude to muscle them across than on melody. For that matter, it had been years since Gateway had even contributed a new song.

Mouse knew that he himself couldn't front a band the way Gateway could, but Gateway couldn't organize a band the way Mouse could, and Mouse felt superior because of it: he could always find another singer to sing his songs, but Gateway would have to hire himself out in order to find work. Gateway was nothing more than a hired player.

He stomped snow from his sneakers when he reached the sidewalk on Grand. It was still more than three miles to the credit union.

Traffic was crawling along the boulevard, car tires muddying the congealing snow into brown slush, and he was the only pedestrian on the block. He looked at the traffic passing him on Grand. Where is everyone going, he thought. What is everyone doing? He imagined that people believed in their lives in some way, that they did the things they did for some reason, but he honestly could not imagine what the reason was, unless it was just money. He felt the package in his jacket and wondered if that was really what it was all about, if he had been mistaken about the transcendence of music all along and the rappers had always had it right. Cream. Cash. Dollar dollar bill y'all.

It took Mouse more than half an hour to reach the bank. He stepped into the Telephone Federal Credit Union north of Lindell Boulevard and filled out the paperwork to open his own private checking account, since he had decided never to use the Apples' account again. He remembered something Amiri Baraka had written—that if you played James Brown in a bank, the whole environment would change—and he tried to blot out the Muzak that the credit union piped in by playing "Money Won't Change You (But Time Will Take You On)" over and over again in his head. Despite James Brown's sentiment, however, he did feel changed by the money, by the fact that money would now become the driving force in his life. Everything was different now, because of the money the Bad Apples wouldn't make, because of the little money they had made. He walked out of the credit union with ten temporary checks, a new account identification card in his own name and fifty dollars in cash. He felt like crying.

He stood on the street for a long time, letting snowflakes caress his face, looking up and down the sidewalk at the storefronts, the campus buildings of St. Louis University. He had walked for miles today and gone nowhere, and now he was being called by Gateway to a pointless rendezvous at Boxcars. Might as well get it over with, he thought. Might as well finish this thing and be done. He headed for Washington Boulevard to catch a bus downtown.

The Delmar bus was half-empty, and Mouse sat down in the back, next to a window. The seats were mildewed, and the whole bus stank of perfume and urine, but the heater was mercifully powerful and Mouse unzipped his jacket. He was determined to break the old pattern with Gateway, in which Mouse made a decision Gateway didn't like, then Gateway melted down, and in the aftermath of Gateway's collapse they renewed their friendship. Not this time, he thought.

When the bus crossed Jefferson, the buildings suddenly became older and emptier, and there were vacant lots where office buildings and manufacturing plants had once been, making the area feel desolate and forsaken. The sheer size of the buildings emphasized their hollow sadness. They were sometimes fifteen stories tall and a block long, with dark, gaping windows staring onto the empty street below. There was no oppressive dread, as there was in many areas of North or East St. Louis. Here, there was only loneliness, the ghost of prosperity.

Mouse stared through the grimy, scratched plastic bus window. He imagined the scenes that had surrounded these buildings when they were new, the pride and hope each one had embodied, the fading luster as each had gradually lost its purpose.

He got off at Fifteenth Street. Boxcars was almost directly

across the street from the bus stop. It was an unlikely place for a nightclub, a storefront that shared its walls with an abandoned five-story brick office building on one side and a men's clothing store called Levin's on the other. Levin's had a gleaming white tile facade three stories tall, and at street level offered window displays of mannequins dressed in business suits. Boxcars was only two stories tall and its facade was chipped black tile, forming a ragged, angry rebuttal to the clean white optimism of the clothing store.

The whole neighborhood felt uncanny with such weird contradictions: respectable old shops that survived from the garment district's heyday adjoining seedy pawnbrokers, sex shops and hulking shells of businesses. A newly renovated cell phone store sat next to a towering, empty parking garage; a plasma bank and a check-cashing center bookended a sewing machine repair shop that had been in business for sixty years. Across Fifteenth Street on Washington, an elegant eight story whitestone building with green metal window framings was entirely vacant except for a private gym that occupied the whole bottom floor. The sight of people in bright workout clothes sweating and pumping energetically in the bottom of a stately, dilapidated structure whose true purpose had vanished made Mouse feel broken.

Boxcars would not open its doors for another hour, and it would be two hours after that before the first act went on. Gateway would probably arrive twenty minutes before the show, which meant Mouse had time to kill. That was all there would be from now on, he thought, endless time to kill. His shoes were soaking wet and the temperature continued to drop. He wandered aimlessly up the street, looking for a place to keep warm.

Two blocks from Boxcars, he came to a shop whose trimming had been freshly painted and whose interior seemed incongruously warm and homey: a Christian Science Reading Room. It was the only occupied space on its block. The building next to it was gated and barred, and the building next to that had sheets of plywood nailed into its window sills.

Mouse hesitated in front of the Reading Room. Through the window, he saw wood-paneled walls and simple armchairs, a selection of books and newspapers fanned invitingly across tables. He wondered if it actually was a reading room, if you could go in and sit down and just read one of the books. No one was inside. He tried the door. It pushed open and he went in, activating a chirpy electronic chime. A decorative fountain in one corner burbled pleasantly, next to a water cooler with an attached paper cup dispenser. Mouse took another step in and looked at the books laid out on a table.

They were all by Mary Baker Eddy: *Science and Health with a Key to the Scriptures*, a book of quotations, a book of hymns and several pocket guides and pamphlets. There were current and back copies of the *Christian Science Monitor*, and some questionnaires about health and spirituality. Mouse opened the hymn book to a song called "Abide Not in the Realm of Dreams," which exhorted him to find meaning in "this very day" in the key of G. He thumbed through a few more hymns and then turned his attention to the *Monitor*, scanning the week's headlines.

He felt a strange sensation: a welcoming calm, the first moment of peace he'd had all day. It was a strangely contradictory feeling, since the vibe of the room itself suggested obsession and paranoia. It was unnaturally clean, not even a mote of dust, a dried footprint or a stray speck of mud on the floor, even on a snowy day like today, but Mouse found that this ruthless cleanliness meshed with his own misgivings about the world, and some part of his psyche felt at ease here: it was as if they were trying to scrub all of life's impurities away, not as metaphors but as facts, an attempt to forget that the outside world even existed. The titles of the books seemed self-consciously authoritative, peculiar and well-meaning.

He heard footsteps from behind a closed inner door. He put down the hymnal. The door opened and an alarmingly clean-cut white guy in a cheap blue suit and red tie came out. He was five and a half feet tall, a hundred and forty pounds, and his short, sandy blonde hair was combed to the side with such mathematical precision that he could have been wearing a plastic Halloween wig. He smiled broadly.

"Hello. Please come in."

I already been in, Mouse thought.

"May I help you with anything?"

"Uh, yeah. I dunno. Be honest, I'm supposed to meet someone up the street later, and... what does that mean, 'Reading Room?'" He pointed to the white letters painted across the plate glass window. "Can I sit here and read a book?"

"Yes, you may," the clean white guy said brightly, as if this were the best idea he had ever heard. "The Reading Room is provided by the Church of Christ, Scientist, as an oasis of prayer, reflection and meditation in this busy world. You can read our books or one of the Bibles there on the table, or you can just pray and be quiet. I take it you're not familiar with our teachings?" Mouse shook his head no. "Well, they're outlined in *Science and Health with a Key to the Scriptures*," he picked up a copy of the book, "and we've got a number of other publications here that tell about the Mother Church, about our practices and our mission. We have over two thousand branches in eighty countries worldwide."

"But I can jus sit here and read? I don't have to do anything?"

The man laughed congenially. "You can just sit here and read. It's not a library, so all the books stay here, but you're free to take the pamphlets with you or a copy of the *Christian Science Monitor*. That's our award-winning newspaper. We also offer copies of these books for sale, in case you wish to take them home, but you're not obligated, at all. The Reading Room is a community service of the church, to promote Christian Science and, more importantly, to advance an attitude of peace, serenity and prayerfulness. We want to give that prayerful attitude a prominent place in every community, and this is one way of doing it." He hadn't paused once, hadn't hemmed and hawed and searched for words. He was like a friendly robot delivering a programmed message. His smile, though broad, continuous and apparently unmotivated, seemed genuine.

"And I can sit down here and read till it's time to meet my friend?"

"That's right."

"Alright." Mouse stepped sideways and hesitated in front of an armchair, testing the man, waiting for him to add a qualification or ask for a donation. The man said nothing, so Mouse sat down. He picked up the copy of the *Monitor* again and began reading one of the articles, with one eye cocked toward the smiling white man, who hovered over him. "Thanks."

"I'll be in the back, if you have any questions or if you'd like to pray about something together. My name's Dale." He extended his hand and Mouse shook it.

"Uh, Mouse."

"Mouse. That's an unusual name."

"You know. It's a nickname."

"I see. Well, Mouse, help yourself to anything, and call if you'd like to purchase one of our books to take with you. I'll be happy to help you, in whatever way I can." Dale turned and walked back to the inner sanctum with military precision, then shut the door behind him.

I could walk outta here with an armload of books and be

halfway to the river before that Ken-doll's the wiser, Mouse thought. But then, who'd want an armload of these weird-ass books? The giggling trickle of the decorative fountain and the perfectly comfortable warmth of the air relaxed him. He looked for closed-circuit cameras, but if someone was watching, they were doing it discreetly.

He opened *Science and Health with a Key to the Scriptures*. In the first paragraph, a phrase particularly caught his attention: "Praying, watching, and working, along with self-immolation, are God's gracious means. . ." He was not sure what was meant by self-immolation, but it was such an odd turn of phrase that he kept reading. The whole book was like that: it took the basic ideas he had learned from his mother and the Baptist Church when he was growing up and twisted them so they cocked in a different direction. Some of the ideas were off-putting. Mouse had never been religious outside of his feeling for Gospel music, and the mumbo-jumbo here about Jesus's intentions for Mouse's life seemed distasteful, but some of the other notions were captivating, especially in their appeal to the incontrovertible facts of the physical universe. Existence itself provided proof to the Christian Scientists of a complex moral system that governed not just human but all natural behavior of every living and non-living thing.

Though he hadn't been looking for it, Mouse realized that this was exactly what he needed: to sit in a quiet place and become engrossed in a thought that was all about how to live and nothing about his life. He slumped down in the chair and held the book up to his face, blotting out the rest of the world. He read one page after another, taking in some of the information and letting other bits slide out of his brain. He didn't notice when the sun set and the streetlights took control of the night. He didn't notice that the snow outside was falling heavier and faster. He was even able to forget about Gateway and his new job and Shauna and his sister and the apartment in Soulard and the Bad Apples and his mother sitting in Brooklyn with the curtains drawn, surely fretting about his safety and well-being. There was no clock in the room, no one else arrived and Dale stayed in the back, quiet, so that Mouse became aware of himself again only at seven o'clock, when Dale came out to close the Reading Room for the night.

"Interesting, no?" Dale said cheerfully, putting on a gray, knee-length overcoat.

"Yeah." Mouse wondered if it had been his own muddled state of mind that had made the ideas in the book seem so clear, or if the ideas themselves held a crystal vision. "You here every day?"

"Every day but Sunday. Let me give you something." Dale retrieved a pamphlet from one of the tables and handed it to Mouse. "This is a schedule of Sunday services and other activities at our church. The address is there on the back. It's in Lafayette Park, if you know that neighborhood. We'd be glad to have you."

"Thanks," Mouse said. He looked the pamphlet over, then folded it and put it in his back pocket with all the other forms, receipts and business cards he had acquired that day.

They walked outside and Dale locked the door behind them. He rolled down a metal shutter and padlocked it to a pair of iron rings set in the walls of the building. Though it was nighttime and the street was deserted, Dale did not seem to fear Mouse, which was a relief. Without quite realizing what he was doing, Mouse walked Dale around the corner to his car.

"Pretty bad storm," Dale said cheerfully. He opened the car and got an ice scraper out of his glove box. "Can I give you a ride anywhere?" He scraped snow from his front windshield.

"Naw." Mouse pointed toward Boxcars with his thumb. "Like I said, I gotta meet my friend. But thanks anyway."

Dale cleaned and dried the scraper with a towel from his car and returned it to the glove box. He shook Mouse's hand again. "It was nice to meet you."

"Yeah, same here."

"I hope we'll see you again."

He got into his car. After a few tries, the engine turned over. Mouse stood by while he let it warm up, and then he drove off, down the snow-covered emptiness of Washington Avenue.

Mouse felt peculiar. He had spent the whole evening reading what he was sure was a cult book, and yet he felt calm and energized, and his anxiety about Gateway had almost disappeared. He walked back to Boxcars.

The neon lights were on, and a lone car was parked at a meter out front. He went in and found the bartender and a single customer watching an old kung-fu movie, without sound, on a battered television bracketed to the wall, while 1970s Philly soul music washed over the room from giant speakers in the corners. He pulled up a stool and ordered a Bud Light.

Boxcars was resolutely and intentionally low-rent. The chairs all came from thrift stores and garage sales and nothing matched. The wall decorations—unpleasant mixed-media creations—were by local artists of dubious talent, and along the ceiling the air vents and pipes were exposed and painted a reddish orange that did not go with the dark blue of the walls. The homemade stage, at the back of the room, was constructed of sloppily measured two-by-fours and raw plywood that had never been varnished or painted. The attraction of the place was that no pretensions were possible. The clientele were all struggling in some way and formed a grim camaraderie, and the drinks were cheap and generous.

"Still a show tonight?" Mouse asked.

"Your guess is good as mine," the bartender said. "You see

how it is out there."

Mouse drank his beer and watched the kung-fu movie. He began to think that he had worried about Gateway all day for nothing, that he wouldn't show up, that their problems would still be waiting for them tomorrow. Beyond closing the Apples' bank account and deciding how to split up the piddling royalties they might earn in the future, there was really nothing to talk about anyway. It was over. Their tour van had broken down seemingly for good last month, and it was rusting away in Mouse's mother's driveway: maybe Mouse would float Gateway a few dollars for his part in the van, but it could hardly be considered an asset any more. Their amps and mikes and mixing board could be a bone of contention, but Gateway had borrowed money from the band against his share in the equipment twice in the last year, and he had never repaid the loans, so Mouse considered the equipment his. After sitting in the Reading Room all evening, the clot of hatred that had been moving toward Mouse's heart now loosened, and he felt that he should make a clean break. His brother-in-law Marvin often advised his clients that divorces cost a lot of money because they were worth every penny, and Mouse began to feel the worth of his divorce from Gateway more than its cost.

He ordered another Bud Light and felt more relaxed. An hour passed and a few stragglers wandered into Boxcars, but the weather was keeping people away and it looked more and more like Gateway and Oscar would miss the gig. Mouse ordered a shot with his third beer and descended into a reverie about all of the people who had ever played in the Bad Apples, the stellar horn players who had left to take jobs at theme parks, the guys who had defected to Red Giant (an old-school funk band that had been the Apples' main competition in St. Louis for many years), and all the deadbeats who had flamed out or given up or just gotten older and quit.

The front door flew open with special violence and Gateway and Oscar strutted in. "The party has arrived!" Oscar shouted, and Boxcars' few patrons gave him a Bronx cheer.

Oscar was a good guitar player and a good-looking kid, twenty-three years old with reddish skin and short dreadlocks. He had joined the Apples the year before. He idolized Gateway, and Gateway was glad to have a disciple, but Oscar and Gateway reinforced each other's worst habits. It was through Oscar that Gateway had gotten back into drugs, and Gateway had filled Oscar's head with half-baked Black nationalist theories and fantasies of stardom.

Oscar led the way in, carrying an acoustic guitar case whose battered surface was entirely obscured by a riot of bumper stickers. Gateway followed, wearing what looked like a brand new black leather coat and a flowing red scarf. For all the talk of his craziness and his weekend-long bender, he looked remarkably put-together.

"Fuckin freezin out there, Jim," Gateway shouted at the bartender. "Set us up a round." Gate was almost to the bar before he realized that Mouse was sitting there, hunched into his drink. "Shit! Mouse motherfuckin Watkins. Comin out of his castle!" Gateway's speech was clear, but his eyes were wild and predatory, and he licked his lips in an unsettlingly reptilian way. Mouse figured he was speeding or cranking.

Mouse said, "Gotta come outta the castle to see how the peasants live." Mouse had not intended to be belligerent, but his tone rose to meet Gateway's.

Oscar strolled past Mouse, adopting a put-on gangsta lean that he had probably learned from movies, since he had grown up in the affluent suburb of Clayton. He intentionally bumped Mouse's shoulder, then stood behind Mouse while Gateway approached.

"Bud Light here wanna know how the peasants livin,"

Gateway said to Oscar.

Mouse stood up. He didn't realize how drunk he was until he swayed against the bar. Gateway stuck his chest out at him and exchanged a look with Oscar. It seemed that Gateway had found a new partner-in-crime, a replacement for Mouse, and he didn't need Mouse to rescue him any more. This notion unexpectedly angered Mouse.

"I'm waitin," Mouse said. "What're these 'things' we gotta settle?"

"I'm takin over the Apples," Gateway said. "I'm gonna keep sellin the songs."

"No you aint. They aint your songs."

"As much mine as yours."

"Yeah, but still not yours. You caint do it without me."

"That aint what Oscar says."

"Oscar don't count for shit."

The bartender set draft beers in front of Oscar and Gateway. He nodded at Oscar's guitar. "You can set up and play whenever you're ready." The bartender stood across from Mouse, trying to will everyone to be civil.

"You not the only one with a lawyer in the family," said Gateway. "You aint gonna ruin my earning potential jus cause you quittin."

"Earning potential? Who taught you that?"

"Shared copyright does not imply shared rights control," said Oscar. "It only implies shared compensation."

Mouse looked from Gateway to Oscar. Their pupils were pinning from whatever drugs they had taken, but their speech was as clear as could be.

"Catfish Crunk wanna sample 'We Hold These Grooves To Be Self-Evident.'"

"Fuck that. We shouldna let'em have 'Afrobatics,' and they damn sure caint have 'Grooves.'"

"Yeah, well, I'll send you a check, cause we already set up the contract. I jus asked you down here to give you a chance to sign on, but we doin it with or without you."

"That's my song. You didn't have nothin to do with it."

"That's a Bad Apples song, and if you aint part of the band, you don't get to say." He exchanged a look with Oscar. "I'm tired of you messin up the band, messin up things for me. You think you so pure and noble, like you better'n everyone, but that aint how the world is, and you aint takin me for a ride no more."

"Takin *you* for a ride?" Mouse said. "You been gravy-trainin me for years. The Apples aint nothin without me! Whatchyou *ever* done that I aint done for you?"

"Well, you aint never done this for me."

Mouse didn't understand what he meant, since Gateway waited nonchalantly for a moment before throwing a lightning quick uppercut. His fist caught Mouse's chin, a glancing blow, but Mouse was drunk enough and surprised enough that he staggered back into Oscar, who pushed him forward into Gateway, who landed a much heavier punch to his abdomen. Mouse doubled over.

"All right, all right!" the bartender yelled. He raced around the bar, and a customer helped him separate the combatants. "You're outta here. Bad enough it's the slowest fuckin night of the year."

The bored bar patrons manhandled the adversaries out the door in a scrum. They heaved Mouse and Gateway into the night, where they tumbled into each other and then splayed across the slippery sidewalk. The bar crowd went back inside. Mouse and Gateway were left alone with Oscar in the swirling snow and ice. They picked themselves up and stared at each other.

Mouse couldn't believe Gateway was cutting another deal

with Catfish Crunk—maybe he had still more deals for other songs already lined up! Now Mouse might have to go begging at Marvin's door for legal help. They were *his* songs, but he didn't know enough about copyright to understand how the division of ownership might affect his ability to stop Gateway from using them. But that problem would have to wait for later: as long as Gateway stood poised in front of him, drawing strength from his little pal Oscar, Mouse could not turn away. He was addled and confused, and from the looks of things, the new, fraudulent Bad Apples had a plan for him.

Behind Gateway's pulsating pupils burned rage and indignation, as if Mouse had attacked him. Mouse suddenly realized that there was no reasonable way for either of them to handle the breakup of the band, and that this was probably how it had to end, absurdly, in a show of dumb bravado. Every breakup probably ended with some kind of violence—physical, emotional, artistic— and lawyers and court orders. But the songs! He couldn't sell the songs!

A steady breeze was swirling snowflakes down Mouse's collar. His bared knuckles, raised to mirror Gateway's, were chapped and freezing, and even the adrenalized sweat in his palms felt clammy and cold. The streetlamps looked as unreal as freshly shaken snowglobes.

"Come on, man," Oscar said. "We aint gotta stand out here with this fool."

Gateway stuck out his chin. He tested his footing on the icy sidewalk.

"Either you believe in the Funk or you don't," Mouse said. "Catfish Crunk aint Funk."

"You so full a shit, Mouse. Look at James Brown. You think James Brown believed in the Funk? Them old songs of his made more money as samples than they ever did as songs." Gateway spat on the sidewalk. "You sayin James Brown didn't believe in the Funk? He invented it!"

"Yeah but 'The Payback' is funky. 'My Lovin' aint!"

"You so fuckin stupid sometimes it make me wanna scream. 'Jawbreaker' was the first song we ever sold, and it made us money, Mouse." His tone turned from anger to pleading. "Why you gotta be so stubborn all the time? Why's everything your way or no way?"

"Cause I don't want some punks stealin my music."

"It aint stealin if they pay for it. And we wrote the songs, motherfucker, that's our music. I dunno what world you livin in, man. You got this idea of purity or somethin, but that shit don't exist in the world. What's gonna happen now with all them songs we wrote? Nothin? We talkin 'bout gettin paid, 'bout not workin at fuckin Anheuser-Busch. You twisted, Mouse. It's like you losin somethin if somebody pay you for your music. You think James Brown ever turn down a dollar bill over some shit like 'rap aint real music?' What is that shit, man? You broke up the band the first time we ever got a song on the radio."

"That wasn't nothin we did."

"Both our names on 'Jawbreaker,' we wrote that song sure as we wrote 'Afrobatics.' That's how the world works."

"It aint how I work."

"I keep forgettin. You work for Bud Light."

Mouse wondered how Gateway knew about his new job, how he could have negotiated a deal with Catfish Crunk in the last four days while he was on a bender. Maybe he'd been negotiating behind Mouse's back for a long time now. Then, a surprising new thought occurred to him: maybe Gateway aint lost touch with reality, after all. Maybe I have.

Mouse felt the whole weight of their friendship, the gravity of thirty years, screwing them into place on the sidewalk. Gateway became mesmerizing in his righteous rage, like a messenger angel sent from on high—but what was the message?

Dimly, at the edge of his awareness, Mouse heard a car engine coming up the street behind him. It drew closer and closer, until it stopped right beside them, its engine purring smoothly. Gateway feinted a punch at Mouse, and Mouse bobbed backward.

Oscar turned toward the car. It idled beside them for a long time, and then Mouse heard a door open.

Gateway feinted again, but this time Mouse held his ground, daring Gateway to hit him.

"Jesus Christ," a woman said. "What are you guys, five years old?"

The voice was familiar, but in his agitated state Mouse couldn't place it. He finally took his eyes off of Gateway and turned. It was Shauna. She was standing on her driver's side runner.

"Come on, Mouse, let me give you a ride a home."

Mouse felt his whole world condense into the socket around his right eye. His right foot lost its purchase on the sidewalk and he slipped on the ice. He hit the ground flat, and his head snapped back into the sidewalk with a sickening smack. Gateway had suckerpunched him! He suddenly couldn't move, and he heard Shauna's distant voice coming closer, yelling.

He saw little dots of green light racing away, into the blackness in front of his eyes. His brain was hammering his skull from the inside. Everything seemed chaotic and broken. When he opened his eyes, he felt like throwing up.

Shauna was kneeling beside him, cooing sympathetically while she evaluated him with a nurse's expert touch. He was no longer aware of Oscar and Gateway, and he could not understand what Shauna was saying, but she helped him to his feet.

The objects on the street lost their outlines. He walked with jelly legs through liquifying forms to Shauna's car. She helped him inside and buckled his seatbelt. The blast of warm air from the heater felt like hell itself.

Shauna got in and put the car in gear. Mouse laid his head back against the seat and it slid in a disturbing way. He put his hand to the back of his head and felt blood. Shauna guided the car away from the curb and Mouse oozed involuntarily in his seat like unset pudding. He opened his mouth to speak, but no words came out.

The streets were empty, but the snow forced Shauna to drive deliberately, slowly. Mouse stared through the windshield, trying to have a thought. It wasn't until they had plowed all the way up to Grand Boulevard that he could form words in his mind, and by the time the words got to his mouth, they had turned into a dry pant. "You come. . ." He tried to swallow but couldn't. ". . .all the way. . . from Rock Hill?"

"Looks like."

"For me?"

"For Beanie Rice and the Chickens."

The heater made Mouse sleepy, and he closed his eyes and felt his head droop.

"Hey!" Shauna yelled. She took one hand off the wheel and cupped Mouse's chin, turned his head so that he had to look her in the face. The whole world swam. "You will not go to sleep! You hear me! You will not go to sleep! All right? Hey!" She pinched his nose, and Mouse blinked his eyes hard and felt his tongue, seemingly twice its normal size, stick to the roof of his mouth. He looked up at the dizzyingly high green copper roof of SLU Hospital. Shauna turned off the heat and rolled down Mouse's window. The cold air felt good. She flipped on the radio and turned the volume all the way up, and Mouse didn't know whether to laugh or cry: the song that came blasting out was "Jawbreaker.

Part 2

Work

Every day, Mouse walked home from Busch with a twelve-pack of Bud Light, put it in the refrigerator and started drinking. Though it was insipid, it did the trick. He passed out early and slept until starting time next morning, when he would jump out of bed and race around the corner to One Busch Place. The sprint through the cold morning air would wake him up and by the time he punched in, he was usually alert enough to fake it till the first coffee break.

"Yo! Yo yo Mouse! Hold up! Yo Mouse stop!!"

Mouse stopped the forklift and turned to face his crew leader, Joao. Joao was twenty-eight years old, a wiry, muscular African who had come to the United States as a child from Angola. His family had fled the South African invasion, and Joao had spent three years in a refugee camp before obtaining a sponsorship from the AME Church to come to America. He had lived in St. Louis for more than twenty years, but he still spoke with a Portuguese accent, which lent his commands an alien authority.

Joao was the most industrious person Mouse had ever met. He sent a quarter of his Busch paycheck home to Angola to support his family, and he took odd jobs at night so he could send more. His dedication, and his history as a refugee struggling just to survive, made Mouse's distaste for straight jobs seem shameful.

"How many times I gotta tell you?" Joao said. "The

stamped side goes *toward* the truck."

The palette of beer cases suspended on the end of Mouse's forklift was facing the wrong direction, again. Mouse had to lower the palette to the platform and maneuver the lift to the other side. Joao and four of Mouse's coworkers stood and watched, delaying the whole crew and the truck driver waiting to roll. It was the second time this morning Mouse had made the same mistake, which was exasperating for Mouse more than anyone: he actually liked driving the forklift and was better and faster with it than his crewmates, but he couldn't keep his mind on the simplest details of his task.

"Keep your head in, Mouse," said Joao. "The whole team needs you."

Mouse felt the contempt of the other seasonal workers. Each time he slowed the work of the crew, he jeopardized their chances at permanent jobs. The full-time guys leaned against the refrigerated truck and relaxed while Mouse reversed direction and lifted the beer from the correct side.

In spite of Mouse's indifference, he was a better-than-average beer warehouser. His years of drumming gave him stamina, strength and the ability to do several different things at once without thinking too much about it, and he was quick to learn mechanical tasks. He also perceived patterns in the flow of the work that others missed, and he tackled his job with an order and symmetry that was so ingrained in his nature that he didn't notice how much it set him apart. However, since he was bleary in the mornings, apathetic in the afternoons and defiant all the time, his presence was a constant irritant to those around him.

"If you get your head right," Joao would say, "you could really do something at Busch, but you have to show'em you care, you have to concentrate and keep the mistakes down. Management here pays attention, you know? They see how people really are."

The last thing Mouse wanted was for anyone to see how he really was. His whole identity was now an open question, from his career to his relationships and even his appearance.

In order to stitch up Mouse's head after his fight with Gateway, the emergency room doctor had shaved a wide, ragged swatch out of his voluminous afro, and it had been impossible to make it look right again. Mouse had reluctantly shaved the rest of his hair off, and though his new look fit better with the cueballed brothers on the Busch loading dock, he felt as weak as Samson.

He stared at himself drunk in his bathroom mirror every night, unable to recognize his ears, his face, even the look in his own eyes. He would caress his bald head and wax poetic about the philosophy he'd carried in his 'fro. He'd always worn his whole life's work—his message, his politics, his funk—on the outside of his head, but now, as a bald man, his message remained invisible to the world, trapped inside his head, where it could hurt him most.

Mouse had received encouragement in his new life from an unexpected source: his brother-in-law Marvin. Marvin was delighted by Mouse's sudden change of circumstance and took an avuncular interest in his life, and once Marvin got behind him, Jackie followed suit. Though Soulard was too bohemian for their tastes, they thought Mouse's new apartment a world better than Brooklyn or East St. Louis, and they were relieved that he was finally working a regular job, however temporary, since it could lead to "better" things. They had loaned him some nice furniture from their basement, and Marvin had paid a team of professional movers to set him up in his new place. Shauna had helped him buy a queen-sized bed from a secondhand shop on The Hill, and Mouse's mother had given him cookware and place settings. He traded a bass amp for a cheap stereo system, and just like that he was guzzling Bud Light in a furnished two-bedroom walkup near the Soulard Market, exactly as he'd daydreamed it on the day of his interview at Busch.

In order to keep making the rent, however, Mouse would have to find another job that paid at least nine dollars an hour the moment his warehousing position ended. With Marvin's help, he thought, he might get a few interviews for other work; but he could stomach the job he had now only by drinking great quantities of beer every night, and he felt yoked by his family's renewed interest in his life. He was sure that their encouragement would turn to resentment the minute he was unable or unwilling to follow their program.

Mouse usually ate lunch alone in a corner of the Busch cafeteria, his eyes lasered into a book of poetry, his shoulders hunched, consciously warding off any attempts at conversation. Today, the temperature was below freezing and sleet had fallen throughout the morning; no one was venturing out to the restaurants in Soulard, and the cafeteria was full. Mouse bought a ham sandwich and chips from the vending machines and was forced to sit with some guys he didn't recognize at a long aluminum table. They gave him a chance to join their hashing over the Rams' playoff prospects, but when it became clear he wasn't interested, they turned their backs to him and he brooded over his sandwich, trying to ignore their sports prattle.

Joao walked up and took a seat across the table. He scrutinized Mouse's book.

"Poetry?"

"Yeah. Some Arabic stuff I found."

"I'll trade you." Mouse's crew leader set a plastic-wrapped chunk of bread and a paper cup of coffee at Mouse's elbow. Then he took Mouse's book, opened it and read part of a poem. He nodded and handed the book back. "Dessert," Joao said. "I make a big batch of pumpkin bread every Halloween, then freeze it."

Mouse unwrapped the thick slice of orange bread and poked it with his index finger: it was spongy and moist and filled with dark chunks. He ate a piece, then washed it down with a sip of the tasteless coffee Joao had bought from the automat.

"Thanks."

"I like to bake. Reminds me of home."

"Tastes more like cake than bread."

"Better for you than cake, though. No sugar. Just honey and dates."

Mouse felt that he was expected to say something but didn't know what. "Well, thanks."

"I was wondering what you're doing this Sunday?"

"Uh. I dunno."

"I'd like to invite you to come to church with me. There's a service at eight-thirty and one at ten-thirty, and they serve a little meal after each one. Nothing fancy, but I think you'd like it."

Mouse looked at the pumpkin bread more skeptically. His supervisor was recruiting him.

Joao lowered his voice and leaned closer. "Do you know our Lord Jesus Christ? You act troubled sometimes, Mouse, and I wonder if you know that Jesus can help you make sense of things."

Mouse felt sick. Joao's well-meaning attempt to help him felt somehow like a betrayal. "Thing is," Mouse lied, "I kinda been goin to this church already, kinda got my own church, so. . . you know, thanks, but. . ."

"What church do you attend?" Joao's accent made the question seem formal, like a cross-examination.

Mouse jostled his brain for the name of a church. He could think only of his mother's baptist church in Brooklyn and Saints Peter and Paul Catholic Church around the corner in Soulard, but both these lies seemed fraught with difficulty, if Joao pursued them. Then he remembered the Christian Science Reading Room downtown, and he said, "Church of Christ Scientist."

"Hmm. I've heard of them, but I'm not familiar with their teachings."

"They believe in science and health and clean livin, like that. It's a regular church."

The chime for the next shift sounded. Mouse finished the slice of pumpkin bread and took his coffee with him outside, where the sleet had turned to snow. Joao gave him a friendly clap on the back as they walked.

"I'm glad to know you have a personal relationship with Jesus," he said. "We'll have to talk more, and maybe we can visit each other's churches."

"Alright."

"You know, I love to learn more about our Lord, about different ways of finding him and thinking about him. I know he has a plan for my life." He smiled at Mouse. "He has a plan for your life, too."

After their conversation about Jesus, Joao made a special point of looking Mouse in the eye and giving him encouragement, which irritated Mouse. He would now be forced to maintain a falsified churchgoing persona with Joao, and Joao would feel connected to him because of their supposed mutual faith. He was furious with himself for not having the internal fortitude to tell the truth.

Mouse had this problem in every phase of his life these days. He was unsure what the truth was any more, so he played chameleon, mimicked the views of those around him, said things he thought would get him through the day with the least effort and controversy. He had no regard whatsoever for the accuracy of what he said, and then he hated himself for lying and hated the other people for forcing him to lie. He had no opinions or feelings about his work, no opinions about himself. He only wished to be left alone.

"Mouse! Yo yo stop Mouse! Hold up!!"

Mouse cringed. He had stopped paying attention and picked up yet another palette of beer cases from the wrong end.

"Hey Lorenzo," Joao said. "Why don't you take the lift for a while?"

Mouse stepped out of the forklift. Lorenzo smirked as he climbed behind the controls, and Mouse took his place with the rest of the crew on the other side of the palette. His crewmates refused to look him in the eye. He made a big cloud of steam with his breath.

The first time Mouse saw the helicopter landing at One Busch Place, he assumed there was a medical emergency. The second time, he asked Joao and was dumbfounded to learn that the chairman of Anheuser-Busch often flew his own private helicopter to work from his estate outside St. Louis. Mouse didn't even own a bicycle, and his boss was flying a private helicopter.

He learned about the rise and steady expansion of the Anheuser-Busch empire from the abundant promotional literature placed throughout the plant. Especially prominent in the break rooms were fliers detailing the company's charitable works and the professional opportunities available to all workers, no matter their race, creed, gender or color. In the locker rooms were placards trumpeting the fabulous historical successes of the Busch family and its plans for continued international dominance of the brewing industry. Oddly, none of the pamphlets mentioned that Anheuser-Busch had recently been bought by Belgian beer giant InBev and was now merely an arm of a multinational brewing conglomerate. That little detail, Mouse thought, would send a mixed message about America's favorite beer—better to keep the Bud Light patriotic.

The promotional materials included stories of the company's founders that reminded Mouse of the chronicles of great religious figures. One pamphlet even described how Adolphus Busch, the patriarch, had obtained the recipe for Budweiser from German-Catholic monks. The dominant theme, which was repeated in every poster and notice, was that the Busch empire would continue to expand and prosper and all you had to do to share in their success was hitch your little wagon to Busch's majestic team of Clydesdales and let them carry you.

The postings of actual available jobs gave Mouse a somewhat different impression. There were almost no positions for which he qualified. They needed engineers, lab technicians, metal machinists, steamfitters, horse handlers and other technical personnel with vast amounts of education, experience or both; salespeople, field representatives and tour guides for their breweries, positions that required genuine enthusiasm; and management positions, such as the one Bobby Grant had worked forty years to obtain. There was only one permanent position on the Busch job board that Mouse could reasonably apply for: warehouse technician, the job he was already doing, for the third shift, which meant overnight from ten-thirty in the evening to seven in the morning. The overnight warehousers were responsible for filling up palettes with beer orders, so the palettes would be ready the next morning for the first shift warehousers to load and ship. Even thinking about it made Mouse feel heavy.

His crewmate Lorenzo carried a copy of the warehouse

technician job description in his pocket, and he would take it out and hold it up for his coworkers to see. "I'm gonna get that job, y'all," he would say. "That's my job, so aint no reason for y'all to even apply. I'm more qualified than y'all and hungrier than y'all and faster than y'all. Third shift be my shift, baby."

"That's the attitude, Zo," Joao would say. "Of course, the job's open to everybody. The whole city, the whole world. Anybody can walk through those gates and apply."

"It don't matter. Could be the King of Beers hisself come and apply, cause caint nobody load up a palette faster than Zo. Might as well give me them orders to fill right now, and I'll just work all night."

This kind of talk would continue for some time, with all the temporary crew members but Mouse joining in, each person telling how he was most qualified and why he was going to get the single available job over the other applicants. The talk often evolved into the dozens, with even the white guys joining in and Joao officiating and using the game to pace the work. Mouse was too sullen and contemptuous to play along, and he made himself the butt of everyone's jokes by standing off.

He didn't understand how his crewmates could get so excited about competing for the lowest possible position in one of the largest companies in the world. They were begging to be fleas biting the ass of a giant Clydesdale. Some of the men had families to support, and some, like Joao, were immigrants who desperately wanted their slice of the American pie, but the fact that a company whose head man flew a helicopter to work could generate this kind of enthusiasm among the poorest and least qualified workers in the city depressed Mouse. They should just land that helicopter on our backs, he thought.

"You think you so above it all," Lorenzo said to Mouse one day, "but I seen how much Bud Light you been buyin up at the company store. You supportin the company one way and another just like the rest of us. Mm-hm."

After that, Mouse stopped drinking Budweiser.

"What do you care what they think?" Shauna asked Mouse one night.

"Like I'm tellin you, I don't care."

"Obviously you do, or it wouldn't be bothering you so much."

Shauna was in Mouse's kitchen frying chicken breasts. Mouse sat on the bare hardwood floor in his living room sorting through his compact disc collection, reliving the memories attached to each album, each song, the places he had purchased them. The fire in the fireplace popped and shushed and made him sweat.

Shauna was a good cook, and as long as her hospice patient in Soulard stayed alive, they had a nice arrangement: she worked overnight at her patient's house three days a week, and she came to Mouse's apartment in the evenings, before her shift. He would just be getting home from Busch; she would fix dinner, and they would make love. Afterward, Mouse would walk her to her patient's house.

"I brought that nice bottle of white wine," she called. "Or do you want beer?"

"Wine's good."

Mouse felt aggrieved by the stacks of plastic cases all around him. Most of his CDs were scratched and old and skipped when played, and many of them were too obscure to have resale value, especially now, when everyone just loaded there iPods up with tunes from the internet instead of buying discs. He'd collected them on the road, buying the recordings of other struggling bands to help keep their music alive, to help ensure that control of the music industry stayed out of the hands of the crass corporate mega-labels and in the hands of the musicians who made the music. But this political act had left him with boxes full of mediocre music and now that CDs were a bygone technology, they were little more than trash. Most of the bands had split up, anyway.

What was it they had all been dreaming of, Mouse wondered, all these bands whose haplessness cluttered his living room? He found Funkadelic's *One Nation Under A Groove*, the last commercially successful album of the Parliament/Funkadelic collective. Was that what he'd wanted to be, a famous psychedelic funkateer wearing chartreuse bell bottoms and rhinestone-studded sunglasses? It seemed ridiculous now.

Shauna came back into the living room. She turned over one of Mouse's empty storage boxes, set a candleholder on it and lit the candle, then brought out two plates of steaming chicken, mashed potatoes and boiled spinach. She sat down and raised her wine in a toast, "To the world's sexiest bald man."

Mouse touched the top of his head. Shauna always exposed Mouse's debilitating self-absorptions with just such inscrutability: on their surface, her comments could be taken either as mockery or encouragement, and Mouse never knew by her tone which they really were. He clinked her glass and drank.

"You know, you only have the job for two months," Shauna said. "It seems like a waste of energy to make up a lie every time anybody asks a question. And then you have to keep the lies straight in your head." She drank a long swallow of wine. "Why not tell them the truth?"

"I don't want them knowin me at all, that's the point. That aint me they see at Busch." He tore into his chicken breast.

Mouse felt deeply embarrassed about being a Busch warehouser. If he ever told his crewmates the real truth, he would have to introduce himself as a failure who had squandered his youth, missed his chances; a martyr for a cause he no longer believed in; a man who had never done anything manly or even worthwhile, whose energy had been spent furiously leaping and grabbing at one longshot after another, like a monkey lunging at rotten fruit in a cage. He looked at the scratched CDs of defunct, unknown bands strewn around his living room: that was the truth, a truth he couldn't even begin to tell the insanely optimistic Joao or the snide Lorenzo.

"I just wanna avoid confrontation," Mouse said. "No reason to bring up a lotta issues they don't care about. Only thing matters at Busch is movin them cases of beer."

"Then why do you sit here and piss and moan about the conversations you have with these guys?" Shauna finished her glass of wine and refilled it. "You're just hurting yourself, the way you handle these people."

"Can we drop it?"

"Nobody at that place is gonna think poorly of you if you say what you really think. You don't go to church? So what? You're not a career warehouser? Hell, half those people are temps like you, barely have jobs, probably all messed up somehow or other, and I bet they never did *anything* for themselves, not like the Apples. You're not a failure, Mouse, that's all there is to it. You think I'd hang out with a failure?" She drank half of her second glass of wine. "You know that *Cutting Edge of Funknology*? That's one of my all-time favorite albums, by anybody. I was still listening to that still a month ago, even before I met you again."

The Cutting Edge of Funknology was the Bad Apples' fourth album, produced twelve years earlier on Mouse's and Gateway's own label. Mouse thought it their best effort, the only CD he wouldn't change at all, if he could do everything over again.

"Maybe," he said, "but nobody at Busch wanna hear about

that. It's like, if you so great, why you here loadin beer? You think you better'n us? That's they attitude."

"And you'd rather pretend to be the kind of loser they are than admit to being the kind of loser you think they think you are? That's messed up, Mouse."

"That's how it is."

"That's not how it is! You're not a loser, and nobody thinks so but you!"

Mouse imagined a Renaissance artist that nobody had ever heard of, some great master, whose paintings were as good as Michelangelo's but who died unknown, whose canvases were lost to the garbage heap of history. Would such a painter's genius matter?

"Maybe you oughtta call yourself Joseph."

Mouse made a face.

"Well?" Shauna said. "Mouse is a stage name, and if you're not gonna be on stage, maybe you should stop reminding yourself that you used to be."

"It aint a stage name. It's a nickname. I like my name."

"All right. Just a suggestion. I'm only trying to help."

All anyone does any more is try to help me, he thought, but nobody has the slightest idea what I need. He didn't know himself, so the help that was proffered needled and vexed him. To change the subject, he asked about Shauna's hospice patient, a topic she could discuss at great length without much prompting; and as she divulged the intimate details of her patient's last days on earth, Mouse drank great gulps of wine.

He watched the way Shauna moved her hands when she spoke, making fast fluid arcs like a sheet billowing on a line; the childlike animation in her features; her gray-green eyes pulsating hypnotically, widening and narrowing as she became excited. He admired her gracefully curved lips, which were the same vibrant strawberry color as her hair and seemed liquid and cool, like fresh brushstrokes. There were tiny reddish brown freckles scattered across her forehead and around her ears, but otherwise her skin was pure and pale, supple and unlined despite her age and nicotine habit.

As with everything in his life, he didn't know whether his budding relationship with Shauna was good fortune or ill. Despite the fact that she could be abrupt and difficult, she was enthusiastic about their affair. He imagined that she was deeply lonely and liked the convenience of a ready-made boyfriend, a more or less known quantity from the past: he was a project that got her out of the house and made her contemplate the course her life had taken. He assumed she was working out some mid-life questions of her own, and that once she found the answers she would disappear again, as she had before.

Still, she was less flighty than Mouse had initially assumed. She had spent a whole weekend buying fabrics and sewing new curtains for every window in Mouse's apartment. She had hand-formed, fired and glazed two ceramic roses for the chandelier in the dining room, to replace missing originals. She had installed a massaging jet showerhead in Mouse's bath. Being a homeowner had made the once reckless Vita DuPlease crafty, handy and practical, and she was full of ideas for improving Mouse's apartment. She was also not shy about spending money on him: she paid for the food they ate together, for all the materials of her housewarming projects, and she even bought bottles of whiskey and gin to leave at his apartment, most of which he drank himself. He was glad for her generosity, and her company.

They finished their dinner and stacked the dishes in the sink, and Shauna led Mouse into the bedroom. They took their time removing their clothes, kissing each other on the neck and lips and nose, caressing each other's whole bodies gently. Shauna never let her eyes stray too long from Mouse's, and her gaze held no challenges, only warmth and acceptance. When Mouse had known Shauna as Vita DuPlease, their sex had been gymnastic and outlandish, with S & M props, game-playing and role reversals—theatrical sex more for the sake of breaking taboos than connecting emotionally. But now Shauna leaned toward simple, predictable gestures, expressions that her earlier self would have considered dull. It was the opposite of the sex they had had in their youth, sedate in its movements but wild in its effects, creating a space of intimacy and recognition that Mouse felt was a gift. Making love with Shauna was the only thing Mouse did that wasn't psychologically jagged and fraught with anxiety, and though she made it clear that she would do anything he wanted her to do, all they ever did was face each other and move quietly in and around each other and stare into one another's eyes.

After they were finished, they lay silent, nestled together in their blankets. Shauna's watch alarm told her it was time to go. They dressed in heavy winter clothes and walked downstairs.

This was the earliest, coldest winter in St. Louis memory, and flurries were falling again. The blacktop of Menard Street was obscured by a pristine layer of snow, as yet unmarred by tire tracks. Shauna put her arm through Mouse's and snuggled close into his body as they walked. Her hospice patient lived only a few blocks away, and they were soon at his door. She kissed Mouse extravagantly, her lips still tasting of chicken and wine and sex, and told him to be good to himself and go to bed early.

When he returned home, Mouse put a copy of *The Cutting Edge of Funknology* into his CD player. He didn't listen to the Apples' music much and hadn't heard this old album in years, so the cleanness of the production surprised him. He tried to imagine it from Shauna's perspective, the attack of the horns on the opening track over the modified rhumba cadence of the extra percussion, the toms and bongos and djembe all insinuating themselves around a square drum pattern, the bass playing triples and the scratch guitar filtered through a wah pedal, oscillating around the horns as they came in again before the opening verse. The whole album was a heady stew of saxophones and midi-strings, Latin percussion and slap bass, an exuberant declaration of absurdity in the face of privation, the most elaborate, expensive and technically produced of the Apples' albums, the one Mouse had known would put them over the top.

After a favorable mention in the St. Louis *Post-Dispatch* and a splashy feature in the *Riverfront Times*, the band had built some momentum around *The Cutting Edge*. They headlined a bar tour of the Midwest and newspapers were calling for advance interviews and writing reviews comparing them to the biggest stars, but just when they seemed poised to break into the big time, their bass player was jailed on a domestic violence charge and Gateway nearly killed himself on a drug overdose and wound up in rehab. There had never been any trouble in the band before, but as they approached the brink of success, their personal problems seemed to multiply, they fought among themselves and the black hole of imminent achievement sucked them in and spit them out. The band had almost collapsed completely, and by the time Mouse had picked up the pieces, people had forgotten about *The Cutting Edge of Funknology* and their momentum was lost. They were forced to start again, practically from scratch, now with drugs and domestic battery attached to their names. Even the smallest taste of success had proven more bitter than their steady diet of failure.

Mouse hit the stop button halfway through the album. He turned out all the lights and took a bottle of Henessey to bed with him.

Every Saturday morning, Mouse slept late and then wandered half-conscious to the Soulard Farmer's Market for coffee and candy-sprinkled doughnuts. Winter was the off-season anyway, but the persistent snow and ice was keeping even die-hard suburbanite regulars off the freeways and away from the Market. Only the locals from Soulard or Lafayette Park bought groceries there now, and the enclosed center arcade became listless, the sounds muffled by thick plastic insulation around the windows. The vendors complained that the central heating wilted their vegetables (which, in the wintertime, had already spent many days on ships and trucks), and customers complained that the quality of the produce didn't warrant the high off-season prices. Mouse liked to listen to them complain, and he liked the subdued atmosphere and the homemade preserves and fresh-baked bread that the farmers' wives sold to make ends meet.

This morning, the heat of the arcade was stifling, and Mouse took his candied doughnut and coffee outside, where the temperature was below freezing. There was no middle ground this winter between fever and chills. The radiated heat in Mouse's apartment was always broiling, but if he shut the valves or opened a window, the frigid air iced his blood. The Busch loading docks were kept at thrity-eight degrees year-round, but the work made Mouse sweat through his winter clothes, and he took his coat off and put it back on again like a nervous habit throughout the day. Most irritating, the season's bitter cold seemed to emphasize the constant stiffness in his muscles. Though he lifted and shifted heavy crates all day, the work was neither as various nor as subtle as drumming, and he never felt loose the way he did after even a single set behind his kit.

He walked up Lafayette to Eighth Street and looked for the blonde woman he had seen on the morning of his job interview with Bobby Grant. He had seen her smoking on that balcony a few times since that day. He always nodded a greeting to her and she always stared at him sphinxlike. The very fact of her fascinated Mouse, the fact of all these people closed up in their beautiful apartments, the simple yet unexplainable lives they were living. He eavesdropped on their conversations at the Market, watched them coming home from work and sitting in the bars and clubs, laughing and drinking. Now he was one of them, yet his neighbors felt alien and strange, and he had to remind himself not to stare.

He waited for several minutes below the blonde woman's balcony, sipping his coffee. The woman did not appear.

At the corner of Eighth and Allen, he noticed that the chapel door of Saints Peter and Paul Catholic Church was open a crack, and he decided to look at the church's towering stained glass windows from inside. He finished his doughnut and opened the door.

Beyond the nave, a cavernous sanctuary opened, lit solely by muted light filtered through the stained glass saints. The arched, buttressed ceiling was more than thirty feet high; the chapel's flowing design and gray stonework suggested cool serenity, but the air inside was doughy and warm and Mouse began to sweat. The play of sanguine, saintly colors across the chapel's stonework floor made the heat seem almost tropical.

A couple of elderly white women were kneeling at the wooden altar down front, praying silently. Mouse took a seat in a red-cushioned pew a few aisles in from the door. He thought about the characters bent in postures of agony in the windows, the way the milky sunlight shining through them added myth and magic to the scenes of their deeds. Not everyone's deeds ended up decorating churches: he imagined how Joao would look up there, sainted for future generations to revere, an inky black man on a sparkling yellow forklift hoisting a blue-and-red crushed-glass case of beer. He wondered what the mysterious blonde woman who lived around the corner did for a living, how she would look in an edifying stained glass scene: an alabaster figure with a green telephone in her hand, staring into a glowing orange computer monitor, her free hand on a variegated glass keyboard, her mouth open, issuing divine human resource commands. Saint Heather of Systems Management.

The actual scenes in the windows were moments of ministry, compassion and suffering, yet Mouse realized that without the stained glass artists to depict these holy moments, he would not have been contemplating them, and he wondered which was more important: the saints or the artists. The saints performed sacred deeds, but their effects were local; it was the artists who moved people with visions of the deeds thousands of years later, thousands of miles away.

He stared around the chapel, admiring the detail of the masonry, imagining what it must have been like to build this church, hulking and delicate at once. He wondered if slaves had built it, if it had been the French or the Americans or Germans. A lot of people had left their fingerprints on Soulard through the centuries: the French founders with their architectural styles, the German immigrants with their brewhouses, the Natives with their mounded earth, the slaves. . . he wasn't sure what the slaves had left in Soulard, except their blood, now invisible under the stones of the church. He imagined being a slave here and thought how much better he had it now, drawing a paycheck from Anheuser-Busch, than his forebears, getting cracked with a whip. This thought did not comfort him.

One of the elderly women at the altar stood, crossed herself and turned. She tottered down the aisle toward Mouse. When she passed him, she lifted her quavering right hand, as if in blessing, and a bell rang ten times. Mouse stood and followed the old woman out.

Ten o'clock in the morning, and he had nowhere to go but back to bed. He watched the woman shuffle along Eighth Street to a purple 1960s VW station wagon. He walked aimlessly back to his apartment.

Mouse picked up Shauna's pack of Marlboro Lights from his nightstand. Half the people he knew smoked, and in the clubs there had always been cigarettes, reefers, blunts and anything else people could set on fire and inhale, but he had never been tempted to light up, until now. Occasionally, on their after-dinner walks, he would share a cigarette with Shauna, more out of companionship than anything else. He didn't want to become addicted the way she was, but now he took a cigarette from the pack and held it between his second and third fingers. It would give him something to do for seven minutes; he calculated that he would need to smoke a hundred and twenty more that day to take him to bedtime.

He stepped from his sweltering living room onto the front balcony, lit the cigarette and leaned on the railing. Now, to the people passing below, *he* was one of the mysterious Soulard residents with a mysterious life and unfathomable choices, standing on his balcony smoking. A door opened just up the street; from the house on the corner, a woman in a beige skirt and stylish fur-trimmed wrap emerged and walked down the sidewalk. She seemed about Mouse's age, with creamy caramel skin and tightly platted hair, and she carried a brightly wrapped package with an enormous bow. She opened the door of a Mercedes sedan and placed her package on the passenger seat.

"Hey there," Mouse called. The woman looked up.

"How you doin," she said in a perfunctory way, discouraging conversation. She walked around her car and opened the driver's door.

"You live here?"

"That's right."

"I didn't know any sisters live up in here," Mouse said.

"I didn't know any country brothers lived here, either."

"What?! Why you call me country?"

"Why you shoutin out fool things on the street, Country?" She shook her head in disgust and got into the car.

Mouse watched the Mercedes drive away. He took a long drag on his cigarette and felt like an idiot. Mouse Watkins, Funkateer, would have known what to say to a woman like that; Mouse Watkins, beer warehouser, was a plain fool.

"Why do you even have to define yourself by your work?" Shauna asked.

They were sitting across a cafe table from one another in the Bread and Butter Grill on Soulard and Ninth, eating brunch on Sunday morning. The warm chatter and the heavy clanking of silverware ebbed and flowed around them, creating a friendly arrhythmic cacophony that pleased Mouse. Waiters and cooks shouted orders back and forth behind the counter.

"How do you define yourself?" he asked.

"I'm a lot of different things. An artisan. A feminist–"

"An artisan?"

"I built those chairs on my back patio with my own hands. I made your beautiful curtains." She spread butter on rye toast. "I'm a cook. A daughter."

"You been a nurse for twenty years."

"I'm a nurse."

"If you at a party and someone turn to you and say, what do you do? You say I'm an artisan, a feminist and a daughter? No. You say I'm a nurse."

"Well, you've been a drummer your whole life. I don't see why you can't introduce yourself as a drummer. The fact that the Apples broke up doesn't mean you're not a drummer any more."

Mouse leaned forward and enunciated every word clearly. "The drums are my enemy."

"The drums are your whole history, Mouse, and there's no reason to deny that. That's why I fell for you in the first place, remember? That night we went out for drinks after you and Gateway got your first four-track, back in like, what, 1985? You had this look in your eye when you talked about music, the drums—it was like nothing else mattered."

"You see that look in my eye now?"

"I know it'll take time to get over the Apples and figure out what you're gonna do next, but this big melodrama is stupid, and it bores me, to tell you the truth. Why don't you just relax? You don't have to define yourself as anything right now. You're making up your mind, you're a young man, you've gotta lotta options. You're in transition." It was not lost on Mouse that Shauna's hospice company was called Transitions. "You don't really mean the drums are your enemy."

"They aint my friend. They aint never helped me, and they caint help me now."

"God, Mouse, you just don't let up, do you?" She had barely started eating her omelet, but Shauna threw her napkin down on her plate and stood up. "You can't concede the slightest little point, or even try to see things a different way." She took her coat off the back of her chair. "Call me when you wanna talk about something else. Anything else." She turned and left the restaurant.

Mouse had not understood that Shauna was really angry, and now that she had walked out, he felt empty and exposed. He had no options: he couldn't race down the street after her begging for forgiveness—that had become his main role in their relationship; he couldn't sit there dour and uptight by himself and finish his breakfast with his relaxed, convivial neighbors staring at him; he couldn't return to his empty apartment and its dense atmosphere of foreboding and fear. He hadn't even touched his eggs, but now that Shauna was gone he felt so awkward and out of place among the jabbering Sunday brunchers that he couldn't imagine staying. He couldn't do anything.

A waiter came to his table. "Is the lady done with her breakfast, sir?" The waiter took Shauna's plate, which felt to Mouse like a piece of his own heart.

"Mouse! Hey man, what's happenin?!" It was Chester, a white trumpet player with the St. Louis Symphony who occasionally sat in with bands around town. Chester and another white man approached Mouse's table. "Good to see you. You ever met my brother?" Chester introduced his brother Pete. "Pete's up from Atlanta for the weekend."

"Hey, how you doin?" Mouse stood up and they shook hands.

"Pete's thinkin about takin a job with Weyerhaeuser, right up the street. I'm talkin him into it."

"What kinda job?"

"Knife sharpener," Pete said.

"For Weyerhaeuser? Aint that a paper company?"

"Yeah. I sharpen blades for Georgia-Pacific right now, but Weyerhaeuser's hiring toilet paper specialists. It's the same money, but I could come back home to St. Louis with this job, so I'll probably take it."

"I don't get it," Mouse said. "You sharpen knives for toilet paper?"

Pete explained that he sharpened the blades on a giant wheel that processed pulp into tissue. "That's just my specialty, you know. The same pulp gets made into everything: paper towels, writing paper, card stock, what-have-you. How the paper turns out depends on the kind of blades the pulp passes through—how it's processed, see?"

"And you specialize in toilet paper?"

"Your ass can thank my rotors, man. It's gotta be soft enough for a baby's bottom, but it still has to hold together and be strong. You don't wanna wipe your butt with business cards, right? But you don't want your finger pokin up your ass either. It's delicate, man—you gotta sharpen those blades right to make the paper come out just so."

"I never thought about it."

"Hell, I can make pulp into anything—a lot of guys can do the heavier stuff, even paper towels—but it takes the right touch to make bathroom tissue. I'm the guy with the most experience cranking toilet paper at Georgia-Pacific, and that's why Weyerhaeuser is bringin me on."

The pride in Pete's voice astonished Mouse. "You fellas wanna pull up a chair?"

"Naw, man, we're just headin out," said Chester. "I wish I'd seen you earlier, we coulda joined you. You oughtta come by sometime, tell me how the gig at Busch is workin out."

"How you know about that?"

"Gateway called me up, wanted me for a holiday gig up in Quad Cities. How come you quit, man?"

"He bookin the Bad Apples, or he got his own thing now?"

"You and Gateway not talking?"

"I dunno, man. It's weird right now. You take the gig?"

"I couldn't. We're playing *Messiah* that weekend." Chester's brother looked bored. "Seriously, Mouse, come by some time. You know, Gateway's workin it pretty hard around town. Maybe you can drop by and we can jam a little and you can tell me about it."

Chester and Pete left, and Mouse sat and stared at his breakfast. Gateway was continuing the Bad Apples without him, and the guy who made toilet paper for a living was proud of his job. Life was unspeakable.

He picked at his eggs for a while but didn't have the stomach to eat any more. He paid for brunch without finishing it and made the short, slow walk back to his apartment.

Love

Mouse woke up early on Thanksgiving morning, still drunk from the night before. He felt used up. He rolled out of Shauna's bed and tiptoed into her bathroom.

In the mirror: eyes bloodshot, gray-black stubble on his chin, deep creases across his cheeks and forehead. He looked like the derelicts the kids used to taunt on the streets of Brooklyn. He blinked hard, and when he opened his eyes the bathroom swam.

He and Shauna were due at his sister's house for Thanksgiving dinner at eleven o'clock: it would be the first time Shauna would meet Mouse's mother. Mrs. Watkins had promised to behave herself, and several of Marvin's and Jackie's friends would be there to help deflect any trouble, but Mouse knew that his mother hated the fact that her only son was dating a white girl. His mother was the kindest soul he knew, but she was bitter with the wisdom of her life, and he wasn't sure which he feared more, what his mother might say or what Shauna might do. He turned the hot water in the shower all the way on and waited for steam to appear.

Shauna's hospice patient in Soulard had died, and Mouse had been spending more time at her house in Rock Hill. Shauna's house was an unusual single-story white stone bungalow squeezed between more typical two-story red brick homes. Hers was the only house on the block with no backyard fence, and she had a gravel driveway instead of concrete; her lawn was unruly, and her home's lack of pretension made Mouse feel at ease, in spite of her neighbors' relative affluence. Rock Hill was not nearly as rich or as white as nearby Webster Groves, but it was an expensive town occupied by white collar commuters, where the phrase "respectable community" was still code, and Mouse did not always feel welcome walking its quaint streets.

Shauna had inherited the house when her father had died, at a time when she was growing tired of the party scene downtown. To her, Rock Hill represented stability and respectability, and becoming a homeowner had completed Vita DuPlease's transformation into Shauna Duprey—the same sort of transformation that Shauna was now urging on Joseph Watkins.

Mouse stepped into the shower and let hot water splash across his face. He fingered the scar at the back of his head where his stitches had been. Shauna had accompanied him back to SLU Hospital to have them removed, and as the doctor had snipped and tugged, Shauna had entertained Mouse with horror stories about the many gruesome skull fractures she had seen during her time as a nurse. The scar was still tantalizingly soft and fresh. Mouse's fingers were constantly drawn to it, to this strange new lumpen growth that was now a permanent part of him, and he wondered if his hair would ever grow back right. He thought of Gateway every time he touched the yielding, fleshly scar: it was as if Gateway had tattooed his name on Mouse's head with that sucker punch.

The hot water revived him and he began to believe he might make it through the day. Not only would Shauna be meeting his mother for the first time, but the party promised to be generally awkward, since Jackie's and Marvin's friends tended to be rich and patronizing, and Mouse never knew what to say to them. Mouse thought the fact that he was worrying about what to say to them was, in itself, a sign of doom.

One of the unexpected consequences of not playing drums

was that Mouse now thought too much, and obsessively. He spent most of his energy fearing the future, worrying about the present and compulsively rejecting the ideas of those around him. When the Bad Apples had been gigging, when there had been a future he could imagine, he had never wasted a second wondering what other people might think or do, what he should say or how he should act. He had walked with the confidence of a sleepwalker, sure that his dreams were reality, and he had rarely stumbled, much less fallen. Now, dreamless, he thought about the reality that other people had made and how he could fit into their plans. It disgusted him. He finished his shower and toweled off.

The main hazard for the day was Shauna's high-spiritedness, which was her most charming and vexing quality. She was like a free-form jazz player, where her life was the music and her mind was the instrument, and she couldn't keep her improvisations inside the meter everyone else was playing. The result was sometimes exhilarating, but it was also tiresome, because Mouse could never relax around her. He always had to be "on," ready for her next sudden departure from the music he thought they were reading together. Their relationship, though, did not really suffer because of it, and Shauna brought many more good things into Mouse's life than bad.

Shauna was relentlessly positive about Mouse and often told him how smart and handsome he was and how much he had accomplished in his life; and though he didn't believe these compliments, they were welcome relief from his self-flagellating internal monologue. She didn't worry him about his next job, or when he would start looking for it. She herself had quit her job at Transitions Hospice when her last patient had died, and she was comfortable with the idea of moving from job to job without a plan. Of course, as an experienced nurse, her services were always in demand, but she applied the same even-tempered attitude she had about her own work to Mouse's, and it made him feel that he had time to make a decision, that his whole life was not riding on his next paycheck.

Most of all, Mouse liked reminiscing with Shauna. Reliving their youthful follies helped him understand how far he had come and how much more he knew about life and music than he once had, even if it had all come to nothing; and, through reminiscing, Mouse began to understand the irony of Shauna's situation. Just as she was encouraging him to become a square-job-working taxpaying upstanding apartment-living member of the community, she herself was looking for something more daring to do. Scattered around her house were community college catalogs, art school pamphlets, online design course printouts. She was weighing job offers from Barnes Jewish Hospital and SLU, but she often talked of becoming a graphic designer or opening a clothing boutique instead. She was sick of nursing and bored with suburban tranquility: Shauna's transition to the suburbs had not entirely killed Vita DuPlease, and Vita wanted to live again now, through Mouse.

He slipped into the robe and houseshoes Shauna had bought for him and walked into the kitchen. Shauna had remodeled the house herself, laying the shiny black-and-white kitchen tiles on the floor and painting the cupboards and cabinet doors a deep purply crimson—the color of blood. He opened a cabinet, shook coffee into a filter and poured water into the pot.

He didn't feel quite drunk any more. Now, he felt thin and ready to give, like an old rubber band stretched around a package too big for it to hold. He sat down at the table, took up a pen and doodled on some scratch paper while the coffee brewed. He drew a sketch of Shauna lying naked in bed, with a sheet wound around her mid-section, her hair fanned out across her pillow; but it looked like a police artist's crime scene drawing, and he tore it up and threw it away. Much in Mouse's life reminded him of death these days, and he'd been relieved when Shauna had quit the hospice, so that he no longer had to endure the details of her patient's slow expiration.

The floorboards in the hall creaked. Shauna shambled into the kitchen. "What're you doin up at this hour?"

"Couldn't sleep."

"You look awful." She yawned and turned the coffee pot off. "Come to bed. You don't want coffee yet." She held out her hand, but Mouse remained seated. "Something wrong?"

"Naw, not really."

"What is it? Just tell me."

Mouse shrugged and looked away. "It aint nothin. I don't usually bring girls home to meet my family, is all."

"I can imagine. I've seen some of your groupies."

Mouse stared blankly.

"It'll be okay. Come on." When it became clear that Mouse was not going to follow her back to bed, Shauna pulled up a chair and put her hand on his. "I've already met your sister. It'll be fine."

"My sister aint my mother."

"Well, so? It'll be a beautiful dinner. We'll talk about the weather, we'll eat, we'll come home. Don't think of it as such a big occasion, alright? Forget about Thanksgiving. It's just a nice meal with a little decorative turkey, and pumpkin pie at the end."

"Blackberry cobbler."

"Okay, blackberry cobbler. We'll make nice."

"That aint it, though. I guess I shoulda said: I don't usually bring white girls home to meet my family."

Shauna blanched. "You didn't mind introducing me to your sister."

"Like I said, my sister aint my mother."

She pulled her hand away. Her eyes burned cold. "No, I don't think so," she said. "This isn't about your mother."

"I'm tellin you it is. You don't know how she feel about white people." Mouse wanted to forget the whole thing, the holiday, this conversation, everything. He wished Shauna would go back to bed and leave him alone.

"All right, then, enlighten me."

"The thing about white people. . ." He didn't want to say these things, but he didn't think Shauna understood the potential difficulty with his family, the resentment his mother felt, the awkwardness it created for him. "White people aint gotta live with black people, but black people gotta live with white people."

"That's ridiculous. We have a black president. Everybody in America lives with black people."

"Naw, we got a black president on tv. He don't live down the street from you. This here's still a white country."

"Okay, so America isn't Zimbabwe. I don't see what that has to do with Thanksgiving at your sister's house."

"White people can go they whole lives and never think about black people, but black people caint pretend y'all don't exist, cause you own everything. You say how it is and we gotta take it. That's my mom's attitude about white people, and it aint every day you even see white people in Brooklyn, so it's a double bind for my moms if you there at Thanksgiving. It's gonna be a problem."

"So I'm just one of the white people?"

The iciness in Mouse's voice surprised even him. "Look in a mirror."

Shauna wilted and slowly let all the air seep out of her lungs. "That's how you think of me?"

"Easy now." Mouse suddenly had trouble breathing, as if Shauna's long sigh had emptied the whole kitchen of air. "I'm explainin 'bout my moms."

A single tear rolled down Shauna's cheek. She looked into her lap and began fidgeting, pressing her thumbnails into the skin of her thighs.

Mouse went on, panicked, hoping that if he talked enough he would eventually say the right thing. "Everywhere my moms go, her whole life, she gotta deal with white people sayin how it is, sayin what to think—she aint gonna like dealin with it in her own family, that's all. It aint nothin personal against you. It's like, if a white person went to her church, that's her sanctuary—the holidays, her family, her church—that's her true self. It's gonna be like we bindin up her soul or somethin."

Shauna stared at Mouse without blinking while tears streamed down her cheeks. For the first time since they had met at Sweeney's, she seemed not just angry at him or offended by him but genuinely vulnerable to him. She sobbed once and then controlled herself, wiped her eyes on her pajama sleeve; but when she spoke, her voice cracked. "Since when did you ever care about pleasing your mother?" She sobbed again and then let herself cry.

Mouse wasn't sure if Shauna was accusing him of being a racist or a poor son, and he was confused by her anguish. "It aint about pleasin her," he said. "I thought you oughtta know, it's somethin we about to run up against, that's all."

"No, it isn't."

"I think I know my own family."

"This isn't about your family. It's about me."

"How is this about you?"

"It's about you and me."

"How is this about you and me?"

"Admit it, Mouse."

"I aint gonna say somethin that aint true."

"No? Why should today be any different?"

"Meaning what?"

"Just get it over with, Mouse. Say you're ashamed of me. Say you don't want me at your family's Thanksgiving. Say you don't wanna see me any more." She snuffled. "Sometimes I think you don't care about me at all." She brought her heels up onto her chair, wrapped her arms around her knees and wept uncontrollably.

Mouse didn't know what to do. Her posture, curled into herself, all elbows and knees and arched back, made it difficult even to touch her, and he felt inadequate to comfort her. He was the one with the problem.

He got out of his chair, knelt beside her and put his arms around her. Her knees stuck into his chest. He rubbed her back, a gesture that felt childish and useless.

"I've stood up for you," she sobbed. "If anyone asks why I'm with you, I tell them how great you are. I would never make excuses to keep you away from my family."

The fact that Shauna's only living relative was an elderly aunt in San Diego made this assertion moot, but Mouse thought better of pointing this out. He continued to rub her back.

"Don't you love me, Mouse?"

No matter what conversation Mouse thought he was having with Shauna, she was always having a different one with him. "I– I– I guess I hadn't really—we only been goin out for like three and a half weeks."

"We've known each other half our lives! It's not like we're kids and don't know what we want."

On the contrary, Mouse thought, it was exactly like he was a kid and didn't know what he wanted. His life had collapsed into mundane details. All of his relationships were ruined or in jeopardy, and his casual acquaintances, the hundreds of people who might have recognized him if he'd ventured out to the clubs, never phoned him or sought him out and never would. He lived like a hermit now, and he felt alone, and a stranger, even with Shauna. He smelled her skin, kissed her knee. Love?

She uncurled herself and put her feet on the floor on either side of Mouse, rested her hands on his shoulders. He felt enthralled by her misery.

"I'm gonna tell you something, Mouse," she said. "You're upside-down. You don't know if you're coming or going. You don't need me to tell you that, but I know something you don't. Your energy is clear and bright in spite of all that confusion, and that means this chaos you're feeling is just the surface. Underneath, you know exactly what to do." She touched his chest. "In here, you know what to do, and you have to trust yourself to do it." She moved her hands to Mouse's cheeks and cupped his face. "I trust you to do it. I'm so happy you came back into my life, Mouse, and I want to be with you. I don't want our relationship to be temporary. I don't want to be just another thing you can cast aside once you've figured it all out." She kissed him. "I want to be the thing you figure out."

Mouse could not imagine that someone might love him for something other than his music, or that Shauna could even use the word love after such a short, tempestuous affair. "If I never play music again, you still wanna be with me?"

"Of course."

"Why?"

"Is this a test?"

"Naw, I really wanna know. Serious. Why you wanna be with me? Why you 'love' me?"

"I don't know." She sat back and thought about it. "It doesn't make much sense, does it?"

"You bustin me?"

"You asked an honest question, it deserves an honest answer. I haven't tried to put it into words before."

Mouse fought to keep silent while Shauna contemplated her feelings. He feared he might talk her out of liking him, and he would be exiled to Soulard, completely alone.

"I guess I like the way I feel with you," Shauna said. "I always liked the way you made me feel, even when we were kids."

"That's what I thought," Mouse said. "You just relivin the old days through me. That's why I wanna know about today, not the old days, right now. I wanna know what's in it for you today. Right now."

"I mean today. I mean right now. I don't need some trip back in time, Mouse. I don't need to feel young. You make me feel the same way now as you made me feel back then, and it has nothing to do with age or Vita DuPlease or anything else but you. I didn't know I was missing that feeling—when we were young, I didn't even know what it was—but now I feel like we should've been together all along."

"What feeling you mean?"

"Like I'm myself. I feel like you can see me for who I really am and that it's okay to be that way. Like I don't have to be a version of myself with you. I can be my whole self."

This struck Mouse as extraordinary, even delusional. He had no special insight into Shauna's character. He didn't even know who she was half the time. Her assertions often baffled him and her reactions dismayed and enraged him. She was not the easiest person to get along with, she didn't even try most of the time, but Mouse recognized a compulsive honesty in Shauna that she probably recognized in him, an unwillingness to pretend to be different than she was for the sake of convenience. Perhaps she was forced to pretend with everyone else, and maybe that's why she had become a hospice nurse, to be around people who didn't have time to play games, who wouldn't waste their energy on everyday lies.

"And what about you, Mouse? Don't you wanna be with me? Are you really ashamed to have me over for Thanksgiving?"

"I aint ashamed."

"Then what's all this about your mother?"

"Like I said—"

Shauna shook her head no. She would not take his concern about his mother's feelings at face value.

She was right that he'd never worried about offending his mother before. He thought about all the ways he'd defied his mother over the years, and he wondered why he should want to appease her now, why he so wanted to avoid this dinner. The idea of his sister's house decorated with gourds and Indian corn deflated him, and the image of his mother at the head of the dining table made him weak with scorn. But he couldn't quite comprehend the force of his feelings.

Shauna touched his thigh, lightly, letting her fingers brush over his knee. Her touch was like a magician's flourish, coaxing a rabbit from a hat, alluring the impossible into being, and this simple touch rippled through him. He felt a tremor rise from his legs into his gut, as if his whole body were nothing but water trembling from its surface into its depths. He was ashamed, but not of Shauna, not of her whiteness or her hotheadedness or anything else about her. He was ashamed of himself.

He didn't care at all what his mother would think of Shauna: in the face of his family, their success and accomplishment and unwavering convictions, he felt embarrassed even to exist. He couldn't stomach their problem-solving suggestions and secret condemnations. If he had become a pop star, he could have invited them to the Grammy Awards and movie premieres, they would have walked down the red carpet, hobnobbing with celebrities, so proud that he had made good, that they were associated with the Mouse Watkins, he could have invited them to Thanksgving at his mansion and had the servants make them a feast; but because he was an abject failure, they could only grudgingly offer him their help and hope he wouldn't humiliate them with his inappropriate behavior in front of their guests. Shauna was just one very minor strike against him, one more way that he didn't measure up to their expectations. He refused to be one of them but he couldn't be anything else, couldn't get away from them or impress them, so his very presence in his family was untenable.

"I'm sorry," he said.

He had wanted Shauna to bear the burden of his shame, and she wouldn't do it. Now he was sorry so out of proportion to his offense against her that he wished he could be swallowed whole into the earth, and even that would not have been penance enough. "I'm sorry."

Shauna took him into her arms, and he began to shake. "I'm sorry," he said again.

"It's okay, baby."

"I'm sorry."

"I heard you. It's all right. Why don't you tell me what's going on?"

The tremors shaking his body became more violent. He buried his face in Shauna's breast and trembled. He felt he was having a seizure, like a mass at the core of his brain was boring through the top of his skull. His mouth felt full and his teeth chattered. "I'm sorry." He said it over and over again, a wail in place of weeping, "I'm sorry I'm sorry I'm sorry," and Shauna wrapped her arms tighter around him and whispered, "It's okay it's okay it's okay." He felt himself breaking. The grip of will that had been holding him together slipped, and he cracked inside like an ice cube dropped in warm water.

When he could no longer even groan the words I'm sorry, he cried, a prolonged choking wail. He lost himself in a fit so black and empty that whatever had been Mouse Watkins collapsed like a dead star imploding in the vast hollow coldness of his interior space.

"I'm sorry I'm sorry I'm sorry," the words peeled out like vomit from the center of his soul.

When Mouse recovered himself, he was lying curled in Shauna's arms on the kitchen floor. The morning sun was shining through the window, and Shauna was petting his face and shushing him, a feverish child. He felt weak and bewildered. Shauna smiled at him kindly.

"Are you okay? Why don't you sit up and I'll get you some water."

He sat up and looked around. It seemed as if someone had removed every object from the room and replaced it with an exact replica. Shauna poured a glass of tap water and handed it to him. He drank. The water tasted dense with minerals. He felt profoundly sleepy and foreign, as if he himself had been replaced with a replica. His thoughts were foggy, and a hope suggested itself: that he would never have to be himself again.

Shauna knelt beside him and kissed him on the forehead. "Wanna lie down? Wanna sit on the sofa?"

She helped him into the living room. They sat next to one another on her sofa, and Mouse had a strange sense of dumb well-being.

"Wanna tell me about it?"

He shook his head no.

"But you're all right? No pain, no nausea, headaches?"

He shook his head no and drank another sip of water. He could almost see the air, it seemed so thick. The edges of every object were so clear and fixed that they became mysterious. He had entered an alternate dimension in which the realness of objects was amplified. He did not feel the urge to characterize, describe or create; he did not feel time passing. Thought itself seemed primitive and unnecessary.

Shauna took his empty glass and set it on the coffee table. She pulled him into her body, and they sat half-lying in each other's arms. Mouse couldn't tell if he was dreaming he was awake or he was actually awake and thinking that he was dreaming he was awake or if being awake was a trick of the dream. He noticed that he was smiling. He nuzzled his face into Shauna's stomach and stretched across the sofa.

"We need to get ready," Shauna said.

"Just let me lie here a minute." A ray of sunlight fell on his face.

"You've already been asleep for over an hour."

"Oh." He blinked and looked out the window. The sun was higher and brighter now.

"How do you feel?"

"What happened?"

"You tell me. You fell so hard asleep. I was worried about you."

Shauna's living room seemed small and ordinary again. Mouse sat up and shook the sleep out of his head. His euphoria had disappeared, and he felt heavy and thick.

"You okay to go to your sister's?"

He nodded yes. "I'm glad you comin with me."

Shauna hugged him tight. "Me too."

Shauna and Mouse were the last to arrive at Jackie's house. They hung their coats on the rack behind the door. "It smells delicious," Shauna said, as she squeezed both of Jackie's hands.

The living room was festooned with elaborate, handmade autumnal decorations. Marvin offered them glasses of wine and introduced everyone.

In addition to Mouse's mother, the guests included two couples: Zack and Chloe, and Oliver and Sharisse. Oliver was an attorney in Marvin's law firm and Sharisse was secretary for a Montessori school in Frontenac: they had met and married in college, where Oliver had been a second-string receiver on the football team and Sharisse had been a cheerleader. They were the Beautiful People, Mouse thought, just like Jackie and Marvin, and they delivered high-handed declarations about this, that and everything.

Zack and Chloe were a white couple who owned a piano shop near Forest Park. Even in a freshly pressed suit, Zack looked hangdog, in sharp contrast to the waifish Chloe, who was chic and sharp. In their business, he was the technician and she was public relations, but they both spoke unpretentiously and seemed like regular folks.

Mouse was thankful that Zack and Chloe were there, so that Shauna didn't have the pressure of being the only white person at the party, but Mouse also knew that Jackie had her own reason for inviting them, and it wasn't racial. Everyone at the party was about forty years old, financially successful, and—most importantly—childless. Jackie and Mrs. Watkins had been carrying on variations of this conflict for years: Jackie wanted to prove to her mother that she could live a fulfilling life without children, and Mrs. Watkins wanted to prove to her daughter that she could live a fulfilling life without "improving" herself. The conflict was complicated by the fact that Jackie actually wanted to have children but Marvin refused, and Mrs. Watkins actually wanted to leave Brooklyn and find an upright man—each of them wanted for themselves what the other wanted for them, but they were entrenched defending opposite positions. Out of spite, neither could rise above their long history of unforgiving self-righteousness to see what Mouse thought was obvious: that they agreed on all points.

The group made small talk about the inclimate weather until Jackie ushered everyone into the parlor for a recital. It was a tradition at Jackie's house that every occasion began and ended with music. Above and beyond cooking sumptuous food (all from scratch), Jackie also prepared a piano piece to play at every gathering, and she took great pains to select just the right music. She never repeated herself. Mouse had been to countless holidays and birthdays at Jackie's house for decades, and outside of Christmas carols and "Happy Birthday," Jackie had never played the same music twice.

They sat around the grand piano in leather director's chairs. Jackie asked if Chloe would turn pages for her, and she sat down at the piano bench with Chloe sitting to her left.

This year's selection was Brahms's Rhapsody in G Minor, a Romantic piece that was much more serious and dramatic than Jackie's usual taste: she preferred light Classical melodies, so the disquieting grandeur and minor key of the Brahms surprised Mouse and set an ambivalent mood that resonated with his own feelings. He was still strung out and exhausted from his breakdown earlier in the morning, and he relaxed into the subtle changes of the theme as it developed, as it carried him away from his own melancholy into a more majestic, shared one. The fact that Jackie was spending her energy to express such beautiful, sweeping restlessness consoled Mouse, and he wondered if she had made this unusual choice especially for him.

Shauna tapped Mouse's thigh and looked at him wide-eyed. He smiled. It was easy for him to take his sister's talent for granted, to forget how impressive her playing was. Though Jackie wasn't technically brilliant enough to perform professionally as a concert pianist, only true connoisseurs of Western Art music could distinguish her failings. Her grace, feeling and expertise, combined with the sheer volume that the parlor grand produced, could be overwhelming. Mouse put his arm around Shauna and allowed himself to drift away with the music. He closed his eyes and could almost imagine that it was the nineteenth century, and as the music ebbed and flowed, becoming by turns violent and delicate, pushing forward and drawing back, he felt the teeming fetidness of his own little estuary drawn by tidal forces into a larger, fresher, more turbulent sea.

Jackie finished and everyone applauded. "Thank you very much," she said.

She turned to Chloe. "Would you or Zack like to play something?" Jackie addressed the rest of the party. "I asked them to prepare a piece for after dinner, but as long as we're all gathered around the piano, maybe we should hear a little something right now?"

"I don't know," Chloe demurred. "I only prepared the one piece—it's Chopin's E-flat waltz, you know?" She hummed a fe bars, then looked to Zack, who held up his hands to indicate that he didn't want to play.

This was the Jackie Effect, which Mouse's sister had even on her friends, even on other talented musicians. Chloe couldn't have been a slouch player if she had prepared a Chopin waltz, but something about Jackie's presence, her attitude more than her virtuosity alone, told everyone that they weren't in her league, and no one wanted to invite unfavorable comparisons to her or have to apologize for not meeting Jackie's standards. Jackie simply wasn't generous the way most musicians are with one another.

"I understand," Jackie said superciliously. "But maybe just a favorite piece, or something you could sight-read?" She pointed at the shelves all along the parlor walls, which contained thousands of sheets of music.

"Maybe." Chloe looked to Zack for help. "It would be hard to follow that great piece you played with something we were just sight-reading, though."

"It's not a competition," Jackie said. Mouse was sure that, in Jackie's mind, it actually was a competition, one that she'd fixed for house odds. "What about you, Zack?"

"I guess I could play the Ravel I use to tune my pianos," he said. "But the mood is so totally different from what you just played. I'm kind of enjoying that, just being in that mood."

Mrs. Watkins hefted herself out of her chair with a groan. "I guess they's only one thing to do," she said. She hobbled to the keyboard. She suffered from arthritis in her hips and knees and was considerably overweight, but she always seemed a little more arthritic in front of groups. Now her limping and puffing became a stage show for Jackie's guests. She shooed Jackie and Chloe away from the bench. Chloe, relieved, quickly took the seat next to her husband, but Jackie refused to yield.

"What's your plan, mom?"

"You want somebody to play a little somethin right now, right? Well, nobody else here wanna play this piana." She looked around the room. "Mouse, you wanna play?"

"Naw," he said. "Whyn't you play somethin, ma?" Mouse was enjoying his mother's mutiny against Jackie. Though Jackie had first learned how to play from her mother, she had long since lost interest in her mother's simple repertoire of spirituals and doo-wop ditties.

"What are you going to play, mom?"

"I dunno. I'll think up somethin."

Jackie would not yield the bench.

"C'mon, now, let me in there," Mrs. Watkins said. She waddled right into Jackie, and Jackie backed down. Mouse's mother sat at the keyboard and Jackie crossed her arms and fumed. "Now let's see here," his mother said. "Aw right, I got somethin. This'll be a good song for Thanksgivin. Y'all join in if you know it."

She began with a series of showy glissandos and then plunked out a gospel chord progression. Jackie's refined parlor was transformed into a church meeting hall by a rollicking rendition of "Old Time Religion." Mrs. Watkins couldn't quite find the time—she slowed down and sped up unconsciously—and her singing was flat, but her energy was full and propulsive. "Gimme that old time religion/yes that old time religion/gimme that old time religion/it's good enough for me." By the time she got to the second verse, Oliver and Sharisse, the Beautiful People, were singing along with gusto. Oliver had a booming baritone that his wife's alto harmonized with perfectly, and Mouse decided to help his mother keep time by clapping out a regular beat. Shauna clapped with him, Zack and Chloe followed, and before he'd even thought about it, Mouse was singing along, too, taking a tenor line between Oliver and Sharisse.

All the carefully attenuated melancholy of Jackie's performance disappeared. Even Marvin joined the singing, and the mesh of their voices, the robust sound of their ragged harmonies, made Mouse's heart light. He felt a wave of nostalgia for the old days when he and Jackie were kids sitting at his grandmother's spinet. "Make me love everybody," they sang. "Make me love everybody/make me love everybody/and that's good enough for me."

The song seemed to go on forever, with Mrs. Watkins shouting out the next repeated line at the start of every verse. They sang "Gonna take us all to heaven," "It's a beautiful mornin," "Thank God for Thanksgiving," "We all happy together," and "Gonna eat us some turkey," before coming back to the start and "Gimme that ol' time religion," which they sang twice more.

When they finished, everyone clapped and hooted, a veritable ovation next to their polite applause for Jackie. While they congratulated Mrs. Watkins and themselves on the rousing spiritual, Jackie went into the kitchen for another bottle of wine and refilled everyone's glasses. She called attention by clinking her glass against the bottle, and everyone became quiet and looked to her.

"To that old time religion," she toasted with stern propriety, and Mouse couldn't help but admire the deftness of her tactic. By toasting a Negro spiritual stiffly, with etiquette-book snootiness, she made the whole scene seem quaint and she put the song, the style and the religion it represented back in its place as a tolerated but derelict family friend at the posh celebration.

"Amen!" Zack shouted joyfully, not understanding Jackie's maneuver at all. "To that old time religion!"

Jackie announced that dinner would now be served. She led her mother by the arm into the dining room.

Sharisse actually gasped when she saw the Versailles table laid with Jackie's magnificent feast. Mouse realized that his sister must have hired a secret helper to set out the food while they had been gathered around the piano. The table was brimming with artfully arranged silver serving dishes filled with mouthwatering treats, and the food was still steaming. He listened for signs of activity in the kitchen but heard none. He wondered how much a covert maid cost on Thanksgiving day.

Jackie preened while her guests cooed over the pumpkin-orange tablecloth and rust-colored napkins, the hand-calligraphied name cards, the silver place settings and crystal goblets and china, the lighted candelabra and the gourmet meal itself. The hostess directed them all to their seats—the four couples across from each other and Mrs. Watkins at the head of the table—while Jackie herself remained standing.

"Before we get started," Jackie said, "I'd like to explain a little bit about the dishes. I thought it would be nice this year to have a traditional Thanksgiving meal, a meal that the Pilgrims might actually have made from the provisions available in Plymouth Colony. So I did a little reading about the diet of the Wampanoag Indians and the Puritans, and the local climate and game animals of seventeenth century New England, and came up with this menu."

"What a terrific idea," Sharisse said. Mrs. Watkins looked bored.

"Oliver and Marvin helped out by supplying venison from their bowhunting trip to Minnesota," Jackie continued, "so you can all thank them for that."

"Hear hear," Zack said. He raised his glass to the preening attorneys.

"I had to buy the turkey at the supermarket, though, so maybe you boys can aim at some birds next year." Jackie smiled expansively. "There are two kinds of sobaheg—that's the Wampanoag word for stew—there's duck sobaheg, and squash with sunflower seeds and ground acorns." She pointed at the tureens and serving dishes around the table as she named their contents. "Indian cornbread, seethed whitefish, lobster, boiled onions, peas, artichoke hearts and green beans. We have two kinds of sauce for the turkey—onion and cranberry—and a sweet prune sauce for the venison. Now, they wouldn't have had potatoes at that first harvest meal, but I know my mother would throw a fit if there were no mashed potatoes and gravy, so that's the only exception here." She sat down. "If Marvin will do the honors and carve the bird, I think the rest of us can dig in."

To his surprise, Mouse was enjoying himself. His mother's

"Old Time Religion" alone had been worth coming for, and whatever else he felt about his sister, he couldn't deny that she knew how to lay a table. The food was perfect, the wine delicious and plentiful, and Mouse and Shauna were seated across from Chloe and Zack, so that Mouse did not have to force conversation with the Beautiful People.

Marvin and Oliver spent much of the dinner boring Mrs. Watkins with talk about their law firm, and Charisse and Jackie found a wealth of chatter in the politics of hair styles. Far from suffering through the dinner or feeling embarrassed about himself, Mouse found that he had many musical touchstones in common with Zack, and they spent the meal discussing everything from Duke Ellington and the tap dancing Nicholas Brothers to Twiggy's bubblegum pop records.

"I used to love those British girl groups when I was a kid," Zack said. "The Orchids and the Breakaways. I think the first single ever bought with my own money was a Cilla Black record."

"Yeah yeah, I know about her," said Mouse. "She was real square in her rhythms, but she could really sing. You know, I found a Chantelles record in a used bin at Vintage Vinyl couple years back, and I really dug it."

"The Chantelles were Motown, though, right?"

"That was Chantelles number two. They's also a British group. I found this song 'Another Time, Another World'—you know that song?" Mouse sang a bit of the lyric, drawing a stern glance from Jackie. "It just tore my head off. Matter a fact, I wanted the Bad Apples to cover it, to funk it up a little, but my partner said people'd think we was gay or somethin. He always thought that way, but I still like those records. That was actually the last stuff I really dug, somethin I hadn't heard a million times already, was those girl groups."

"I felt that way the first time I heard Emitt Rhodes. You

know? A whole new take on the same old thing."

"Yeah yeah," Mouse said. "But the original girl groups, Motown and whatnot, that's what I like. Dixie Cups, Socialites, Martha and the Vandellas."

"I've got some great McKinleys records I bet you'd love," Zack said.

"I never even heard of them."

"A Scottish sister act. Jimmy Page played on some of their singles."

The conversation took Mouse back to the feeling of his early days, when there had still been whole worlds of music left to discover. Now, obscure genres like British 1960s blue-eyed girl-group soul were the only genres he hadn't exhausted yet, and he felt like he'd found a fellow searcher, a record bin diver, in Zack.

"You should come by the store, Mouse," Chloe chimed in. Chloe and Shauna had been talking about the difficulties of owning a small business—Shauna had been discussing her idea of opening a clothing boutique—and Chloe had already invited her to see their piano shop. "You two should come together. We've got a bunch of old records —we get them from estate sales where we buy pianos—Mouse could have a look at those and you can see what we do to actually manage the business day to day."

"We find the most amazing records at these estate sales," Zack said. "They sell them in big boxes for practically nothing. They don't even know what they have."

"That sounds fun," Shauna said.

She smiled at Mouse, and he felt, for the first time in his life, that he was in an adult relationship. His girlfriend was with him at his family's Thanksgiving party, making friends with another couple. He drank his wine, and a calming wave of warmth and tenderness for Shauna washed over him.

After dinner, Jackie served homemade pumpkin pie and blackberry cobbler, along with soft cheeses and dessert wines. When everyone was completely stuffed, she offered espresso with bittersweet chocolate and bourbon.

They retired to the living room to sip their after-dinner drinks, and Mouse and Shauna were finally forced to mingle with Sharisse and Oliver, around whom Mouse felt exactly as he feared he would: embarrassed, awkward and inadequate. Oliver was a man's man who liked golf, business and hunting, and Sharisse talked about the shopping trips she took to New York with her girlfriends. Fortunately, Shauna carried the lion's share of the conversation, and Mrs. Watkins, who had drunk enough wine not to care about anyone's feelings, frequently interrupted with tart observations about Sharisse's extravagance, so that Mouse had something useful to do in diverting her. When Shauna slipped out for a cigarette, Jackie came over and saved him by asking Oliver and Sharisse about their charitable foundation, which raised money for Alzheimer's research.

At last, everyone gathered in the parlor again to hear Chloe perform Chopin's Waltz in E-flat Major. She apologized ahead of time—"I've had way too much wine," "it won't match Jackie's piece," "I didn't have time to play much this week"—and though her performance *was* clumsy, Mouse enjoyed it.

Mouse wondered, as Chloe played, if he could actually hang out with Zack, who was in the music business but not show business, who had no musical or record industry ambitions, who just wanted to fix and tune and sell pianos and talk about all the great records he liked. Was that anything? What would satisfy him?

Chloe soldiered through her piece, stood up red-faced and bowed sheepishly at their applause. Zack stood up and hugged her and gave her a kiss on the side of the head. They seemed happy.

God

On the Sunday after Thanksgiving, Mouse woke up drunk for the fourth day in a row. He felt as if he were tumbling through empty space, like a lunar module that had overshot the moon and lost contact with Earth. Opening his eyes only caused the room to spin at the same nauseating velocity as his head.

Shauna had flown to San Diego to visit her aunt for the remainder of the Thanksgiving holiday, and the brief respite of calm he'd felt at his sister's party had deserted him the instant Shauna had left. He'd found little to do over the vacation but drink: without Shauna, he was misery consoling itself. He had stocked up on liquor and stayed in his apartment alone, to make sure he didn't find trouble in the bars; but drinking in his apartment had become trouble enough, and his body felt as thin and tattered as a Civil War flag.

He had spent years at a time stoned, lost in a haze of shabby clubs, and he had flirted with harder drugs, but he had never felt so near the brink of self-destruction as now. His only reliable hiding place was drunkenness, and that oasis of calm was becoming less peaceful and more costly, not only in how much alcohol he had to drink to get drunk but in the toll it took on his mind.

He sat on the edge of his bed in boxer shorts, the room unmoored and pitching. He steadied himself, got up and wavered into the living room, feeling his way, his eyes open only a squint. His bones felt pierced with night.

He found the cassette tape mix he had made of the darkest songs in his music collection—War's "Slippin' into Darkness," Sly Stone's "Asphalt Jungle," Funkadelic's "March to the Witch's Castle"—the nastiest grooves, the evil doppelgangers of funk party vibes. He turned the music up and opened the French doors to his balcony. It was still pitch dark out and freezing, and he stood shivering in the frigid wind. The spinning in his head made him want to vomit. Outside, sickening yellow streetlamps lit the old brick buildings like crypts, the shadows on their walls phantoms of hell, calling to Mouse.

He closed the balcony doors and lay flat on the floor, letting the slow desperation of the music soak into him. The muscles of his back ached, and his jaw burned from grinding his teeth all night.

He tried to remember a time of happiness, but his mind returned obsessively to the band and Gateway, the wraith haunting his waking dreams. He wished something besides the passage of time would help him see clearly. Why was it so easy for Gateway to sell out the vision of love and brotherhood they had cultivated for so long? Mouse knew funk music didn't matter in the long run—nothing mattered in the long run—but it had once meant everything to him and Gateway to share their vision of the world as joyous and peaceful, as a place where music and dancing were the highest expressions of the ideal of love that united all people. But even thinking such a thing seemed hopelessly naive to Mouse now. People would never unite under the banner of love, and funk music would be no one's anthem. Gateway didn't care about Love or Justice or the Funk, anyway, he only cared about getting paid; and no one knew or cared about Mouse's vision anyway. His music was a local trivia question, his movement was dead, and the Bad Apples were just rotting scraps on the compost heap of St. Louis. Every thought flitting through his mind afflicted Mouse, and the events that had led him to the floor of this apartment seemed to bear no relation to the person he once knew as Mouse Watkins, Funkateer. His life was botched, squandered and unredeemed.

He dragged himself into the kitchen and poured three fingers of bourbon into a dirty glass; but the smell of it made him recoil, and a wet wretch welled in his guts. He slammed the glass down and crawled back into the living room and sprawled on the floor.

When he awoke again, the cold winter sun shone so pale its light seemed filtered through Mouse's own despair. His stereo was clicking. The cassette player's automatic shut-off mechanism had failed. He got up and pressed stop, turned the cassette over and pressed play: the tape bunched in its plastic case. It made a warble and the spools stopped spinning. He pressed stop and took the cassette out, but the tape caught in the machine and unwound out of the case.

Mouse's heart burned black. He tried to wind the tape back onto the little plastic reels by hand, but it twisted and jammed. He spent long minutes unwinding the tape and straightening it again, rewinding it until it jammed then unwinding it and straightening it. Some of the music on the cassette existed only on that tape—you couldn't get it in digital downloadable format because it had been taped off of vinyl that no longer existed—and Mouse felt frantic and broken. As he worked the cassette with his fingers, he played the songs in his head, and as he failed and failed again, the music itself seemed to slip away. Winding and unwinding, flattening the tape till it jammed, winding and unwinding, twisting and stretching, winding and unwinding, winding it till it jammed, twisting and stretching, winding and unwinding, flattening it, twisting and stretching until it jammed, flattening it, winding and unwinding, twisting and stretching. All at once it became clear that its ruin was permanent, and he screamed, out of his guts.

He hurled the cassette with such force that it cracked a window pane in his balcony door. He snatched the tape player from the fireplace mantel and lifted it over his head. The cords attached to the back yanked the system off the shelves, and the CD player and tuner and two speakers crashed to the floor with a bang and clatter of shattering plastic and clacking metal.

Mouse stood poised with the cassette machine above his head, ready to slam it against the wall, but the uselessness of the gesture overwhelmed him. He brought it down gently instead and set it back on the mantel. He looked at the CD player at his feet. Now it was hopelessly broken, too.

He returned to his bed and covered his head with a pillow. He wished he could think nothing, but random memories lit the darkness of his mind like a deranged vaudeville show, without meaning or continuity. He fought to replace the past with blank blackness, but the effort became too great and the images appeared anyway in twisted forms, so he gave in and watched them swarming by, one memory after another, until one impression in particular lingered longer than the others—and then other memories built around it, until it became a feeling, a sense memory—and his whole mind slowed as he tarried in the unexpected feeling of calm that washed over him. The Christian Science Reading Room on Washington Avenue. It was the last place he had felt completely composed without being drunk. Its random appearance in the slideshow of his memories felt like a revelation.

He remembered the strange guy who managed the Reading Room, the weird books he'd read there. Dale. He remembered Dale's odd manner and cheap suit, and this new focus relieved him of some anxiety. His heartbeat slowed. Dale had told him of a Christian Science church in Lafayette Square, not far from Soulard. Mouse looked at his clock. Eight-thirty. Sunday morning.

He found a phone book listing for the First Church of Christ, Scientist, on Park Avenue, less than two miles away, and he threw on some blue jeans, a polo shirt and his Bud Light jacket. He walked downstairs to the street. The morning was cold and gray, and he started marching.

Mouse encountered no one on the sleepy streets until he came to the center of Lafayette Square. The Lafayette Square neighborhood was built around a thirty-acre park in its center, latticed with ancient elms and alderbush groves, where patches of snow and ice clung to the shadows beneath the trees. The decorative fountains had been emptied for the winter, elaborate gazebos and a bandstand waited for the next party, and a bronze statue of George Washington stood guard on a little hill. A white woman in a thermal exercise suit was jogging through the park with a dalmation on a leash, and some Sunday drivers cruised the periphery. The homes surrounding the park were at least as old as the homes of Soulard but had a more stately sensibility. Where most of the houses in Mouse's neighborhood had been divided into apartments, the Lafayette Square houses had remained single family homes, and many of them looked freshly restored and painted.

He came to the corner of Mississippi Street and Park Avenue and saw a white wooden steeple two blocks away. He walked to the stark white double doors of the church and slipped inside, into a brightly lit, brown-carpeted foyer. Stifling heat and off-key singing swaddled him.

Racks on both sides of the doors held books and pamphlets. A bulletin board displayed photographs of new church members, alongside thumbtacked fliers announcing upcoming activities. Mouse tiptoed to the chapel doors and peered through a small square window at the congregation.

From the pulpit, a fifty year old white woman wearing a turquoise pantsuit directed the singing, while another woman pounded out chords on an upright piano. There were sixty or seventy people standing, singing from hymnals, the most droning, joyless singing Mouse had ever heard in a church. He timed his entrance to the end of the song, opened the doors a crack and slid into the back pew as everyone else sat down.

The woman at the pulpit announced the publication of a new booklet that provided an introduction to Mary Baker Eddy and Christian Science, and she urged everyone to take some to give to their friends. After this announcement, she stared at the congregation for a few seconds with a smile in her eyes, as if she were enjoying some private accomplishment of her own that the worshippers represented.

Mouse was sweating profusely, but he didn't want to call attention to himself by rustling around taking off his jacket. He had never felt so devoid of funk in his life: every single impulse he had was filtered through a censoring thought, so that he couldn't even remove his jacket without thinking about it first. He hated himself for this, and in an act of defiance against this stupidity, he flamboyantly removed his jacket. A woman in the next pew eyed him peevishly, and the minister found him and gazed directly at him with her twinkling eyes, so that he felt exposed. Exactly what he had to hide he didn't know, but he was sure that the minister had found it out.

"The message we're called to hear today," the minister began, "is about the Mind and how our individual minds participate in the one Mind that is the font of the universe. Aspects of this message may be familiar to you, but it's important to have a clear understanding of your relationship with God and his divine order, and today's passages from the Bible and *Key to the Scriptures* will clarify your thoughts and return you to the proper contemplation of the Great Mind and your place within it."

The minister listed the Bible passages she would be reading, from the books of Amos, Jeremiah, Acts and Isaiah, and the section of commentary by Mary Baker Eddy, and then she read with exactly the same intonation and cadence that she had used while speaking extemporaneously. If Mouse closed his eyes, the minister sounded as if she were speaking Bible prophecy off the top of her head, conversationally. He had never heard anything like it. In his mother's Baptist church, the preacher read the Bible with special reverence and feeling, trying to channel the power of God through the words; but this minister made the Bible seem like notes someone had jotted down on a napkin, and the aplomb with which she read had an exhilarating effect on Mouse, of bringing something obscure into the light. She did not read the passages one at a time, one book at a time: she read for ten minutes straight, flipping back and forth between and among books, so that her reading constructed a new coherent passage out of discrete bits of both the New and Old Testaments. It seemed like a revolutionary way of interpreting the Bible, making new connections out of old randomness.

The minister turned to Mary Baker Eddy's book and read large portions of text about the mind. Mouse was impressed by how directly the reading spoke to his own confusion. Mary Baker Eddy's idea was that all of Mouse's thoughts and memories were preserved perfectly intact for all time, exactly as he thought them and remembered them, because his tiny brain was part of a vast cosmic Mind that recorded and understood everything. His confusion was illusory, as were sin and illness, all the results of his too-tiny mind, the limited power of which could cause any single person to become lost in the complexities of life. In order to clear up this confusion, Mouse needed to integrate the small wattage of his brainpower into the infinite lamp of the Great Mind, and in trusting the order of the God of Creation, his own internal order would be revealed. He also learned that he had an obligation to keep his thoughts pure, since every thought of every tiny mind was part of the thoughts of the Great Mind, and he could either contribute to the healing clarity of the whole universe or cause strife for himself and those around him by fostering illusions.

The sermon helped explain the sense of paranoia and obsession he had discerned earlier at the Reading Room: if every thought that passed through your mind either augmented or perverted the order and goodness of the universe, you had to remain constantly vigilant, policing yourself so that only good, orderly ideas passed through your mind. This also explained the uptight rectitude of the Christian Scientists: even their brains were clean and well-ordered, seemingly the opposite of Mouse's mind.

When the minister stopped reading, she spoke directly to the congregation about her own experience of Mind, in the form of a testimonial about a time when she had thought she was ill but had been healed by overcoming the illusion of sin. She delivered her testimonial in a folksy but assured way, never hesitating or missing a beat; and Mouse remembered the way Dale had spoken at the Reading Room, without a pause, without hemming or hawing or misspeaking. The Christian Scientists had a verbal facility and confidence that made their thoughts and their words seem one and the same. It was virtuoso speech. Even if all the words they used were common, the fact that neither the minister nor Dale ever paused amazed Mouse. They were friendly automatons.

The Christian Science attitude felt opposed to funkiness, yet since he had stopped believing in the Funk anyway, Mouse had fallen out of the Flow. The mysteriously fecund swamp that the Funk offered at its most positive had turned into a fetid morass of stagnation in his mind, so that the paranoid order of this sermon appealed to him. Christian Science was a system of belief, a program to follow, where the Funk was much more vague, an atmosphere and an attitude rather than a set of doctrines. The Funk relied on belief in the goodness and joy of life no matter what the circumstances, no matter the specific struggles of the individual. The Funk was an expression of the gladness of being alive, the absurd yet inherent worth of living, but if you stopped believing in that worth, it was nearly impossible to continue to be funky. The Funk was a self-fulfilling prophecy of love that required the lover to love first, to give love in order to receive it; and the Funk implicitly viewed life as a state of grace, but one that knew grace as a response to living and not a gift from a Supreme Being. It was head-bobbing hip-swaying Taoism. Christian Science, on the other hand, fit the believer into a ready-made system, and this pre-existing, deterministic aspect of the faith appealed to Mouse. Christian Science was there waiting for you, no matter whether you believed it at any given moment or not: it was true through your belief and your unbelief, and this submission of individual believers to the Greater Truth made Mouse want to submit, to be part of a larger Mind.

After the sermon, the worshippers stood and sang another tune, off-key and in badly fluctuating time, as if they were being punished. It was the best argument against the church Mouse could imagine: a faith whose believers took what should have been the very essence of joy and turned it into cruelty toward each other and their own eardrums. At the end of the song, the minister announced that everyone should stay for the potluck in the basement, and then they all joined hands and said "peace be with you." The woman who had earlier looked at Mouse peevishly took his hand and squeezed it, and the tone in her voice when she wished him "peace" made

Mouse believe she genuinely wanted him to have it.

The pianist played and the congregation gathered their things and headed out of the chapel, chatting. Mouse sat down again and watched each person pass his pew. He was surprised at the many different ethnic types and colors: blue-black men and women with the wide faces and high cheekbones of Africans, older Latino couples, a young Korean man.

When the minister came to Mouse's pew, she held out her hand. Mouse stood up and took it—it was cool, soft and dry—and she held his hand firmly the whole time they talked.

"Welcome," she said. "Is this your first time with us?"

"Yes, ma'am."

"I'm Dottie."

"Oh. Uh, I'm Joseph."

"Joseph, it's good to see you. I hope you'll come down to the fellowship room and have some food. We can get to know you and welcome you more personally."

"Thank you, ma'am. Uh, reverend."

"Call me Dottie."

"Alright, thanks. Dottie."

She let go his hand and turned to an elderly Chinese woman who was passing at her elbow. They talked about the woman's weekly Mahjong game as they left. Only Mouse and the pianist remained in the chapel, and the pianist continued plunking out chords clumsily, enthusiastically, while Mouse put his coat on and walked out to the foyer.

He followed the minister and the Chinese woman down a flight of stairs to a tidy basement room, where fold-out tables were set with a motley assortment of home-cooked dishes: fatty meats and strange vegetable casseroles, fried rice, a plate of cheese enchiladas, spaghetti and meatballs, hot dogs and bags of potato chips. The smells were riotous, and Mouse thought that if a church of immigrants were going to host a potluck, some Great Mind should coordinate the menu. Twenty or more people were standing around with plates of the miscellaneous cuisine, talking politely in strange accents.

Mouse got a hot dog and a cup of fruit punch, then stood in a corner and ate and drank quickly. He did not feel like an intruder, exactly, but he did feel ill at ease. He wanted to hear more about the Great Mind, but he wasn't sure what or how to ask about it. He quickly ate his hot dog and hurried back upstairs and then stood for a while in the lobby, reading pamphlets. He found one that looked appealing, on the Science of Mind, and took it. The pianist came out of the chapel and he asked her, "Do I gotta pay somebody for this, or can I take it?"

"Help yourself. Here." She found a particular flier and handed it to him. "It's our service schedule and phone numbers, in case you have questions."

"Thanks." Mouse put the pamphlets in his jacket pocket and walked back outside.

It was snowing heavily, but the air was dry and a few people were out taking the air in defiance of the weather. Mouse wandered into Lafayette Park, aimlessly, lost in his own thoughts, until he came to the little pond behind George Washington, which was frozen over. He stared at the dark ice for a long time, trying to see the pond and himself as things that both contained and expressed the perfect order of the Great Mind.

The next day, Mouse bought a King James Bible from the Reading Room, along with Mary Baker Eddy's *Science and Health with a Key to the Scriptures* and *Rudimental Divine Science*. He began attending services on Sunday mornings and Wednesday nights at the church in Lafayette Park.

He did not entirely believe or even understand all of the church's doctrines, and he got queasy when they talked about health and well-being as signs of one's relationship with God, since that seemed to blame sick people for their illnesses; but he felt calm when he read Mary Baker Eddy's books, and calm was worth more to him than understanding. The alien feeling of the church helped put his thoughts in perspective in a way that the down-home earthiness of the Southern Baptists never did. Mouse had always loved the rhythms and feeling of Gospel music, and nobody could shout and stomp a groove like a Baptist choir, but he felt that those rhythms were dead inside him, and those grooves served an idea of community that didn't hold any more. It was false, the same way the Funk had become a Fake. He could blot out his toxic thoughts when he attended Christian Science church, and the fact that most members of the Lafayette Park congregation were recent immigrants made him feel less foreign in his own skin. The context of the Eternal Mind put his failings in music and worries about jobs into a perspective that made them seem almost insignificant.

To Shauna, Mouse's interest in Christian Science was at first laughable, then baffling, then contemptible. "You know it's a nutball cult, don't you?"

"Naw, that aint true," said Mouse. "They Christians like the rest of 'em."

"They're fruit bat Christians."

"Why you always do that? You don't like somethin, you gotta put it down, call everybody names. Why I caint jus go to church and see what they say?"

"Because Christian Scientists aren't harmless like Episcopalians, Mouse. They kill people."

"What?!"

"These are the people that let their children die because they don't believe in medicine. If somebody gets sick, it's a punishment from God, and they'd rather let God take their babies to hell than give them penicillin. They probably don't mention that in their services."

"Why you gotta be so bitter?"

"Did you hear what I said? They kill their children!"

"I dunno. These people don't seem like that."

"Let me tell you a story," Shauna said, as if Mouse were a child she were scolding. "A story you may remember from the papers. We had a baby boy come into SLU Hospital one time, this is maybe fifteen years ago. High fever, screaming in pain, screaming nonstop. Okay? The parents wanted us to x-ray him for a broken bone in his neck, so we did, and while he was there we ran some blood tests and did a spinal tap, totally standard procedure for his symptoms, and we found he had meningitis. No broken bones. Now, meningitis is dangerous if you let it go, but if you catch it in time, you can treat it with acetaminophen and antibiotics, not that big a deal. It doesn't have to be fatal, it's not usually fatal, but guess what? These nutjobs refused treatment, and a week later the baby died, and the parents were charged with child neglect and homicide. Remember that? It was all over the news for a while. That's Christian Science."

"So what happen? They in jail?"

"No, they got off because they really really believed that their own sin caused their baby to die. They really thought they were doing the right thing not treating him, and that's why they're dangerous. I mean, it was a bacterial infection, not a sin! They let their baby die! And they're not the only ones, just the only ones I know about. So this is the basic belief system of your homicidal playmates."

"You don't gotta be so angry, still," Mouse said. "I mean, people pray all the time when they sick, right, and they don't always get better."

"They pray *and* they take the medicine."

"Okay, but look here. I dunno what I believe, I jus know I feel more peaceful when I go there. It aint like I kill babies cause I go to church."

"No, you just give money to people who kill babies. You just buy their books. You're not involved at all."

Mouse found it hard to believe that such well-intentioned people were murderous, and he continued to attend services. He thought it at least within the realm of possibility that they could be right, about everything. What he liked about the Christian Science Church was not that it made sense, but that he didn't have to think about whether it made sense or not while he was there: according to their tenets, all the bad things in Mouse's life were illusory, brought on by his own imperfect and too-tiny mind. Failures were simply errors of mind, not fate or competition or bad timing. It wasn't much to cling to, but it helped Mouse stop drinking himself to sleep every night, and that was enough. Moreover, he never ran into anyone he knew at Christian Science church, and the one thing he wished to avoid above everything was meeting people from the music scene and having to explain how and why the Bad Apples had collapsed, or having to hear what horrible thing Gateway was now doing with the new Bad Apples. Mouse couldn't even face the thought of the band going on without him, and he felt that his name had become a joke in his old community.

"I brought a bottle of champagne," Shauna said, as she picked Mouse up in front of his apartment one gloomy evening. "And some cheese and fruit." Mouse got into her car and they drove toward the interstate. "I thought we could make a real evening out of it."

Zack and Chloe had invited them to Salerno & Sons, the couple's piano shop, to go through a crate of old records Zack had bought at an estate auction. In the weeks since Thanksgiving, Shauna and Chloe had become friends. Shauna would take Chloe out to lunch and they would discuss Shauna's business ideas, or they would stroll through Forest Park on Chloe's afternoon breaks, smoking cigarettes and having intense heart-to-hearts. Mouse had heard a lot about Chloe. Like Shauna, she believed in an ill-defined New-Age-meets-Hindu mysticism, and Shauna admired how scrupulous and perceptive Chloe was. Shauna could not say enough good things about her: Chloe was the first new girlfriend she had found in years who wasn't a nurse or a patient, and Shauna interpreted their friendship as evidence that she was making good decisions. She had found Mouse, and now through Mouse she had found Chloe. Because of Shauna's warm feelings toward Zack and Chloe, Mouse felt that, if he didn't actually have a good time tonight at the piano shop, he would have to pretend to have a good time, which irritated him and made him feel like an adult.

Interstate 40 was dirty with slushing snow and crowded with slow-moving cars whose headlights made the thin fog glow gray. They passed Forest Park, an amorphous mass of deeper blackness in the darkness of early night, and turned onto Skinker Boulevard. Skinker was the westernmost major street of the city before you reached the wealthy suburb of Clayton, and the prestige and value of Forest Park extended to the Skinker-Wydown neighborhood's tidy homes and upscale shops. Thick old elm and oak trees and lush shrubberies lent the neighborhood a pastoral air, so that the narrow, snaky streets seemed almost like manor lanes and the homes like provincial estates. Only the closeness of the houses to one another marked the neighborhood as suburban.

Salerno & Sons was at the corner of Skinker and Northwood, immediately west of Forest Park, at the edge of this prosperous district. It was a low brick building that fit snugly into the wooded rise sloping up behind it. Through its giant display windows, facing the street, Mouse saw the unmistakable sign of success: an inventory of pianos worth hundreds of thousands of dollars. Shauna parked in the blacktopped lot beside the shop.

Chloe was waiting for them at the front entrance. She wore a chocolate brown dress that seemed hand-tailored to her figure, a little brown sweater over it and a long strand of pearls.

"Oh great, I am so starving!" she said when she saw the champagne and finger foods Shauna had brought. "How have you been, Mouse?"

She gave Mouse's arm a squeeze and kissed him on the cheek, which took Mouse by surprise. His impulse was to kiss her, too, but that seemed incredibly awkward, so he reached out to touch her arm, but she had already turned to lock the door behind them.

She ushered them through a four thousand square foot showroom, whose overhead track lighting was pleasantly dimmed, accenting the swooping lines of the grand pianos. Original art hung all around in gilded rococo frames. They walked through a section of black grands and stained-wood uprights to a small nook of electric organs and keyboards, Shauna and Chloe happily chatting about their plans for Christmas while Mouse trailed behind. At the back of the showroom, a stately mahogany conference table was strewn with papers; beside this conference table, an antique mahogany desk held a computer, a calculator and a credit card terminal. Chloe gathered the paperwork from the table into a stack, turned off the computer and said, "It's playtime."

While Shauna set out the wine and cheeses, Chloe retrieved glasses, silverware and a bottle of cognac from the storeroom, and Mouse contemplated the pianos. He remembered a time when he would have walked around the entire showroom and tried every instrument, when he would have hammed up his playing to entertain and impress the owner, when he might have composed a song on the spot about Salerno & Sons. The ghost of his former zeal fluttered over him.

He strolled around, looking absently at the art on the walls, waiting for a piano to call to him. He found a nine-foot Steinway D in its own niche, swathed in shadows, and he sat down and tested the foot pedals. He let his fingers hover over the keys, then felt the texture of them, so porous and soft, so accepting of his touch. He played middle C, then a scale. The action was gentle, invitingly springy. He poked through his brain for a song to play and glided through the gospel-tinged vamp that kicked off Donny Hathaway's "To Be Young, Gifted and Black." He was amazed at how easily he found the right keys, how supple and agile his fingers felt across the keyboard even after a long absence from playing, how his spirit lifted into the clean vibrations of the piano.

He played the song's simple chord progression, adding embellishments; he felt as if he had been released from the prison of his mind back to the freedom of his body, and he felt more fluid and alive with each chord change, with the velvety roundness of the Steinway's sound. The idea that he had given up music forever had been firm in his mind for months, but his relief at playing was so palpable he thought he might cry, and he lost himself in his own ornamentations, in gospel glissandos and variations of the melody in his right hand.

Someone touched his shoulder and he jumped. Shauna and Chloe were standing behind him. Chloe was now wearing faded blue jeans and a dark blue sweater, and he wondered how long he had lost himself in the music. They were looking at him strangely. Chloe applauded.

"That was really great, Mouse," said Chloe. The look of admiration in her eyes gave him an intense feeling of sadness.

"Aw, that aint nothin."

"I've never heard you play piano before," Shauna said. "I had no idea."

"You musta heard me play sometime. Back in the day."

"No. You were always noodling with that guitar at my apartment and you only ever played drums on stage."

"Yeah. Well. I dunno. Whyn't we eat somethin?"

"I'll pour us some champagne," Chloe said, "but I'd love to hear you play some more."

"Naw, you should play somethin," he said. "I liked that piece you played at Thanksgiving."

"I can hear myself play any day. Besides, when was the last time you tickled the ivories of a concert grand?" Chloe went back to the conference table to pour drinks.

Shauna rubbed Mouse's shoulder encouragingly. She said, "I can't believe you can do that and don't want to. If I could play like that, I'd never do anything else."

"It was jus some chords, really."

"And this is *just* a keyboard, really. Now I remember why I slept with you all those years ago. Your fingers on the keys just now felt like they were massaging my heart." She blushed. "Or something. Even Chloe felt it, and she hears people play all day long. Your emotions come right through the music."

Shauna meant her remarks as a compliment, but Mouse felt dismayed. Of course that was why Shauna had slept with him all those years ago, and of course that was the main reason anyone would want to be with him now: his music. Despite her objections to the contrary, Mouse thought that, if he never played again, Shauna would not want to stay with him—no one would—and he felt a desperate desire not to be alone, to please her. He looked at the piano with a renewed sense of obligation. He wished music hadn't become so complicated in his imagination.

Chloe returned with the bottle of champagne and three glasses on a wooden serving tray. She set the tray on the floor beneath the Steinway and handed Mouse and Shauna each a glass.

"If Zack saw me doing this, he'd have a fit. You must absolutely positively not spill the champagne on the piano, okay? Cheers."

"Zack aint here?"

"He got tied up at the Adam's Mark tuning their piano. He'll be along later. So! I've got some sheet music in the back, if you need something to play, but it's mostly classical. Do you play classical?"

"A little, but I aint great at reading."

"Well, why don't you play whatever you like, then. You don't mind, do you?"

"Naw, not if you play, too, I guess."

"Deal."

Mouse had once enjoyed stripping down a funky jam to its bare bones, to a single guitar or piano: not everybody could be funky just exposed with a solo instrument, but he didn't have the confidence to put one of his own compositions across now. He looked out the window at the cold night sky, at patches of snow in Forest Park, illunined by soft yellow streetlights. The scene had a Christmas feel, and he settled on "Linus and Lucy," the theme from *A Charlie Brown Christmas*, his favorite animated show as a child. You couldn't kill the ebullient bass line of that song, and there were so many great licks in it that it was impossible to play without feeling as animated as the characters in the cartoon. Mouse attacked it with verve, and as he pounded out the first break, the bright abrupt sounds from his right hand filled the showroom like a giddy laugh.

Shauna and Chloe put their drinks down and danced beside the piano, imitating the goofy head-bobbing of the cartoon Peanuts Gang. Mouse let the groove carry him, and he extended the song into a long dance number, inverting and then transposing the main riff, always emphasizing the bouncy bass line. When he finally ended with a flourish, Chloe and Shauna plopped down on the piano bench on either side of Mouse simultaneously, with their backs against him, as if they had planned it, as if they were all in a movie musical. They were laughing out of breath, and the softness of the women's bodies breathing hard against him bathed Mouse in warmth and life, and he closed his eyes to intensify the feeling.

They drained their champagne and Chloe crawled under the piano for the bottle and poured another round. Mouse stood up, made a sweeping bow and gestured toward the bench. "All yours," he said to Chloe.

Chloe sat down at the keyboard. "I think if I weren't tipsy I wouldn't be playing this. In fact, I know I wouldn't."

She played a series of dissonant chords with the sustain pedal held down, so that the long decay of each chord muddied the ones that followed it, and she repeated the pattern several times. The chords were weirdly opposed to one another and filled the room with anxiety. Mouse tried to let the music tune his ears, without success; but then Chloe started singing and the chord pattern became more conventional. She sang in a warbling, amateurish falsetto that was nevertheless engaging, and she committed such feeling to the song that she won Mouse over. The lyrics concerned a bird called the nuthatch (which the song rhymed with thatch, catch and match) and explained what a mixed blessing it was to see the bird, how sad to see one coming and even sadder to see it go. It reminded Mouse of a Tin Pan Alley ballad, it seemed so strange and out of time, and the lyrics were disturbingly intimate. He had never heard anything quite like it.

She finished the song, stared at the keys and took a big swallow of champagne.

"What was that?" Shauna said admiringly.

"I wrote that for my dad when he was sick. He was a birder, and his favorite bird was the red-breasted nuthatch, so I sang that for him when he couldn't go bird-watching any more. Sorry it's so depressing. I always forget."

"It was beautiful. Have you written any others?"

"I only have songs about birds." She turned to Mouse. "My dad died of cancer. He was sick for a long time, so every week when I visited him, I'd write a new song for him about a different bird. They're not all depressing, though."

She handed Mouse her wine and played a short, snappy number about a cardinal who didn't want to be red any more. Mouse liked her playing: its spry goofiness made it feel innocent.

"I am so hungry!" she said. "Why don't you play something else, Mouse, so we can end this session on a more positive note, and then we'll have some food."

Mouse sat down again and tried to think of a song they could all sing together. He landed on Fats Domino's "Blueberry Hill," put on his best old-school soul croon and led them through a clumsy version of the song in which they forgot the words, corrected each other halfway through verses and then made up new words. Instead of "I found my thrill/on Blueberry Hill," Shauna and Chloe sang "I got these thighs/from blueberry pies," and Mouse brought his whole forearm down across the keys to end it.

They ate all the food Shauna had brought and finished off the champagne, and Chloe gave Mouse a tour of the shop.

The showroom featured an equal number of new and used pianos, running the gamut from undistinguished American uprights and assembly line Japanese brands to exquisitely hand-crafted Italian models. The workshop in the back, where Zack repaired old treasures, was a junkyard pianist's never-neverland, a riot of cabinets, casters, pedals and strings. Mouse was especially interested in a Frankenstein upright that Zack had created from leftover bits of a dozen different pianos.

By the time Zack arrived, wearing denim coveralls and carrying his tools in a big wooden box, they had started on the bottle of cognac and the party was in full swing in the workshop. Zack sat down on a creaky bench with a heavy sigh and ran his fingers through his messy black hair. "Somebody pour me something, will ya?"

"Tough day?"

"Those jerks at the Adam's Mark. They've got some cabaret singer from Berlin staying in the hotel, and he goes to play the Chickering in their lounge and complains it's out of tune. So Thompson Brothers have their account, and they call them up. Next day, the cabaret guy plays it again, it's still out of tune, they call Thompson Brothers back. Day three, it's still out of tune and Cabaret Guy throws a fit. The hotel thinks this is the biggest disaster ever."

"Was it Clancy or Conrad Thompson?" Chloe asked.

"Which one you suppose is drunker? Finally they call us, and I tune it right for a change, but the manager is standing over me the whole time, and Cabaret Guy shows up and berates me in German, like it's my fault the Thomspson brothers can't tune." Zack drank his cognac. "For what it's worth, we now have the Adam's Mark contract." Chloe kissed Zack on the forehead and topped off his drink.

"'Thompson Brothers' is actually brothers, right?" Mouse said.

"Right."

"Who's Salerno & Sons?"

"I'm 'Sons,'" Zack said. "My dad was Salerno. He left the

business to me and my brother Anthony, and I bought Anthony out a few years ago. The store's had the same name for fifty years, so Chloe and I decided to keep it."

Mouse wondered what it would have been like to have a father who'd left him a business. To have any father, for that matter, to have had a tiny little head start in the world.

After they'd shared a round of drinks with Zack, they sat down on the workshop floor and unloaded crates of records. They divided the haul into fourths, and Zack explained that they would re-sell most of the them on the internet, but they would cull out rare items to keep for themselves.

They played the records they wanted to hear on a turntable at the back of the shop: most were schmaltzy pop from the 1950s, and Mouse was reminded of the simple fact he had learned rifling through used bins at record shops across the country, that the vast majority of recorded music, no matter how popular it might have been in its time, became trash. Perry Como's *The Songs I Love*, Johnny Mathis's *Heavenly*, Rosemary Clooney's *Love*—who would want these songs now? He wondered if he himself had ever produced a single song of lasting value, and what it meant to be successful, to sell a lot of records, if your music ended up at the bottom of a discards crate anyway.

"Hey, Mouse," said Zack, "that's not Clooney's *Love* album, is it?" Mouse handed it over, and Zack slipped it out of its sleeve. "It's in mint condition!" He told Mouse the album was a rare collectors' item that had been out of print for forty years. "They released it on CD a few years ago, so it won't be quite as valuable now, but this is a real find!"

By the end of the evening, Mouse had found only two records that he personally thought were interesting: a 45-single called "Hearts of Stone," by Otis Williams and the Charms, and a 33 1/3 album called *Dance with Daddy G* by Gene Barge.

"That Gene Barge might be worth something," Zack said. "He was a great saxophone player in other people's bands, but I didn't know he had his own records. What's that other one?"

"Otis Williams and the Charms," Mouse said. "Doo-wop, early fifties maybe. Forties? They had that song 'Ivory Tower' that Pat Boone ripped off."

Mouse got up and set the "Hearts of Stone" single spinning on the record player. Otis Williams' silky smooth tenor belted out "hearts of stone will never break." The background harmonies washed over them, like a secret message not just from another century but another planet. This feeling, Mouse realized, the bounce and boldness of the Charms' arrangement, so clear and simple and free, was why he had always wanted to make music, and here was this record, this perfect slice of doo-wop, at the bottom of a dusty old crate. It gave him the dimmest glimmer of hope that he had made the right choices in his life—hope not for himself or his own music but for the value and meaning of pop songs, for the idea that what he had tried to do had at least been worthy, even if unsuccessful. The Charms had succeeded. The Charms had wound up in the bottom of a discards bin, it was true, but they were alive again right then and there in the Salerno & Sons workshop. Their song had traveled fifty years forward in time.

Chloe cleared a wedge of space among the decrepit piano parts and invited Mouse to dance. Zack and Shauna got up and joined them, and they danced around each other. They played the flip side, a poppy song called "The One You Love," and shimmied like teenagers at a house party.

Out of the three hundred records they started with, they found five that were worth more than their original cover prices and one, the Rosemary Clooney album, that was potentially a collectors' item. Chloe offered Mouse the Charms single and *Dance with Daddy G*, but he declined them. He said his days on the Soul Patrol were over. Shauna took a Dean Martin album and two Nat King Cole singles.

"Oh, hey, Mouse, I almost forgot to give you something." They stood at the door saying good night, and Zack reached into the front pocket of his coveralls. He pulled out a folded-up piece of paper. Across the top in bold black letters it said, "LEARN TO PLAY THE DRUMS!"

"It's this music clinic I thought you might be interested in. I mean, as a teacher. Chloe and I do a piano class for them. St. Louis Parks and Rec has been offering group music lessons during the summer for years, but then somebody from the school board realized that if they got Parks and Rec to do the clinics throughout the whole school year, the district could cut its music programs and save money. So now the schools and the Parks Department have pooled their resources to teach these after-school classes year-round. It's their first year trying it, and I know they're looking for people."

"Alright. Thanks."

"Right now, there's only one drum teacher, guy named Ricky Hart, and I think they're looking to expand the program."

"Ricky Hart? I thought he move down south."

"You know him?"

"He was the drummer for Ebony Kings back in the day. I seen him around town all the time, maybe ten, fifteen years ago, but he quit the band and went down to New Orleans."

"I guess he's back. Anyway, pay isn't great, but they need good musicians. I don't know if you teach or what, but you crossed my mind last class I taught."

"Yeah, that's cool. Thanks."

Shauna looked over Mouse's shoulder at the flier and hugged him. "That might be fun, right?"

Mouse put it in his back pocket, and they hugged and

kissed all around and said good night.

When they got back to Mouse's apartment, Mouse realized that he had spent a whole evening in a piano shop playing and listening to music, and he was not completely miserable. He thought of Chloe's odd ditties about her father's favorite birds: surely Chloe had had no illusions about selling those songs or performing them in front of millions of people, and perhaps that should always have been the proper place for music in Mouse's own life. The distance between the doo-wop bliss of the Charms and Chloe's warbling, though, was vast, and Mouse had spent his whole life trying to make and sell pop records like the Charms'. His ambition had not been to write tweetering Audobon rhymes for a lone dying man.

He recalled the Reverend Dottie's sermon from the previous Sunday, about dissatisfaction and envy. In her readings from the Bible and Mother Eddy, Dottie had argued that dissatisfaction with one's lot in life was the result of the mistaken belief that we were separate from God. If everything was God and each one of us was an aspect of the perfect expression of God, then no one thing was better than any other. Thinking that something was better or worse was an error, a way of fracturing God off from himself. Since God is not fractured but whole, any comparison between ourselves and others was naturally false.

As he lay in bed listening to Shauna's gentle sleeping breath, Mouse meditated on God's supposed wholeness, but he could not convince himself that he was a perfect expression of God, nor that there was no difference between Chloe and the Charms, nor that his dissatisfaction was an error of belief. The world was filled with differences, and saying that everything was a perfect expression of God could conceivably justify slavery or war or any other evil. Why would the Charms ever have made "Hearts of Stone" if they had been perfectly satisfied with their lives? Was the song itself, then, an error in God's eyes, because it was an expression of dissatisfaction?

When he finally fell asleep, he dreamed, not of the Reverend Dottie reading from Key to the Scriptures; not of the Charms singing four-part harmonies; not of drumming behind the Bad Apples as they tore up the stage in front of a packed house of concert-goers. When he dreamed, he saw Chloe sitting at a piano, singing off-kilter songs about birds to her dying father. And he saw her father, an audience of one, overcome with love.

Fate

"Y'all've been hearin a lot these last couple weeks about some pretty technical stuff. Practice techniques, economy of movement, tricks for stayin on time. But since this here is the last week before Christmas, I thought we'd take it easy and talk about some advance concepts, stuff the pros talk about when they jus kickin it, give y'all something to chew on over the holidays. For that purpose, we have a special guest, Mouse Watkins. Caint nobody lock in a groove like Mouse, and he been playin on CDs and giggin round the Lou since before most a y'all been born. So give it up."

Eleven boys in their early teens were sitting in a semi-circle of fold-out metal chairs around Ricky Hart's drum kit, in the gymnasium of Vashon High School in North St. Louis. It was the intermediate drum section of Ricky's semester-long Parks and Recreation percussion clinic. The boys had brought their own percussion instruments, from bongos and djembes to single snares and marching tom sets, and most were members of their high schools' marching bands. One boy held only a pair of drumsticks, and he stared hungrily at Ricky's gleaming hi-hat cymbal.

The gymnasium smelled like old socks and felt like a damp cave. The heating system wasn't working properly and cold sieved around the outside doors. The Vashon High cheerleading squad was practicing at the other end of the gym, learning a new dance routine, and the music from their boom box started and stopped unpredictably, playing hometown star Nelly's first rap hit. Most of the boys were more interested in the cheerleaders than the drum clinic.

Mouse had called Ricky intending only to talk about his old friend's life after he had quit the Ebony Kings, to ask if he was still gigging and whether he was making a living teaching drums. Ricky had seized the opportunity to beg Mouse to teach a session of his clinic. Ricky taught three classes a week, ranging from Introduction to Percussion at the middle school level to Jazz Technique, and he had confessed to Mouse that it wasn't always easy to come up with good lessons. This was the first semester the program had existed, and the school board had not yet certified a curriculum, so Ricky was making it up as he went along.

Mouse had taken the bus up Grand Boulevard to Martin Luther King Drive and walked through a sleet storm to Vashon, where he now felt distinctly foolish, confronting a class of pimply boys, like he was back in after-school detention. He hadn't sat behind a kit in nearly two months, and it was clear to him that whatever talent he had as a drummer had amounted to nothing: he was not sure, under the circumstances, what he could say about drumming that would help someone just starting out. "Talk about your life," Ricky had said. "Tell stories about the band or the famous people you met along the way."

"Alright," Mouse said to the boys. "I'll start out by sayin I was the leader of a funk outfit called the Bad Apples the last twenty years. The Apples was straight-ahead funk, from the Sly Stone/Kool and the Gang school. Not as trippy as P-Funk, not as hard as James Brown. I guess we was like Spinners meets post-psychedelic O'Jays with the feelin of Harold Melvin and the Blue Notes, if you had to narrow it down." The boys stared at him stone-faced. "Kinda takin things from each one and makin our own thing."

Ricky laughed. "Mouse, you jus gave everybody a lesson in Greek. Who knows the O'Jays?" Four boys raised their hands. "How 'bout Harold Melvin?" No hands. The boys were bored and fidgety. "How 'bout Catfish Crunk?" Every boy's hand shot up. "Well, Mouse here's the drummer on they song 'Jawbreaker,' which I know y'all know, cause we already talked about it." The boys sat up a little in their seats. "Maybe Mouse could say somethin about that track." Ricky nodded encouragingly.

"To come correct," Mouse said, "I aint never met Catfish Crunk except once at a lawyer's office, when we signed the deal for the song. 'Jawbreaker' was built on a drum-and-bass breakdown from a Bad Apples song called 'Afrobatics,' which was on our sixth album. So they took the part where I turned the beat around at the end of the first solo and laid some effects over it, and that was the song."

"Whyn't you play the break for us?" Ricky said. He turned to the kids. "I want you to think about 'Jawbreaker' while he's playin, okay? Play the song in your mind along with Mouse's drummin and you can get an idea for yourself how to take a basic drum track and turn it into somethin a whole lot more, and how essential the drummer is to makin a whole soundscape like 'Jawbreaker.' A drummer, mind, not a drum machine or a Roland."

Mouse sat down at Ricky's kit, took up a pair of sticks and stared past the cymbals at the kids. The sticks felt good. He played a quick roll on the snare, and he was surprised at how good it sounded, the same reaction he'd had playing the piano at Salerno & Sons. After twenty years of constant playing, two months off felt like an eternity, but Mouse noticed only a slight clumsiness in his feel. His hands felt strong and light.

He stood up again. "Here's a good example of how many different possibilities you find in drums," he said, sounding to his own ears now and even feeling somewhat professorial. "Ricky's a great drummer, but he use a whole different style than me, a whole different set-up for a different kinda feel. His basic kit is two rack toms here and a floor tom, where I use one rack and two on the floor, in different figures. His cymbals are all bigger, especially his crash and his ride, and his hi-hat is in different ratio to the others than mine. And that's just in terms of basic set-up, which give each drummer a whole different feel. He play more with the shank up on the hi-hat, where I really want a thicker rimshot."

"Right," Ricky said, "and I bet my snare is tighter than yours, too."

"That's right." Mouse played another roll on the snare.

"See," Ricky said, "I'm goin for somethin light that kinda drags the beat with me. Like, I never sit all-the-way deep in the pocket like Mouse does."

"That's cause I'm lookin for a fatter sound with more holes in the beat," said Mouse. "Ricky's got more of a swing thing, fillin more of the sound."

The boys were staring at Mouse with constipated looks, and he realized that they had no idea what he was saying. He looked to Ricky for help.

"Alright, Mouse, before we lose these kids completely, whyn't you go ahead and play it, and we can show'em what you mean."

"Okay, so the 'Afrobatics' groove start out as a bluegrass rhythm called 'Chick'n Pick'n,' but I slowed it down, gave it a heavy bass-drum foundation, and added snare ostinatoes on the eighth notes." Ricky rolled his eyes. "Anyway, somethin like this."

Mouse laid down the groove from "Afrobatics." At first, his mind got in the way, thinking how to emphasize the fundamentals of the beat for the kids, but then he flowed into the groove and lay back on it and enjoyed how much the kids flowed with him. The whole gymnasium turned funky, and the cheerleading coach at the other end of the basketball court stopped the practice and let her girls dance to Mouse's beat. Ricky motioned for the boys to come around the kit and watch Mouse from the drummer's perspective, and Mouse stayed locked in for a few minutes, narrating his movements as he played.

When he stopped, Ricky pointed out that Mouse was playing a matched grip, where Ricky had been teaching them traditional, and he took the sticks from Mouse and sat down at the kit himself. Ricky now played the "Afrobatics" groove the way Mouse had played it but using a different grip and then he dropped down into the groove and added some soloing over the top. He discussed the difference between Mouse's sense of rhythm, which laid back on the beat, and his, which pushed the beat forward.

"See," Ricky said, "the time is the same. We both rock-solid on the beat, but the feeling of Mouse's beat is different, cause of where he put the emphasis. It aint accents and fills, necessarily, it's where you gonna lock in the beat, in the front of the groove or behind it or right on top. I know that don't make a lotta sense right now, but that's what we gonna talk about today, and we gonna have each of you play so you can feel what we sayin. It's gonna make these exercises we been doin come together and your practice time gonna be a lot more fun." He invited Mouse to talk about time.

"The first skill any drummer need is to keep solid time," Mouse said. "That may sound obvious, but you'd be amazed how many drummers slip and slide. You got the bass player pullin you and the horns skatin free sometimes and the singer stretchin out, and if you aint got that solid rhythm and concentration, you can lose the beat. The drums are the heart, and if the heart skips and slows down and speeds up, the whole body get outta whack. So you gotta be solid. But not every solid beat's the same, like Ricky's sayin. Not every three-four is the same as every other. You not a machine."

Mouse was enjoying the kids' attention. He was just dumping the contents of his head: he had never ordered his knowledge in any systematic way, and he was spilling ideas as soon as they occurred to him, without thinking about building a coherent message, but he liked the feeling of being an authority passing along wisdom, instead of being the trained monkey playing to amuse drunks. He suddenly felt that his knowledge might make a difference to these kids, in a way that it would never make a difference to the bar crowd.

One of the kids raised his hand. "Whatchyou mean, not every three-four's the same? What's the difference between one three-four and another three-four?"

"He mean tempo," said Ricky.

"Naw, not tempo," Mouse said. He racked his brain for a time analogy that might make sense to a fourteen year old boy. "Think of it like this. You got a ghetto-ass hooptie doin eighty mile an hour, and next to it you got a brand new Escalade doin eighty mile an hour. It's still the same eighty mile an hour, but the hooptie caint go no faster and the Escalade jus be warmin up. So some grooves is like hCSSptis and some's like Caddies. Even though they in the same time at the same tempo, it all depend on the drummer, how he gonna spend his energy, how he gonna drive the groove. What kinda car you wanna drive, the hooptie or the Escalade?"

"Escalade!" they shouted.

"Then you gotta sit back in the groove and let it ride. Like this."

Mouse played the Popcorn groove, laying back in the pocket almost behind the downbeats; then he followed that groove with the same beat the way he would have played it when he was a teenager, straining with all his might to move it, to muscle energy into the beat. It was a lesson that was educational even for him: by playing in an intentionally amateurish way, he channeled his own eighteen-year-old self into the present and realized how many more possibilities he saw in the beat now than he had when he was a kid, how expansive the time seemed. His feel had relaxed, even in the most propulsive groove. He had traveled a long way from the player he was as a boy, from those skills and that understanding, and he realized that he could now see to a farther musical horizon than he had ever imagined growing up.

When he stopped playing, Ricky had the kids sit behind the drum kit one at a time. Ricky helped each boy play something appropriate to his level that incorporated the "Chick'n Pick'n" idea. He talked about Catfish Crunk and how the boys could form their own groups and play on professional tracks.

Before the clinic was over, Mouse again sat at Ricky's kit and talked to the boys about the feeling of a real drummer versus a drum machine or a loop. Most likely, he thought, none of these kids would ever become a professional drummer or even a competent one, but since digital sampling and electronic beats had become the norm, it was good that they at least understood that drumming was the heart and soul of pop music and couldn't be replaced by computers and click tracks.

At the end of the clinic, the kids gave Mouse a rousing ovation, which felt better than any applause he'd heard in a long time. One of the boys had nailed the Popcorn, and the look on his face and his vibe when he left made Mouse feel satisfied. He remembered the feeling when he himself had first mastered a basic groove, how the whole world had opened because of it, and he wondered if there were still places where he could find new grooves now, and if so, where on earth they might be.

As the last boy left, Ricky fist-bumped Mouse. "That was awesome, man!" The cheerleaders walked past with their colorful miniskirts bouncing, and Mouse thought about that kid who had just nailed the Popcorn, how popular he was going to be when he got his thing together.

Ricky gave Mouse a ride home, and they went for a beer at Sweeney's. Sidney was bartending, and he remembered Ricky from his days with the Toucans, his band before the Ebony Kings. Sidney set them up with a round on the house, and they took a table at the back of the room, away from the dirty little stage.

"You were great with those kids, Mouse," Ricky said. "A little too fast and a lot too advanced, but they responded to you. Best class I ever had, straight up."

"To be truthful," Mouse said, "I aint been in the woodshed in a long while, but I felt it all, you know, right there, and I got a grip a new ideas jus playin the Popcorn again."

"Seriously, you oughtta think about teachin this clinic, I mean, for real. That stuff today—you could stretch that into a whole semester, jus that bit right there. I'm tellin you, man, it's a lay-down gig."

"Yeah, but it's your gig."

"They's plenty to go round. Schools aint got enough money for music programs, and people like you and me, no college, no degree, we work cheaper than they can get a regular teacher. They pay me a hundred dollars a class, three classes a week, alright? Caint get a certified teacher for that scratch, no benefits, no nothin. So I'll take the gig, I don't mind the pay. It's better than workin, you know? And St. Louis Schools is talkin 'bout extendin this program, talkin 'bout turnin all the music programs over to clinics like this."

Mouse calculated that Ricky was earning more than half of

what Mouse himself was making at Busch, and he was working only three hours a week to Mouse's forty. If he skimped, Mouse could live on Ricky's wage, even in Soulard—and he could sleep all day! Mouse's sister Jackie earned fifteen thousand dollars a year working only ten hours a week giving piano lessons. Still, it was one thing to spend an evening banging skins in a high school gym, saying things off the top of your head; it was another to go to that same gym over and over and try to coax a clever drum roll from a distracted boy. He wondered if he could develop a tolerance for bad playing if it meant working only a few hours a week: it was surely better than hefting beer cases all day.

"You play out any more?" Mouse asked.

"Naw, that scene aint for me now. My old lady don't like me runnin round to clubs."

"So you gettin by jus teachin these clinics?"

"Naw, I'm makin child support teachin these clinics. I got two kids down New Orleans, and I'm tryin to do right by them and they mother, you know? I still do odd jobs during the day, and my wife works Monsanto nights, cleanin up. I couldn't make it teachin. It's jus money for nothin, is all. Good gig."

Ricky's attitude about teaching music lessons was diametrically opposed to Jackie's. Mouse's sister believed passionately in teaching children piano, creating a link between the traditions of the past and the music of the future, and Mouse was more inclined to her point of view. Ricky only wanted the money. He had no grand passion to teach, but Mouse thought there might be a middle ground between Ricky and Jackie, that he could perhaps keep the Funk alive into the next generation and still be laid back about it and make easy money. If only he could find the Funk again himself. . . perhaps the awfulness of hearing children play badly all the time could be infused with enough purpose to make it bearable.

When they were ready for their second round, Sidney took a cigarette break and joined them. "You guys goin to the Red Giant show?"

"Red Giant?" Mouse said. "They still together?"

Red Giant had been a funk band for almost as long as the Bad Apples: they had been the Apples' only serious competition in St. Louis for years, and the funk scene was so small that the two bands had become incestuous, sharing horn players, swapping guitarists and going through periods of hot and cold wars over bookings and pay. Mouse had always thought of Red Giant as the Apples' irritating little brother. Their songs weren't as good, their sound wasn't as tight and most of Red Giant's core players were Bad Apple rejects. Two years before, Red Giant had moved to Los Angeles, to try to make it in the burgeoning neo-soul clubs on the West Coast. The last Mouse had heard of them, the entire band was sleeping on the floor of a warehouse in Watts.

"Is Red Giant still together?" Sidney scoffed. "Where you been, man? They got a new CD comin out on Warner Brothers. They're big time. Seven figure contract, big tour comin up. Hell, man, you should see their website, like totally batshit. Sharon Jones and the Dap Kings are *opening*."

Mouse couldn't believe his ears. The Bad Apples were better than Red Giant had ever dreamed of being, and now the Apples were washed up and Red Giant had a major label contract? He wondered if Gateway had heard about it.

"They're havin a release party at Mississippi Nights the twenty-third. It's gonna be a blowout. They're in town for a few shows over Christmas, and then they're hittin the road, tv shows, arenas."

"I'll be damned," Ricky said. "Wonder how they did it?"

Sidney took a long drag on his cigarette. "They were playin a one-off at some dive in Hollywood, and just so happens a young gun from Warners goes in that night. He's tryin to make a name for himself, and he sees Red Giant as a way to stand out with his boss, so he signs'em. That's the lowdown I got from Clark over at Buster's. they're tryin a new social media marketing thing with them, you know, like Red Giant is gonna save Warner Brothers now."

Ricky shook his head. "I gotta go, gotta give it up to my boy Kangaroo, if he still with it. You know if they still the same crew?"

"I heard they picked up some new horn players, and Warners slicked'em out, but I think the main guys are still the same, Slide and J.D. and Kangaroo. I mean, it wouldn't be Red Giant without them guys, right?"

Mouse was struck dumb. He had practically taught Kenny how to play the drums himself, and now Kenny was a hotshot recording artist. "Is the CD out yet?"

"Probably not. It's a release party, dude."

"Nobody gonna release a CD two days before Christmas, Sid," said Mouse. "You gotta give people a chance to buy it and wrap it. I bet it's already out."

"Well, whatever, you can stream tracks from their website, and they're givin away all kinds of audio shit, bonus tracks and stuff. It's all social media now, and the CD is just a tool." Sidney finished his cigarette. "If you guys wanna go to the show, maybe we could carpool over."

"Alright," Ricky said. "I think my old lady'll let me out for the night. You in, Mouse?"

"I'm in."

At six o'clock on the evening of December twenty-third, Shauna was wearing red and green plaid pajamas and a Santa Claus stocking cap, stringing Christmas decorations around an eight-foot Scotch pine tree in her living room. The radio was tuned to a station playing traditional holiday music, and she sang along with every song, which would have driven Mouse crazy if he hadn't been so preoccupied.

He stalked around Shauna's house with Shauna's iPod and headphones, listening to Red Giant's major label debut, wishing with all his might that he could hate it—but it was good. According to the band's website, half the songs were written by a team of songwriters Mouse had never heard of. Only three songs were written by anyone he recognized, and most of the band's personnel had changed since he'd seen them last in St. Louis. They had gone big-time: their sound was slick and funky, their playing was tight and there were a couple of songs that had "hit single" written all over them. A capsule review of the CD had even appeared in *Rolling Stone*, which still carried a charge for Mouse, even though the magazine wasn't the arbiter of taste it had been in his youth. Mouse was eaten up with envy.

Despite Mouse's cajoling, Shauna refused to go with him to Mississippi Nights. She was loaning him her car for the drive downtown, but she was staying home.

"I don't wanna go down there by myself," he said.

"You're taking Ricky and Sidney, for Christ's sake."

"It aint the same." He flopped down on her sofa and watched her drape tinsel on the branches of the Christmas tree. "They don't give a shit. They goin for the party."

"Maybe that's what you should be going for."

"I caint believe you'd say that."

"Well, what?" She stepped onto a stool to reach the upper branches. "Some people you know did good, Mouse. They made it, and you were part of their success. Some of those guys learned music by playing with you. It's something to be proud of."

Mouse shook his head. "That aint it."

"It's not a zero-sum game. You shouldn't go at all if you're gonna be angry." She stepped down from the stool and unwrapped a package of colorful lights. "Here." She handed Mouse the end of the strand, and he helped her unravel it and plug it in. The lights blinked on and off.

Mouse hated the fact that Shauna would not share his torment about Red Giant's success. Red Giant was going to funk up Mississippi Nights, the premier concert club in St. Louis, and everyone would cheer them on, the hometown heroes in their triumphant return. He felt like the dutiful brother of the Prodigal Son.

"Whatchyou gotta do here that's so important anyhow? Come on, baby, come down to the show. I'll help you hang all the lights you want, after."

"I don't wanna go, Mouse. I need a few hours alone."

"What for?"

"Just for some personal things."

"Like what?"

"Like maybe you're not supposed to know."

"Don't bug me out." He flopped back into the sofa. "Serious."

"It's Christmas, Mouse. Snow, mistletoe, presents on the tree?"

"You gonna stay home and wrap my present? That's what so urgent? Come with me. That'll be my present, alright? I don't want nothin else."

"If it's gonna be such torture, then just don't go."

"I gotta go."

"Then go. I'll be here when you get back. You can tell me all about it." Shauna sat down next to him and wrapped her arms around his neck. "It'll be fine. You've been to Mississippi Nights a million times. You'll walk in, you'll see how normal it is and it'll just be another show. Everyone will be happy to see you again, you know? Everybody likes you, Mouse, and you've been a hermit long enough. Maybe you'll even surprise yourself and have a good time." She kissed him.

"Right."

"How many times have I denied you something you really wanted? Huh?"

"Never."

She kissed him again. "Tonight is something I need. Okay? I need to be alone, and you can give me that. It can be your Christmas gift to me."

Mouse sighed. "I guess I'll take that gumball machine back to Sears, then."

Shauna brought her hands to her mouth in mock horror. "Mouse! Was that a joke?!" She threw her arms around him and bounced up and down against his chest. "Oh my god, he's alive! He's alive!"

She slathered his face and neck with kisses. She seemed so genuinely gleeful that Mouse felt lighter himself, but he still wished she were going with him.

Mouse had agreed to be the designated driver, which he thought would keep him out of trouble. The last thing he needed was to get drunk and make a scene at Red Giant's coming-out party.

As he pulled out of Shauna's driveway, snow was falling in fat blue flakes, and he prayed for a white-out. Despite all the early snow this winter, there still hadn't been a storm that had really shut the city down, and out of spite Mouse hoped tonight would be the night for the blizzard, to keep people away from the Red Giant party. He wished he had a more generous soul—it was contrary to both Christian Science and the spirit of the Funk to wish others ill—but he couldn't rise above it tonight. He didn't understand how, in only two years, Red Giant had risen so high and he had fallen so low.

Mouse made a circuitous route around the west side to collect his passengers: Sidney lived in an apartment on The Hill and Ricky's townhouse was in University City. Sid was stoned when Mouse arrived, and Sidney and Ricky passed a joint back and forth as they drove downtown. The smoke reminded Mouse of the reasons he had become sick of the clubs in the first place, why he'd stayed holed up in his apartment for the past two months.

They were an hour and a half early for the show, but the club parking lot was already full, and they had to trawl around Laclede's Landing for a long time looking for a spot. They bumped slowly along First Street—the old cobblestone streets had been restored in the late 1970s, after the Landing had been transformed from a shipping dock into a tourist attraction—and they finally found a parking space under Eads Bridge, right by the river.

As they walked toward the venue, past hip cafes and restaurants just waking up for the evening, a horse-drawn carriage clopped by. "Pierre Laclede gave St. Louis its name in 1764, at this very spot," the carriage driver announced to his passengers. "He named it after the Crusader King, Louis the Ninth." Winter-bundled pedestrians glutted the sidewalks, and the gaslight streetlamps were hung with wreaths and Christmas baubles. Lights from the riverboats made the snowflakes sparkle as they swirled into the rippling waters of the Mississippi.

Mississippi Nights was a brick-and-mortar building just north of the MLK Bridge, a former shipping transfer house for tobacco and other river freight. It was the top rung of the local club circuit (just below the prestigious Fox Theater and the larger arenas), an open space with no seating, where up to a thousand people could throng in front of the stage. The Bad Apples had packed this club a few times: they'd held two CD release parties here themselves, one for their first album, *Supply Side Funkonomics*, when they were still brimming with ideas and promise, and one for *The Cutting Edge of Funknology*, which had almost been their breakthrough. Those shows had represented the zenith of Mouse's career, but the show tonight was merely the launching pad for the new Red Giant. A release party meant something different when Warner Brothers money was behind it, starting with Red Giant's luxury tour bus in the parking lot.

They stepped inside the club. A hundred Red Giant banners hung from the rafters, and a Red Giant music video was playing on large-screen tvs over the bar.

They paid their cover, and everyone from the bouncers and cashiers to the box office manager brightened when they saw Mouse. They rubbed his bald head and told him they missed seeing him around, and Mouse was surprised that he felt so sentimental. He had steeled himself against Red Giant and, in his mind, he thought he was coming in hard, but one step through the door and he was already a sap. The Red Giant banners and their new-school funk bouncing through the sound system, however, reminded him that this was not his party. He was just another familiar face in the crowd, and if he never came back to Mississippi Nights, he would never see any of these people again. As good as their displays of affection felt, he was just the drummer in another band they liked, and their fondness did not extend beyond the walls of this club.

A mob of people already pressed close to the stage. Sidney and Mouse pushed through the crowd around the bar and ordered drinks.

A hulking yellow-skinned black man wearing a Mississippi Nights t-shirt and a humorless grimace muscled over to Mouse. The man would have been menacing enough because of his bulk and demeanor, but he was also decorated with tattoos of knives, skulls and Chinese ideograms from his neck to his fingertips. He gave Mouse a friendly chest bump and shoulder hug. "Where you been at, brother?"

"Stayin down low, Amos. Got me a straight job, and jus tryin to keep my thing together."

"Yeah yeah, alright alright. But you know how I look out for you, G, like family. You disappear all a sudden like that, make people think the worst."

"Naw, it's all good."

"Right on right on. You know Gateway's lookin for you, right?"

Mouse blinked solemnly and scanned the clatter and jumble of the club. "He here?"

"I aint seen him in a while, but he been around all night."

"Yeah? Oscar here, too?"

"I aint seen him. I gotta get back, alright? I jus came to say what's up. Stay straight, Mouse. Look me up 'fore you leave." He gave Mouse a friendly forearm shiver across the chest and returned to his post at the front doors.

"Y'all hear that?" Mouse said, when Sidney and Ricky came up.

"What?"

"Gateway's here."

"It aint no thing, Mouse," said Ricky.

"Whatchyou mean?"

"You didn't know he'd be here? Gate's been pimpin the new Apples all over town, so aint no way he'd miss this gig. He can smell the gravy train."

The crowd surged spontaneously toward the stage, and Sidney and Ricky slithered away from Mouse toward the main floor. People pressed in and the house lights dimmed. The DJ was ramping up the recorded music, working the crowd, and Mouse felt numb and frantic inside. He wished more than ever that Shauna had come along. He had no real friends in this place.

He pushed through the mob to Sidney and Ricky, who were ribbing each other, joshing and jostling. The air was heavy with reefer and cigarette smoke, which made the orange and blue spotlights, sweeping over faces contorted with laughter, seem hellish. The crowd's excitement felt too exuberant to be real, and the fact that it indeed was real made Mouse feel misshapen: this was *his* fantasy, come true for someone else, and the Apples were now a bad dream. Ricky and Sidney downed there drinks and cupped another joint between them. The jubilant crowd jounced and pushed Mouse from all sides. He could barely breathe. By the time the house lights went all the way down and the emcee began his bombastic patter, Mouse felt as if he'd left his body.

The footlights flashed, and a burst of pyrotechnics signaled Red Giant's entrance. The crowd screamed and surged again.

Mouse's old nemesis, J.D. "Kangaroo" Reid, strutted onstage and took command of the club, hopping up and down with the mike in his signature move. He wore a bright red buckskin outfit, like a psychedelic Daniel Boone, with absurdly large red glasses, and the band behind him sported similar red frontier costumes. The drummer, guitarist and bass player laid down a nasty groove, the keyboardist added a fat fill and the horns came in with a tasty lick, and they were off and grooving.

The band was loose in the flow and tight on the One. They had lost the deadwood players from back in the day, added younger musicians with serious chops and become a slick plastic funk outfit. Their roster now included a DJ, who was building out the sound with borrowed beats and sampled riffs, spinning wax behind the keyboard stand. Red Giant had stopped fighting hip-hop and incorporated it, and their sound was slick, thick and greasy.

Mouse felt a tap on his shoulder. He turned and found Gateway grinning at him, grooving to the music. "Hey, man," Gate shouted. He nodded up at Mouse's bald head. "Sorry 'bout your head, Mouse. Sorry 'bout that whole thing." He offered a hand in peace, and Mouse took it ruefully and shoulder-hugged him.

"You never could land a clean punch on me."

"I know, man, I shouldna done that. I'm sorry."

"Alright, well, water under the bridge, you know?" Mouse sighed. It would have been more satisfying to hold a grudge.

"If I'da known you look this ugly bald, I never woulda done it."

Mouse could not take this comment as the light-hearted jibe it was intended to be. He wanted more contrition, a more earnest attempt at reconciliation. This joke seemed to him, instead, just another sign that Gateway and Mouse had completely parted ways.

Mouse pointed to the stage. "Whatchyou think?"

"Solid! You know, before, I wouldn'ta let Kenny or Slide hold my picks, but now they up there slicked out and doin it. Seem like they got ten times better chops since I seen'em last. Like they actually practiced!"

They stood jammed close together by the crowd, listening to the band work out a riff borrowed from Zapp's "California Love." Kangaroo sang a weak lyric about how St. Louis was Party Central, USA.

"I been talkin to the fellas," Gateway said.

"Red Giant?"

"Yeah."

"You been hangin with Red Giant?"

"So what?"

"You usedta call'em Black Midget. You said the Mickey Mouse Club had more soul."

"It's different now. They connected, man, they in tight with Warner Brothers, everybody out there behind'em. They got Rose Stone on they new album. It's the real deal, Mouse. I got the email of they manager, and Kenny said he'd get our new CD to the right people at Warners."

"What new CD?"

"Listen, Mouse, this is the new thing everybody in L.A.'s lookin for. It aint throwback funk and it aint battle-rap bullshit, it's somethin else, a whole new thang. Red Giant jus the tip of the iceberg. They got this whole new social network marketing shit gonna save Warner Brothers. Kangaroo say they throwin money at bands like it's goin' outta style, like the old days."

"You gotta be kiddin." Mouse believed that every trend was the next big thing till the next next big thing came along. It was a marketing joke whose punch line was the bands themselves.

"Remember when New Edition and Boyz II Men come out," Gateway said, "and then all of a sudden they's all them New Jack Swing bands. And then Jill Scott and Eryka Badu got hot and then it was neo-soul sisters? This is gonna be like that! All we gotta do is put together a four-song demo and we in. These guys got the connections to get us in!"

"And why they wanna do that? What did Red Giant ever do for us?"

"It aint like that now, I'm tellin you. We aint fightin for the same scraps any more. We can all get paid." Gateway grabbed Mouse's arm. "Did you see they bus? Man, they got velvet lining on the cupholders!"

The last time the Bad Apples had mounted a tour, half the

band and their equipment had traveled in their oil-guzzling, fume-spewing 1972 Econoline Cruiser, whose back windows were broken out and covered with plastic bags—someone had to stand guard over it whenever they parked. The other half of the band had followed the Econoline in the trombone player's equally broken-down 1980 Cutlass, and they'd spent the entire tour, from Carbondale to Cincinnati to Champaign, sniping at each other, spending all their profits on gas and repairs. Red Giant's luxury bus would remove eighty percent of the difficulty of touring, and Mouse momentarily entertained the fantasy of a Bad Apples tour bus; also, the fact that Red Giant would be playing bigger arenas with better equipment and more skilled technicians would make the concerts sound fresher than the Bad Apples' ever had. The Apples had always used gerryrigged soundboards and middle-of-the-road amps, the best they could afford, which couldn't compete with even house sound equipment in a real arena.

"Listen to it, man," Gateway said. "This could be the sound of our future!"

Red Giant was playing every track from their new CD and mixing in old favorites from their St. Louis records. They had a slick set, laying out new work to full effect while nodding at their older fans by sprinkling in obscure early tunes that would make the diehards feel like insiders. It was an impressive display of showmanship, and the band's new confidence radiated off their core crew like an aura of pure light. Mouse imagined them sainted in the stained glass windows of Saints Peter and Paul Catholic Church, their red buckskin suits shimmering over the chapel. But it was still all show and no soul to Mouse. The new songs were slick metallic synth-dance numbers with generic lyrics and borrowed attitude, the opposite of the mulchy, weird, organic funk the Bad Apples played. Red Giant had the form without the flow.

"Did you tell Kenny we had a new CD?" Mouse asked.

"It aint nothin to put a CD like that together. Rearrange some old songs, lay down a few new tracks, throw in a little scratch and bomb the bass. That's it. Maybe write one new song, like an anthem for the L.A. soul crowd, and we in. We can sell Catfish Crunk the rights to 'Grooves' to finance it—the contract's already written! I bet we could do it in a week."

The song Red Giant was playing ended, and Kangaroo held up his hands for quiet. "I'm so proud to be back here, y'all," he panted, "to debut this record for everybody that supported us over the years." The crowd screamed. "Without you, we couldna done it." More screams. "Now we wanna dedicate this next song to our first manager, Jimmy Rafferty, who happens to be the general manager of Mississippi Nights now. Thanks for havin us back, J!"

The band kicked off its biggest local St. Louis hit, a novelty dance song called "The Devil is a Duck." They had simplified it by slowing it down, having the bass play a straight walk and the horns double the melody instead of playing a second counter-melody, and giving a prominent breakdown to the DJ. They had gutted it and turned it inside out. The song sounded glitzier but dead, like a Justin Timberlake knock-off of a Michael Jackson imitation of Earth, Wind & Fire.

Mouse shook his head. "Bad Apples caint play this kinda shit. We might as well put out a BeeGees album."

"Naw, Mouse, listen to me, listen to me, you thinkin all wrong. We got the phone number of the people at Warner Brothers who can say yes. All we gotta do is give them somethin they wanna hear and ink the deal, and then we do whatever the hell we want."

"You think that's how it'll be?"

"Why not?"

"They don't give you a million dollars and then let you do

whatever you want, Gate. This is it! This is the new Red Giant! This is how they gonna be. If we make the Apples like this, then the Apples gonna always sound like this. If you sell out to make it, you caint never buy yourself back again. You caint never have enough juice to say no."

"You don't know shit, Mouse. Look at Kangaroo up there. He look unhappy to have that million dollars?"

"But they sound like KC & the fuckin Sunshine Band. They caint get off the One. They aint no *funk* left in the groove."

"Look around, man! A thousand people here *gettin off* on how they sound!"

"You jus don't get it, do you?"

"Naw, Mouse, you don't get it. And I'm gonna make it this time, with or without you."

Gate turned abruptly and shoved his way through the crowd. He disappeared into the sea of bouncing bodies and blunt smoke, and Mouse felt like throwing up. He wished he'd never come.

After three encores, Red Giant strutted offstage and the house lights came up. Recorded music came on the sound system and it was clear that the show was over, but the crowd was electric with the band's energy and no one moved toward the exits. They clapped their hands in unison and whoo-hooed for more.

Sidney tugged at Mouse's sleeve. "Come on." He was mush-mouthed and the whites of his eyes were opaque. "Let's go say hi to the fellas."

"Shit, man," said Ricky. "How much you think a red buckskin tunic cost?"

Ricky and Sidney pulled Mouse through the mass of bodies toward the dressing rooms. He allowed himself to be dragged along, feeling numb and wondering what he could say to Kangaroo Reid about the show, wondering if he'd find

Gate already back there, sitting on Slide Randall's lap.

Mouse's connections with the bouncers allowed them backstage into the bowels of Mississippi Nights. The hallway to the dressing rooms was crammed with young men smoking cigarettes, posing, and young girls wearing skin-tight clothes doused with cheap perfume. With a mixture of horror and envy, Mouse remembered the nights he'd had his pick of these girls. The haze of other people's sweat bearing close in the smoke-filled air, the humid walls and floors stained with countless drinks and old bodily fluids, the drugged punks swaying into one another, laughing, the obscene graffiti and seedy band posters made Mouse's stomach turn and his head swim. They steamed through the skanks and pushers and flatterers to the end of the hall, where a bouncer Mouse didn't recognize guarded a door painted glossy black.

"Hey, man," Sidney said enthusiastically. He grabbed the bouncer's shoulder and leaned heavily into him. "Tell Slide that Sidney Purcell wants to see him."

The bouncer shrugged Sidney casually into the wall, where Sidney's body smacked the dirty gray bricks. He let out a heavy 'oof' and looked at Mouse like a scolded puppy.

Mouse held up his hands in a gesture of peace. "Do me a favor," he said to the bouncer. "Please give this message to J.D. Alright? Mouse Watkins come to collect his Buffalo nickel." The bouncer didn't even blink. "We aint makin trouble. We friends from back in the day."

"Everybody's they boys from back in the day, chump."

"Please. Mouse Watkins, Buffalo nickel. Take you five seconds."

The bouncer didn't budge. Mouse threw his hands up. "How bad you want it fellas?" He reached into his pocket and held up a twenty dollar bill.

Ricky said, "I aint payin this guy to let me see Slide Randall. Hell, Slide still owes me money."

"Sidney?"

Sidney looked as if he might whimper. "I'm cashed."

The bouncer's expression had not changed. "Well," Mouse said. He put the money back in his pocket. "Fellas, we gettin big-timed by Red Giant." He turned and marched back the way he had come.

The crowd on the main floor had thinned, and Mouse bolted through the slack-jawed stragglers as if they were blocking dummies on a football field. Amos shouted at him from across the bar, but Mouse kept his eyes locked on the exits. He did not acknowledge the irritated shouts of the people he bumped into; he did not even acknowledge the familiar goodbyes of the doormen and floor managers. He crashed past them, through the front doors into the frigid night air.

The chill wind blowing down the Mississippi felt good after the seedy, smoky, sweaty club. He ran through the parking lot past Red Giant's bus, jumped over the ice-encrusted railroad ties that separated the blacktop from the riverbank and skidded down the snowslicked hill. He slipped, fell to his knees and tumbled into a somersault. He came to an abrupt halt on a thin strand of rock right at the water's edge. His chest heaved and cold air burned his lungs. His steamy breath trailed away fast in the wind, like wisps of spirit leaving his body one ghostly hope at a time.

He followed the line of the MLK Bridge with his eyes, to its pillars on the Illinois side of the river, where only a handful of the brightest lights penetrated the snow and fog, will-o'-the-wisps beyond the water.

"Mouse!" Sidney shouted from the parking lot.

"Why you trippin, man?" Ricky yelled.

Mouse turned. The lights of the parking lot behind Ricky and Sidney silhouetted their figures dark black above Mouse, shadow demons. He felt out of time and place. He wanted to leave them there and leave Shauna's car on the Landing and just walk away down the river. He looked at the icy water lapping at the rocks and wished he could plunge in and sink below the surface and let the current carry him far far away.

He got to his feet and climbed back up the slope, tracing the muddy skids of his own footsteps. Sidney put his hand on Mouse's shoulder and looked into his eyes, but he was so stoned he couldn't even see clearly. He cracked up laughing and accidentally head-butted Mouse. Ricky laughed, too. Mouse slapped Sidney's hand away and pushed him to the ground.

The ride home was intolerable. In addition to suffering the gridlocked traffic inching through downtown in the snow, Mouse was forced to put up with Ricky's and Sidney's antics in the back seat. They were so stoned and drunk that they no longer knew how incoherent they were, but they'd found the same loopy wavelength and everything they did and said became hilarious to each other. They taunted Mouse about things that didn't remotely make sense, then slobbered over him for his pardon, then did it again.

When they reached University City, no one could remember which townhouse was Ricky's, and they spent a few minutes backtracking up and down the street. Mouse finally recognized it and stopped. Ricky fell out of the car and Mouse sped away. After they had dropped Ricky, Sidney fell into a stupor across the back seat, where he lay comatose until they arrived at his apartment on The Hill. Mouse hefted him out to the curb and dumped him on a bus bench in front of his building. He shook and slapped Sidney until he came around enough to walk under his own power, and Mouse watched him stagger to his door and stumble inside.

The drive back to Rock Hill was at least silent, but Mouse

was preoccupied with Gateway and his ideas for reconstituting the Bad Apples as a turntable-driven arena band. He wished he had asked Gate if he'd actually agreed to sell more rights to Catfish Crunk; now, he would have to call Marvin's friend, the lawyer who had negotiated the original deal with Crunk, to make sure nothing else happened without Mouse's approval.

Mouse pulled into Shauna's driveway, to a welcoming light shining through her living room window. Snow had frosted her lawn white, and Mouse's footsteps crunched up to the front door. A two-foot tall mechanical Santa Claus beamed ruddy and cheerful from the porch, waving its plastic arm as if to wipe away the despair of the night. When Mouse passed in front of the Santa doll, it "ho-ho-hoed" at him, as if to say that here, in the suburbs, Christmas truly was the happiest time of the year.

Mouse let himself in, and Shauna got up from the sofa and rushed to greet him. She squealed and threw herself into his arms. Mouse squeezed her tight.

"I'm glad you still up," he said. "You aint gonna believe what happened."

Shauna kissed him, a full sloppy kiss that she pressed into him for so long it literally took his breath away. When she pulled back, her face was electric with delight, and Mouse almost forgot his bad mood. She squealed and kissed him again.

"What is it?"

"You want the news standing up or sitting down?"

"I better take it sittin down."

"I'm pregnant."

Mouse's jaw dropped. The strands of colorful lights strung around Shauna's Christmas tree blinked on and off, one against the other, one after the other, three at once, a riot of cheer. Shauna's eyes had lost their usual hard glint and glowed dewey and loving.

"You sure?"

"Yeah. I felt it awhile ago, but I took the test tonight. I did it three times, to make sure, and they all came out positive."

"Wow."

"I know!"

She hugged herself closer into Mouse's body. Mouse stroked the back of her head.

"But we use condoms every time."

"If you'll search your memory carefully, you'll find that's not entirely true."

"Yeah, but. . . we never. I mean, it wasn't like. . ."

"It takes one little trooper."

"I know. But. . ."

"You're not happy?"

"I dunno what I am. It's so. . ."

"I know."

"Wow."

"Well, I'm happy." She kissed him. "Really happy. Merry Christmas, baby."

"Yeah," Mouse said. "Merry Christmas."

Part 3

Into the Past

"Everybody huddle up," Joao shouted. He stood by a stack of palettes at the back of the loading dock, case after case of Natural Light towering above him. The shushing exhalation of air brakes underscored the heavy metallic groaning of a delivery truck easing away from the dock. It was just before quitting time, and Joao held two clipboards in front of him the way Moses might have presented the Ten Commandments.

"As you know," Joao said, "this is the last day for everybody who's helped us out over the holidays. Except for Zo, of course, who'll start working overnight next week." Lorenzo beamed, giving Mouse an especially vain, triumphant nod. "Tomorrow we go back to our regular teams, so I want to thank you temporary guys and tell you how much Mr. Busch appreciates all your hard work. The holidays are critical to our success, and that means each and every one of you is critical to our success. I hope your experience here has been positive. It's been great to work with you as team leader."

This comment drew applause. Mouse found the reaction weirdly genteel from a group of tough-guy dockworkers who were getting their walking papers.

"I have no control over payroll as such," Joao continued, "but I do have some pull with the guys who sign the checks, and I put in a special request for bonus pay to show what an outstanding job you did and how much I personally enjoyed working with you. For those of you back here tomorrow," he held up his right-hand clipboard, "these extra packets represent congratulations for exceeding our quotas during the holiday season. For those of you moving on to other things," he held up the other clipboard, "these are tokens of appreciation, and also invitations to join us again in the future. When I call your name, get your bonus packet. And thanks again for your hard work." The crew applauded again. This time, Mouse joined them and did not feel as silly as he thought he would.

Mouse's name was last. By the time Joao said "Joseph Watkins," he and Mouse were alone on the dock.

"I thought you could've gotten that overnight position, Mouse. But Zo really went after it."

"Yeah, well. Maybe next time."

"You put in a pool application?"

"Not yet."

"Maybe that's what Mr. Grant wants to see you about."

"Mr. Grant wanna see me?"

"He asked me to have you stop by his office on the way out." Joao put his hand on Mouse's shoulder. "I really meant what I said, Mouse, that it was good working with you fellas. I know you didn't have the best time in the world here, but you're a good worker. You'd be a good forklift driver if you wanted to be."

"Thanks."

Joao clapped Mouse on the back and looked reassuringly into his eyes. "Anyway, Mouse, keep the faith. I know God has a plan for you. Just trust in Him and you'll be fine."

Now that Joao was no longer his boss, Mouse felt no obligation to respond to such sentiments, which he felt were condescending. As they parted company, Joao told him to take care of himself, and Mouse directed his eyes toward the ground and said nothing.

A big blizzard had finally hit on New Year's Day, and the

Anheuser-Busch brewery, like the rest of the city, was half-covered in undulating hillocks of snow. Mouse followed the shoveled stripe of sidewalk from the loading docks to the Bevo Bottling building, kicking the encrusted ice at the path's edges, sending crystal sprays across the concrete. He opened his bonus packet, found a check for fifty dollars and wondered if everyone's bonus had been the same. He folded the check and slipped it into the pocket of his Bud Light jacket.

Since he'd learned that Shauna was pregnant, Mouse had had even more trouble than usual keeping his mind on his work, and he was glad his term at Busch was over. He had a whole new world of choices to make now. He'd seen the way unplanned pregnancies had wrecked his friends' lives over the years, and he didn't want to make the same stupid mistakes they'd made. More than that, he didn't want to do what his own father had done, skipping out and leaving his mother with nothing, but he'd only just gotten used to the idea of becoming a respectable person himself, and as a black man with no high school diploma, he was not really respectable yet. What would he do with a child? He felt completely unprepared and unequipped.

"You don't have to keep the baby," he'd told Shauna.

"You don't have to keep your balls."

Shauna shared none of Mouse's apprehension. On the contrary, she seemed giddy with confidence. The day after Christmas, she had accepted a position in the Obstetrics Department at Barnes Jewish Hospital and had outlined a plan of action to prepare for the pregnancy and the baby. Mouse should move into her house in Rock Hill, she said, so they could pool their resources. She would work full-time at Barnes as long as she could while she was pregnant, and after the baby was born they could each work part-time and share child-rearing duties. Since Shauna could earn a better wage as a nurse than

Mouse could ever hope to make, she even allowed that she could be the main breadwinner and Mouse could be the main parent, though Mouse wasn't sure he liked that idea.

Shauna was unwavering in her conviction that Mouse would make a good father, and she was convinced beyond a shadow of a doubt that their child would be beautiful and brilliant. She had abandoned altogether the notion of quitting nursing and going back to school or opening her own business: she didn't even complain about the medical field any more, as it now served a larger purpose in her life. Her mid-life crisis seemed resolved by the baby, and whatever remnants of Vita DuPlease, Nihilistic Free Spirit, she had been resurrecting in her relationship with Mouse suddenly returned to the netherworld of her past, replaced by maternal zeal. She had quit smoking cold turkey. She was knitting colorful booties and blankets.

The transformation was so sudden that it made Mouse suspect Shauna of ulterior motives, of intentionally entrapping him into becoming her baby's daddy as a way of beating her maternal clock; but try as he might, he detected no controlling selfishness in her behavior and only affection and generosity in her treatment of him. Her attitude about Mouse's uncertain employment opportunities had not changed at all, and she continued to approach his identity crisis with gentle mockery and an aplomb that Mouse himself could not muster. That very evening, for instance, she had invited Zack and Chloe to join them at a restaurant in University City to celebrate Mouse's "retirement" from Anheuser-Busch, a joke whose spirit, at least, Mouse appreciated.

Mouse saw no way to reverse course. Shauna was pregnant and she intended to have the baby: the question was not whether it should happen but how he would react, and she was doing everything she could to persuade him that the baby was the best kind of blessing—unlooked-for. She interpreted providential meaning in every moment, and she would often hum quietly to herself whenever there was a pause in conversation.

Mouse went to his Anheuser-Busch locker and threw his few personal items there into the trash: a soiled undershirt, a bottle of aspirin, a pamphlet from the Church of Christ, Scientist. His prospects in life seemed increasingly bizarre. He had never imagined that he would actually have to work a straight job for a living, and Shauna was giving him the option not to: all he had to do was settle down in a pleasant house in the suburbs, teach a few drum lessons to supplement the family income, change diapers and go to PTA meetings. Outside of becoming an international pop star, it was the furthest distance he could imagine traveling in his life: from the chocolate city of Brooklyn to the vanilla suburb of Rock Hill, from bad motherfucker to babysitter, in less than a year.

Mouse could not conceive of his life without Shauna just now. She was his one source of stability and comfort, so as dreamless as life in the suburbs seemed, it would at least be a life. Without Shauna, Mouse had only his failures to cling to, and by himself he would face an apartment in Soulard he couldn't afford, the scorn of his family and child support payments. His course was set, and even if the situation had been different and he could have figured out how to make a living on his own, he had no desire whatsoever to leave Shauna: he wished only that the changes he had set in motion two months before had not accelerated so rapidly.

Mouse walked across the sprawling Anheuser-Busch compound, which looked almost charming under the snow. In front of the regal matte-brick paddocks that housed the clydesdales, a gleaming red buckboard wagon projected bucolic serenity. The massive brewhouse embodied the outsized greed and ruthlessness of its industrial designers, but the blue-white icing of snow cresting its facade made it seem cheerful, even congenial.

He rounded the brewhouse toward the steel-and-glass administrative headquarters that held Bobby Grant's suite. The character of even this modern structure was improved by the heavy frosting of snow, and Mouse thought the ugliest realities of life might be improved simply by covering them up, literally. Rather than ruin this peaceful vision by going up to Grant's suite, he stood and stared for a while, making this view his final memory of Busch Headquarters, with its full latent beauty expressed by the snow. He turned and strode slowly back up the lane he had taken on the day of his first interview with Mr. Grant, the topiary animals along the sidewalks now hibernating under frosty white blankets, and out onto the street, beyond the realm of the King of Beers. Bobby Grant could wait.

The sun had already set and a long line of road-grimed cars jammed Seventh Street, inching away from One Busch Place, choked by their own exhaust fumes in stop-and-go traffic. At Victor Street, Mouse turned away from the idling, irritated throng of drivers and walked to Menard.

He thought it a disconcerting coincidence that he had taken an apartment on Menard Street and the club where Gateway would debut his new band that night was called the Menard Club. He had gone to the library to look up the word and discovered that Pierre Menard had been a prominent French trader in the late eighteenth century who had become the first Lieutenant Governor of Illinois. There were houses, counties, streets and geographical features all over Illinois and Missouri named after him, and the Menard Club was near the Menard family home, not far from St. Louis; so the coincidence wasn't as extraordinary as it had seemed at first. Still, Mouse felt that the prominent presence of the Menard name in both their lives was uncanny, and Shauna believed that the guiding hand of fate was behind the coincidence. It was serendipity, she said, like everything else that was happening to Mouse right now, but Mouse thought calling it "serendipity" ignored the menace underlying the coincidence.

For example, Mouse had threatened Gateway with a lawsuit to keep him from using the name "Bad Apples," and Gateway had hired a lawyer himself in order to claim the rights to the name. Since neither of them could actually afford a court case or legal fees, they had settled out of court after a volley of nasty letters written by proxy. In the settlement (brokered by a friend of Marvin's), Mouse had agreed to sell their old tour van to Gateway for one dollar and to divide their sound equipment between them; in exchange, Gateway would call his band "The Applejacks" and never perform any Bad Apples songs. Once that matter was resolved, Gateway had wasted no time setting up a regional tour and had then surprised Mouse by inviting him to see the Applejacks' first gig, in the tiny town of Chester, Illinois, on the banks of the Mississippi.

The Applejacks would play a series of shows in the hinterlands to refine their act and then debut in St. Louis in six weeks. Mouse still felt contemptuous of Gateway's newly rejuvenated narcissism and delusional ambitions, and he was still sick of the smalltime club scene, but, with Shauna's encouragement, he had decided to go to their first show. Secretly, Mouse was hoping that the Applejacks would be a disaster, to prove his point that the Bad Apples, no matter their name, were nothing without him; on the other hand, he hoped Gateway would be all right, even if he *was* a sellout—he feared that Gateway had taken the Red Giant show to heart and created a quasi-hip-hop act, and he was embarrassed at the prospect of Gateway rapping and humiliating himself on stage, but he didn't wish Gate any ill, personally. Mostly, he wished never to think about the band again. Music was becoming something else to him now, though what it was becoming was unclear, and he wasn't sure how seeing the first Applejacks show would clarify matters. But Shauna had convinced him that it was important to go.

Shauna's car was parked on the street in front of Mouse's apartment. She had loaned it to him for this trip, which she had practically insisted on. Shauna said that nothing new could arise until the old fell away, and being at Gateway's debut would point Mouse in a fresh direction: he would witness with his own eyes how Gateway's path into the future would differ from Mouse's own, and the end of his former life would open as yet unseen roads into the future for Mouse. Mouse was neither so optimistic nor so sentimental, but there was a practical side of this trip, as well: official documents to sign and deliver, after which he could legally wash his hands of both Gateway's new band and the Bad Apples forever.

Mouse got in Shauna's car and cranked the engine over. He wished Shauna were coming with him, as he always did on important occasions, but she was working the swing shift at her new job at Barnes Jewish Hospital. Everything was changing at once.

He took Russell Street toward the interstate. His first stop would be Gateway's mother's house in East St. Louis. At the lawyer's office, Mouse had been unable to produce the title to the band's tour van, so they had ordered a copy from the Motor Vehicle Division. The new title was waiting at Mrs. Collins' house for Mouse to sign, along with some other Bad Apples equipment that Gateway wanted Mouse to have. The involvement of the lawyers had seemed like a bad dream, a bad way to end a band and a worse way to end a friendship, but at least Mouse's name would no longer legally be associated with Gateway's. Nobody needs lawyers when they agree, Mouse thought.

The rush hour had slowed traffic to twenty miles an hour on Interstate 55. As he approached the crossing to Illinois, Mouse pounded out a nervous rhythm against the steering wheel. He crested a hill near the river and the Jefferson Memorial Arch loomed over the highway, its curving steel panels lit by silvery searchlights. Its reflection outshone the sulfurous streetlamps below—it was a bright string of quicksilver tying the black heavens to the earth. Gateway had always wanted to walk boldly through this towering portal into the stars, as he had put it, but Gateway's vision was too aggrandized for Mouse, who had always preferred the symbolism not of the Arch but of the river, the river that was slowly, steadily sweeping the ground beneath the Arch away. The river was invisible now as Mouse rolled across the Poplar Street Bridge, the surging muddy blackness obscured beneath the guardrails and counterbraces, but he still felt the water's energy sweeping him south toward the sea. He thought of the many nights he and Gateway had gone down to the river—they would hash through the shows they played, fantasize about Big Time success, and, after a certain number of beers, they would run out of ideas and memories and slip quietly into reverie and let the river's eddying undertow carry their dreams into the depths. The fact of the river made dreams seem possible, the fact of the current measuring time in swells and silt, pumping life through the earth like the blood through Mouse's own heart. It made Mouse feel connected to something larger than himself within himself, flowing toward him and away from him into the wide world beyond, the world that might receive his dreams as gifts, as it received the life-giving waters of the river. He'd once believed that the metaphors of the river were real, but like the symbolism of the Arch, they'd turned out to be merely metaphorical after all. The ideas that had driven his imagination in the past promised something different now, equally symbolic but more complex and less liberating. His imagination had been corrupted by the persistence of reality, and the river as a river now seemed more powerful than the river as a symbol ever had, an implacable force that did not respond to human dreams but only returned them to the turbid slipstream of the Unconscious.

He crossed the bridge and took the Tudor Avenue exit into East St. Louis. The road curved away from the highway and deposited him in the South End, a residential neighborhood that had been improved by the recent blizzard even more than the Anheuser-Busch brewery had. The vacant lots between houses glowed serene and welcoming now, though Mouse knew that countless scraps of trash and industrial debris lay hidden beneath the pretty coating of ice and snow. The brick and clapboard houses appeared sturdier and more secure with the snow smoothing the lines of twisted rain gutters and concealing cracked stoops and buckling walkways. Even the abandoned houses looked less ashamed under snug blankets of snow, though the snow's weight on their frail roofs was surely accelerating their collapse. At the edge of his headlights, Mouse saw snowmen with stick arms waving from an empty lot.

He came to Lincoln Park, where he'd played basketball as a boy. The park was one of the few places in the neighborhood where the open expanse of fields was intentional and not a sign of abandonment, but even the generous snow and darkness could not conceal the fact that the basketball goals had no rims.

The Collins house was a long, narrow rectangle set back several yards from Trendley Street, in a neighborhood of shotgun row houses. The roof on the left side of the porch was sagging, and a wooden pole had been jammed vertically between a joist and the concrete floor to keep the roof from giving way.

Mouse parked on the street and walked up to the house, which brought back a thousand jumbled memories of childhood, playing dominoes on the stoop, crashing toy cars around the porch, breaking the living room window with a foul ball. From the looks of its disrepair, Mrs. Collins' porch might soon be as jumbled as the memories it inspired.

He knocked on the screen door and Gateway's mother appeared. She was nearly as broad as she was tall, with a round milky face and a constellation of black moles around her eyes. She wore a blue calico dress, an unflattering cross between a muu-muu and a picnic blanket.

"Bad night to be drivin," she said. "They's still a lotta roads aint plowed yet from the storm."

Mouse stepped inside and heard the humidifier whirring in the corner. In winter, Mrs. Collins always had a humidifier pumping moisture into the house, to combat the chafing dryness of her baseboard heaters. The sound of it, and the moldy smell of the carpet and armchairs, made Mouse feel like a child again. She waved Mouse toward the sofa, offered him a cup of coffee and waddled into the kitchen to get it.

Unlike Mouse's own mother, Mrs. Collins had a job, as the day school cook at the Ninth Street Baptist Church. She'd taken the job when her husband had died of a heart attack, and it had allowed her to pay the bills and feed her children (with school leftovers). Even now, her diet consisted mainly of daycare food—bulk-rate hot dogs, pre-cooked spaghetti and meatballs from giant cans, grilled cheese sandwiches—and her girth demonstrated the effect the food had on an adult body, a body no longer able to turn the starch and fat into new bones and muscle.

"Donald left some papers for you to sign," she called from the kitchen.

"I know. That's why I come."

"Naw, I mean some other papers, too."

"Yeah? Like what?" Mouse was sure they had taken care of everything but the van title in the lawyer's office.

While he waited for her, Mouse studied the four generations of nostalgia crammed into the living room, floor to ceiling. The Collins family had lived in the same house since Gateway's great-grandfather had worked at the Armour Meat-Packing Plant, which had long since been abandoned. Every square inch of wall held stiffly posed family portraits, including Gateway's middle school graduation picture, Gate's face ruddy and bright under a red mortarboard cap.

"Your mama come by the other day," Mrs. Collins said. She carried a tray containing two cups of coffee and a passel of papers into the living room. "She don't call much these days, but I still see her round church." She set the tray on the coffee table amd sat down across from Mouse.

Mouse took a cup and sipped his coffee. "I seen her at Thanksgiving and she talked about you," he said.

"I know. I jus mean when you boys was on the road, we was real close all the time. Now that she know where you are, she kinda settled down a little ad I don't see her."

"She seem pretty calm to me for years now, pretty used to it."

"That's what a mother s'posed to do, though. You s'posed to look like everything's under control, but you never stop worryin 'bout your family. Especially you boys off in God knows where with some groupie doin' God knows what. You know. We aint stupid, jus worried."

"I guess so."

"You got a good family, Mouse."

"I know."

"Anyway, Donald want me to show you these papers here." Mouse picked up the papers. On top was the van's new title, which was still in Mouse's name; under that was a stack of documents that Mouse recognized from the Bad Apples' contract with Catfish Crunk: royalty agreements. He read them and discerned that Gateway had agreed in principle to sell the rights to two Bad Apples songs, "We Hold These Grooves To Be Self-Evident," and "Peace, Love and Hominy." The deal for "Grooves," which had been promised to Catfish Crunk, Mouse already knew about; but the other song had been tentatively sold to a group Mouse had never heard of called the Beat Monks. Each contract was worth several thousand dollars in advance payment plus rights, credits and royalties from the new songs that each band would create out of the Apple originals. The compensation represented a significant increase over the first contract that Mouse and Gateway had signed—the success of Crunk's "Jawbreaker" had inflated the Apples' stock.

"Donald said you wouldn't be happy 'bout these, maybe, but he ask you to look at the money. I know he sure could use that money, Mouse, and I imagine you can, too."

Mouse wondered when Gateway had had time to do all this. He hadn't mentioned these agreements at all in the lawyer's office, when they were hashing over the Apples' meager legacy. All the work was done, all the signatures had been affixed except his own. All he had to do to put nearly five thousand dollars into his own personal bank account was sign his name.

He thought about the end of his job at Anheuser-Busch, and his uncertain prospects for employment, and his baby on the way. With five thousand dollars, plus whatever royalties the songs might generate, he and Shauna could have a tidy nest egg. He could probably start his own home music studio with that much money, the way digital recording equipment worked these days, or go to vocational college for something more lucrative than dockwork; but the thought of Catfish

Crunk rapping and goofing over another one of his songs made him sick. It was one thing for people to pay you money for your own song, because they liked it and wanted to hear it again and again; it was another thing for someone to pay money to change the sound and meaning of your song. Did music mean something or not? Were the songs just advertisements, jingles for sale to the highest bidder? Mouse sipped his coffee. The booty call of "Jawbreaker" was far away from the Black is Beautiful vibe of "Afrobatics," but was there anything noble in being Black and Beautiful if you starved to death doing it?

"He said you can take them contracts with you, if you wanna think about it. He gonna talk to you about'em tonight, anyway."

So that's the reason he want me to see his show tonight, Mouse thought. He don't care what I think about the Applejacks at all.

The wall clock chimed the half-hour. In order to make the Applejacks' first set, Mouse would have to cover the forty miles to Chester, through snowed-over country roads, in less than ninety minutes.

"I gotta go. I aint sure I wanna take these papers, Mrs. Collins."

"You want my advice, Mouse?"

All anybody do any more is give me advice, he thought. "What?"

"About the band?"

"Yeah?"

"I don't know nothin about it, so you do what you want. Bad Apples, Applejacks, Apple Fritters, whatever."

"But?"

"Take the money, Mouse. There aint nothin right or wrong about money. It just is. And these here, these are legal contracts, not some scam, welfare dodge, what-have-you. You know how people gotta make it in East St. Louis, what they gotta do, how everybody two deep breaths from goin under. But this here's somebody sayin you done good and here's your reward. Take the reward, Mouse. You know how long it take me to earn five thousand dollars?"

"How long?"

"Six months. More. And here they gonna hand you a check, and you aint gotta do nothin but sign your name."

Mouse fidgeted and looked at the clock again. "It aint about the money, Mrs. Collins."

"It's always 'bout the money, child. Less you talkin 'bout God or your family, it's about the money."

"Bein funky aint about gettin paid."

"You aint seen a lot of funky brothers down at the homeless shelter, Mouse, have you? Caint be funky without money. Only thing poor people can afford is the blues."

"Not true. Funk is just blues that don't give a damn no more."

"Take them papers with you, anyway. You got some drivin ahead. Maybe you'll do some thinkin, too. I mean, they's some reason you drivin all that way to see Donald's new band, right? The big debut! Cause you still love Donald, and you boys been through a lot together."

"Yeah."

"Well you can do right by him with them contracts. It's okay if you wanna do somethin else with your life, but that don't mean you gotta take Donald's dream away, too."

Mouse shuffled the contracts into order, took a final sip of coffee and stood up. "You heard the new band?"

"Not yet." Mrs. Collins lifted herself out of her seat. "Wait here a minute." She went to the kitchen. Mouse heard the refrigerator open and close, and Mrs. Collins came back with a shoebox.

"Some sandwiches and snacks for Donald," she said. She handed it to him. "Caint be eatin bar food all the time. And, you know, it's nice to have somethin from home."

"He stayin with you these days?"

"He got a place with Oscar over in North St. Louis. They come around here sometime, but I probably aint gonna see'em for a while, with this tour and all." Mrs. Collins escorted Mouse to the front door. "You can eat some of them cookies in there, if you want."

"Alright. Thanks."

Mouse walked out to the street, opened the driver's door of Shauna's car and stopped to look back. Mrs. Collins stood silhouetted on the porch. He had seen her standing on that porch for thirty years, looking out at him lovingly, telling him to "come in out the cold and call your mama if you wanna stay for dinner."

"Hey Mouse," she shouted now. "I always thought you had a bigger head."

Mouse was perplexed, until she ran her hand across the top of her head. It was the first time she'd seen Mouse without his afro. "Gettin smaller every day," he said.

"Make sure you keep it on straight."

Into the Future

Since the blizzard, there had been enough traffic on Illinois' backroads to pack the snow down but not clear it away. Each road was reduced to three slushy tire grooves in the compacted snow. The center groove was shared by both directions of traffic, and whenever two cars traveling in opposite directions met, they had to slow almost to a stop and negotiate around each other, their tires leaving the relative safety of the well-worn ruts to venture onto humps of compacted ice in-between. The rural routes were lonely at this time of evening, but on the occasions when Mouse had to pilot around oncoming cars, he nearly plowed into snowbanks twice and narrowly avoided accidents two other times. His palms started sweating every time he saw headlights approach.

Just outside of Chester, the thick stripe of the Mississippi swerved toward the road, carving a line blacker than the night through the snowy fields; and once the road found the river, it mirrored its curving course through the countryside. Mouse saw the familiar signs of railroad tracks in-between the highway and the river—a line of tall wooden poles with bell-shaped glass insulators on top, guiding wires and glinting moonlight, and every so often a pole flashing a hooded warning light. Railroad tracks could go anywhere men wanted to build them, up mountains or through them, across dusty deserts and plains, over and beyond the greatest gorges and bays, so it puzzled Mouse why railroads so often followed rivers. Even the highway Mouse was on, the Great River Road, took pains to adjust to the course of the riverbed, as if even with steam power and internal combustion we could never quite escape the pull of the river.

A green and white sign pointed toward Chester, and Mouse turned onto a road that had been plowed completely free of snow. He rolled into a sleepy downtown, a three-block row of grocery and hardware stores and mom-and-pop shops. The curbs were mounded with dirty snow, and the asphalt glistened with water that was quickly turning back to ice. Mouse could imagine nowhere less likely for a funk band to debut.

On the far outskirts of town, at the crossroads of two blacktopped lanes near the Mississippi, was a two-story cut-granite building painted bright ochre yellow. A neon blue sign announced "The Menard Club," and a neon martini glass blinked on and off beside it.

The club had sharply protruding ledges and broad window sills mounded with snow. It was lit from below, which threw shadows from the ledges onto its stony face, lending it an eerie feeling more like a nineteenth century orphanage than a nightclub. Mouse wondered what had led someone to open a club in such an unwelcoming place, and why Gateway had booked his band here. Mouse had never even heard of it before, so it wasn't part of the regular circuit—he had played every horrible club within driving distance of St. Louis, but The Menard Club achieved new depths in ambience.

Four cars were parked in the lot, and a few more sat on the street out front. Mouse gathered up the contracts, the van title and Mrs. Collins' care package and walked up the wide granite steps. He pushed open a windowless metal door and went in.

Inside, the club was little more than the cavernous front parlor of an old manor house, redecorated with posters of scantily clad women proffering beer. Two beefy white bouncers in blue uniforms greeted Mouse with grunts. They looked him over dismissively, asked what was in the shoebox and told him that no outside food was allowed. He explained that it was for the band, and the bouncers insisted on opening it and pawing the plastic bags. Satisfied, they collected the five dollar cover charge and stamped Mouse's hand.

A dozen white men in heavy flannel shirts sat at tables horseshoed around the stage. The only women were the two waitresses, wearing matching red cocktail dresses and black tights, chatting up the customers. The sound system blared mechanical 1970s disco, and the tiny stage looked more suited to puppet shows and mimes than funk bands.

Gateway and six other guys were setting up on stage. Mouse knew some of the band. Oscar was there, wearing a bass instead of his usual six-string guitar, and the saxophone player had been around St. Louis for years: a middle-aged white guy named Sherman, who made his living writing radio jingles. The Bad Apples' one-time trumpet player Howard Vincent was there as well, and he greeted Mouse with a hearty "Hey, Brother" and a shoulder hug.

Howard had quit the Apples ten years earlier to get an Information Technology degree from St. Louis Community College. He had then landed a job with a packaging company in the West St. Louis suburb of Creve Coeur and dropped out of the music scene altogether.

"Howie, man, I thought you went straight," Mouse said.

"Yeah, but I kinda got crooked again. It's hard not playin out, man. Feels like your soul gets all tight, you know?"

"What about your job with—what was it?"

"Carustar Custom Packaging," he said proudly. "I'm still doin it. Me and Sophie jus bought a house in Creve Coeur."

"That's a long drive for a gig, Howie."

"Yeah, but to tell you the truth, Mouse, I been losin my

nut a little bit and I didn't really know how to get back with it. I'm lucky Gate called me with this new band. I mean, Creve Coeur to Chester aint too far to drive—to get your mind back, you know?"

"You doin new songs?"

"Some new, some old. I been writin off and on still, and Oscar got some new stuff, and then we got a couple songs that was layin around from back in the day that we kinda revamped. Hope we don't screw'em up too bad for ya."

"Me, too." Mouse clapped him on the shoulder and looked at Gateway, who was checking a vocal monitor. Gate was all business.

Howard pulled Mouse aside and whispered confidentially. "It's weird, Mouse. This here's the first time I been on stage in ten years, and I feel like I'm gonna throw up. I aint never felt that way before."

"Don't sweat it, man. You get in a couple licks and you'll be cool. Just like sex and ridin bikes."

"I thought it was horseshoes and hand grenades."

"Maybe you right to be nervous, Howie, if you think sex is like hand grenades." He fist-bumped Howard and sauntered to the front of the stage, where Gateway held up a finger for him to wait.

"Check check check," Gateway said. "Mary had a pocket full of posies, check check." He sang some falsetto "oohs" and "aahs" and then stepped away from the mike and ooh-aah-ed some more. The sound bounced around the room like a superball, but he seemed satisfied. He jumped down from the stage.

Mouse thought Gateway looked a lot better this evening than the last few times he'd seen him. His eyes were clear, and he scanned the room with a sense of purpose and command.

"Thanks for comin down, man."

"Your moms give you this." Mouse offered the shoebox full

of sandwiches and cookies. "And I signed over the van title. I put it in the box there with the rest."

"And the contracts?" Gateway said. "Whatchyou say, Mouse? You see, I been doin your job."

"I guess you have. Whyn't you say somethin about it with the lawyers?"

"Our lawyer didn't want us discussin these new deals with anybody till the old Bad Apples shit was put to bed and the terms of these deals was settled. Which didn't happen till yesterday."

"He didn't want you discussin'em because they violate the settlement that we jus signed."

"You can change that, Mouse. All you gotta do is sign them new contracts. It's all square."

Mouse watched Oscar tuning his bass, plucking and turning the machines. A turntable was set up next to the keyboards, and a young guy was setting vinyl discs in a stand on the cabinet.

"You got a DJ now?" Mouse said. "Just like Red Giant?"

"That's where it's goin. Mixin up the old with the new to create a whole new vibe. I'm tellin you, we gonna get this together and be ahead of the game for once."

"People been havin DJs for years, Gate."

"They aint been doin it like this." Gateway scoffed. "Man, you been thinkin it's 1974 since we started a band. You always tryin to get back to that vibe you heard when we was little, but it's gone, man, that sound aint comin back. This here's the new sound."

"I wasn't tryin to bring it back. I was tryin to carry it forward."

"Well that's what we doin now. This is that sound for the new generation."

"I never thought I'd see the day you was bitin' on Red Giant."

"I don't mind followin a band that got a million dollar contract." Gateway pointed at the contracts Mouse still held in his hand. "You aint gonna play them songs no more, right?"

"I dunno what I'm gonna do."

Gateway sighed. The Applejacks were all wandering into position on stage and the club manager behind the bar pointed at his wristwatch. Gateway held up his hand to indicate that they'd be ready in five minutes.

"Look here, Mouse. I know you got a straight job now and maybe you don't need the money, but the Applejacks could use five grand. We need equipment, we gonna need studio time. Man, we gotta lay down some tracks soon, cause Red Giant's people be lookin for new bands everywhere they go, and Warner Brothers aint the only label tryin to sign bands like us. Everybody want in on it, and that means bidding wars, high prices—we gotta jump in now, and we could can turn that five grand into fifty or five hundred or five million."

Mouse shook his head. "You and me been playin how long? How many times we heard that same shit?"

"Did you see Red Giant's tour bus? You think that's a rumor, or a fantasy?"

"I think they got lucky bein' in the right place at the right time in Los Angeles, and anyway they sold they soul to get that bus. Aint nobody from no record label trollin Chester, or Carbondale, or St. Louis. Not for real."

"We got the cell number of a dude from Warner who can actually say yes to a contract! He already know who I am, Mouse. I met him!" Gateway glanced over his shoulder at the band, then back at the club manager. "If you don't wanna be part of that, whatever, but don't ruin it for me, man. Sign the contract, cash the check and turn off your radio. All you gotta do is sign, and the Applejacks can make a record, and we'll even cut you in, when we get our million dollars. Whatever deal you want, we'll do it."

Mouse looked at the contracts again. He imagined the horrible track Catfish Crunk would make out of "We Hold These Grooves To Be Self-Evident." He looked at the Applejacks and tried to see them as pop stars: Gateway, a forty year old with mostly gray hair and lines around his eyes, not exactly a pin-up; Oscar, a handsome young kid with dubious chops; Howie, a computer programmer who hadn't been onstage in ten years; a middle-aged saxophonist who wrote radio jingles; and the rest of the band—the DJ, drummer, and keyboard player—were green, nervous-looking kids. The drummer looked like one of the boys in Ricky Hart's high school clinic.

"I dunno," Mouse said. "Lemme hear how you sound."

"Fuck you, Mouse. We aint gonna audition for you. If you gonna do it, do it cause you a friend. Do it cause you wanna help us out. Do it for the dream you had once. Do it cause some of us still have a dream."

"That aint how I see it, Gate. You askin me to sell out everything I believe in for five thousand dollars."

"You already done it once! Shit!" He turned again and looked at the band. "Look, it aint now or never. You can think about it. This gonna be a tight group, Mouse. By the time this tour get back to St. Louis, you gonna wish you had your old job back." Gateway whirled around and hopped up onstage.

Mouse took a seat at the back of the room and ordered a beer. He surveyed the patrons: all white, all men, all with the same severe haircuts and bulging muscles. When the waitress brought his drink, he asked, "What kinda town is Chester, anyway?"

"What do you mean?" She put her hand on Mouse's shoulder and leaned in close. The waitress's heavy, sweet perfume attacked Mouse's nose, then faded back into the ruffles of her cocktail dress, leaving Mouse with a nearly uncontrollable urge to over-tip.

"I mean, this don't look like a crowd that wanna see a funk show."

"I see your point." The waitress laughed artificially and moved closer, so Mouse had a better view of her cleavage. "Most of the guys are guards at the prison."

"Prison?"

"There's a maximum security prison outside of town. That's why this club's here. And the laundromat. And the Great River Diner up on Kaskaskia Street—it's open real late for the graveyard shift. Otherwise, we're just a normal small town."

Mouse thanked her and gave her an extra dollar. Gateway's new funk band was about to debut its act for a bunch of white prison guards.

Gate stepped to the mike and grinned, big, goofy and open, a smile Mouse had grown tired of lately but that could still light up a room. His energy had always been infectious.

"How y'all doin?" Gateway said. "We the Applejacks from St. Louis. We appreciate you comin out in the cold and snow to see our show, and we gonna make you glad you did."

The drummer counted off with his sticks and launched into a hamfisted go-go groove. The rest of the band dropped in, and the horns blasted a five-note melody slightly out of tune. Gateway turned his back to the audience, as if calling a huddle with the band, and he hammered out a sharp rhythm with his scratch guitar, willing the band into lockstep. The keyboardist played the song's simple chord progression, and they ran the groove through a few bars, until they were together. The DJ punched in some noise effects, and Gate turned back to the audience with the same goofy grin and sang.

"We hear to turn this party out/
aint no doubt we got the clout/

this here groove is what it's all about/
and this is how we turn it out."

After a horn break, the DJ took his mike and rapped about how the Applejacks were in town, so now it was safe to party. It was the most tired, generic lyric Mouse could imagine, and the band's sound wasn't exactly original, either, but it wasn't the worst dance music he'd ever heard. It was miles away from the slickness and high production values of Red Giant's show. Mouse saw problems that could easily be fixed in rehearsal, if Gateway could figure them out, and some other problems that experience might solve; but he couldn't see how this band would be different from any other dance band on the minor league club circuit. They would still have to come up with good material, they would have to stay together long enough to develop an original sound, they would have to translate their sound onto record or into a better show just to catch the ear of someone with the money and power to take them to the Big Time. Red Giant had bastardized their own sound, but they'd at least had a sound to sell out. The Applejacks sounded like a better-than-average high school cover band trying to imitate the Bad Apples. Even with Red Giant's connections, this band was not the Next Big Thing. At least, not yet, not the way they played tonight.

Mouse sat through two covers of recent dance hits and an original that sounded a lot like an Eddie Kendricks song filtered through a computer sound effects program. He wondered, if he allowed Gateway to use the Bad Apples' songs, if this band would even know how to play them. Red Giant's success changed nothing. So Red Giant got lucky, and now Gateway was holding the phone number of someone at Warner Brothers. The Applejacks still sounded like a mediocre band filling a weekday slot in Chester, Illinois.

There was one song in the Applejacks' first set that Mouse

thought might make a good single, when the band had honed it and they'd worked out a better modulation at the bridge. It was a bouncy house groove called "Beautiful Butterfly," about an imaginary moment during the filming of the movie *Gone With the Wind* in which actress Butterfly McQueen refuses to utter the famous line "I don't know nothin 'bout birthin babies." Ironically, the song sounded like the deep funk the Bad Apples had always aspired to, and the sentiment seemed closer to the Bad Apples' rejection of the status quo than the Applejacks' aspiration to join it. The song had an irresistibly catchy chorus, but it seemed to Mouse that, even in the new songs he created, Gateway was still a Bad Apple, after all.

When Mouse got up to leave, he gave the unsigned contracts to the waitress and asked her to give them to Gateway. He put on his coat and stood by the exit and waited till Gate looked his way. They had been best friends since they were little boys. Until a few months before, they had spent nearly every day of their lives together for thirty years. They had written hundreds of songs together, played thousands of shows, earned their successes and suffered their failures together, and there was no other reason Mouse could give for being there, for driving more than an hour across snowy roads on a frigid evening when he had somewhere else to be. He should have made Gateway come to him, but he also knew that there was a part of Gateway that needed to have Mouse there for his first show without him. Everything he had once wanted involved Gateway, and now he was leaving all of those dreams with his old friend, to do with what he wanted, in an awkward nightclub for prison guards on the outskirts of a tiny town in Southern Illinois.

Gate finally met his eye. Mouse felt himself turning to a pillar of salt inside. He and Gateway were now separated by what had once bound them together: the music they had made, which no longer belonged to either of them. He raised his fist in a Black Power salute. As Gateway continued to sing, he took his hand off the neck of his guitar and raised his fist in response. For one long moment, Mouse and Gateway stood alone in the bar, fists raised in unison, and then Gate grabbed the neck of his guitar and hammered out a rhythm, and Mouse turned and stepped out into the cold.

It was a silent, crystalline winter night, so clear that the outlines of objects threatened to crack. Mouse sat behind the steering wheel of Shauna's car for a long time listening to his own breath, staring up at the absurdly bright yellow walls of The Menard Club, hearing in the caverns of his own mind the warm mediocrity of the grooves continuing inside.

He was due back in St. Louis at ten-thirty, to pick Shauna up from work, but he did not relish the return trip. He drove across the club's icy parking lot and turned toward the highway.

As he reached the center of Chester, he stopped the car and took a long look back at the brightly lit Menard Club, a yellow candy sprinkle in the vanilla ice cream of the Illinois snow: the ungainly club that had become the mausoleum of his dreams of stardom, the final resting place of the Bad Apples, halfway between the Mississippi River and a maximum security prison.

Back to the Present

Watching the dormant Illinois countryside roll by, Mouse soaked in the tranquillity of snowfields reflecting milky blue moonlight, the ponderous austerity of bare sycamore groves patiently enduring the long season of black-ice streams and birdless skies. He felt solitary but not alone. He did not feel Gateway's presence in the car with him, did not imagine what he should have done or might have been; for now, Mouse felt only that he was driving back to St. Louis, a city empty of dreams and therefore full of promise. He remembered seeing photographs of St. Louis before the Arch was erected, when the city's importance was still real and not merely symbolic. There had been a time when St. Louis was the beginning and end of America and did not need shining silver monuments to prove it. Mouse wondered if he could strip the gleaming steel facade from his own imagination and live in the city as a fact of his life and not a symbol of something else.

It was after nine-thirty when Mouse reached the outskirts of East St. Louis. He decided he had enough time to detour to his mother's house in Brooklyn. In her garage were two plastic bins of Bad Apples paraphrenalia—CDs and t-shirts, scrapbooks of press clippings, notebooks filled with songs—and Mouse was inspired to get rid of the remaining waste from that other life he had led. After his visit to The Menard Club, he wanted to lay the Bad Apples to rest once and for all.

He parked on the street in front of his mother's house.

The front porch light was out, and the windows were dark. Snow had completely buried the front stoop, and no neighbors or church volunteers had come to shovel it off. He trudged through the snow and unlocked the kitchen door.

The air was heavy with the sickly-sweetness of rotting greens. His mother probably hadn't taken the trash out since the blizzard. Mouse tiptoed through the kitchen in the dark, slipped into the garage and flipped on the light.

Mrs. Watkins' garage was a tumult of objects accumulating in layers like the strata of ancient civilizations. A lifetime's collection of chipped ceramic figurines guarded a broken stationary bicycle that was festooned with old Christmas decorations. A pyramid of Mary Kay products, from Mrs. Watkins' failed attempt to sell cosmetics, rested atop a broken sewing machine cabinet. Half-empty paint cans and rusted garden tools were scattered everywhere. Mouse picked his way through this jetsam to the far corner, where his drums were packed away in hard cases alongside the Apples' remains.

He removed the lid from a plastic bin and found multiple copies of each of the band's CDs and a wad of promotional t-shirts. He selected a CD and held it up to the light: it was their only concert album, *Live from the Garden of Eden*, recorded at a nightclub in Carbondale in 1998. The cover art featured Adam and Eve standing under an apple tree, blushing; in the branches above them, instead of fruit, photos of the band members dangled.

He set the CD aside and pulled a white t-shirt from the bin. On its front was a full-color drawing of a steaming apple pie cut open to reveal photos of the band members baked into the filling. A slogan was written into the crust: "Everybody Loves Bad Apple Pie," which Mouse still thought an unfortunate compromise. He and Gateway had quarreled for weeks about that slogan—Mouse had wanted "Bad Mothers Serve

Bad Apple Pie," and Gateway had wanted "The Bad Apples Want to Fill Your Pie." The history of the band was fraught with such disputes, disagreements about album titles and concepts, track ordering, arrangements and instrumentation; late-night songwriting brainstorms, drawing and redrawing artwork for posters, writing and rewriting lyrics and liner notes. Mouse could have imagined no better way to spend his time, and he was still sure that nothing else would come close to the intensity of those arguments, every trivial detail seeming so grave and important at the time.

He laid the t-shirt across his mother's Mary Kay boxes and piled a few more shirts on top. He would give them to Shauna as souvenirs; or maybe, he thought, he would wash them a few times to soften them up for use as swaddling clothes for his baby. This idea surprised him, and he looked at the shirts in a new way, as if he were suddenly holding a piece of the future instead of the past, as if this evidence of failure might somehow be redeemed by his baby. Maybe one day his child would be happy that its father had made these things, and Mouse imagined how he would feel if his own father had been a funky drummer, and he could have grown up playing his daddy's drum kit. He touched his snare drum case affectionately and became so lost in the idea of passing it along to his child that he didn't hear his mother opening the garage door behind him.

"Whatchyou doin out here, Mouse?"

He jumped. His heart spun. He turned to face his mother, who was carrying an aluminum baseball bat on her shoulder.

"Damn, ma! Like to give me a heart attack."

"Whatchyou think you do to me, sneakin round out here in the middle of the night!"

"I aint sneakin."

"And it's freezin out here! Come on inside."

"I aint got time right now."

"You got time to stand there gawkin at some ol' shirt, you got time to come inside."

She went back into the house. Mouse stuffed the t-shirts back into the plastic bin, shut the lid tight and carried the whole container into the kitchen. His mother was setting the kettle on the stove.

"I aint got time for no tea, ma."

"Well I do." She got a single cup from the drain rack and a teabag from the cupboard. "You don't look so good, Mouse."

"Thanks."

"Sit down." She pulled out a chair and sat at her kitchen table. "Tell me 'bout it."

Mouse reluctantly sat down. "Aint much to tell."

"How'd you like Gateway's new band? I went over to Maebelle's house the other day, and she said he was real enthused about it."

"Yeah. He thinkin they onto somethin. Sound like the same old thing to me, though."

Mouse's mother pursed her lips. "He jus doin what he think is right, Mouse. We all gotta do what we think is right."

"I couldn't agree more."

"So whatchyou gonna do now? This was your last day at Busch, right?"

"That's right. Last day."

The kettle whistled and Mrs. Watkins got up to fix her tea. She poured the water, added sugar, stirred, added more sugar, pressed the tea bag with her spoon, dangled it up and down in the water, slurped it loudly, then clanged her spoon around the inside of the cup and slurped again, a ritual whose familiarity and consistency drove Mouse crazy. She sat back down at the table. "Why you don't wanna talk to Bobby Grant 'bout that job he tryin to get for you?"

"What job?"

"They got a permanent job up in the warehouse, and Bobby wanna give it to you. He said you did pretty good on the loading dock, always showed up on time, and he tryin to help you out, but you wouldn't even go talk to him. He called me up and said you didn't go see him like he asked."

"I don't wanna work for Busch, ma. They cold-blooded, and anyway they got bought out by the Belgians. InBev owns Busch now. It's a global empire of bad beer."

"Well, whatchyou gonna do then?"

"I heard about a job over at Schlafly."

"What's that?"

"Local brewery. It's the only other brewery left in St. Louis except for Busch. They brew the beer here, and they sell it here. Local guys. You caint even get it outside St. Louis. It's the Lou, through and through."

"And you rather work for a tiny company like that than a solid place like Busch?"

"They make good beer! Budweiser aint nothin. Anyway, they's this drum clinic I got hooked up with, too, maybe teach some drum lessons for Parks and Rec. I dunno."

"Caint nobody without college get a better job than Anheuser-Busch for better pay. That's what Bobby told me."

"That may be true, ma, but Schlafly's a good company, and they owner don't fly to work in a helicopter. Anyway, I aint even applied yet. I jus heard about the job from some of the fellas at work. Probably be better off teachin drum classes—least that's somethin I know about."

Mrs. Watkins slurped her tea and stared at Mouse over the lip of the cup. Mouse felt the seconds oozing by.

"I gotta go, ma. I'm s'posed to meet Shauna."

"Mouse, I'm glad you come by tonight. I got somethin to say to you."

"Alright."

"You know I always help you out when I can."

"Sure."

"And I know you tryin to do right."

"Yeah?"

"I think you oughtta go see Mr. Grant and get that job at Busch. I'm gonna be here to support you no matter what, but with a baby on the way, you gonna need somethin solid you can count on. Not some drum clinic, some rinky-dink local brewery. You need to do right by your child. By my grandchild."

Mouse was dumbfounded. He and Shauna had never discussed how or when they would tell their families that she was pregnant—he wasn't even accustomed to the idea himself yet—and now his mother was giving him unasked-for advice about it. He'd never expected Shauna to speak to his mother, of all people, behind his back. His family thought little enough of him before; now, with an unplanned pregnancy on his hands, his sister and his mother would have no doubt that he was irresponsible, that he had no idea what he was doing, that he needed them to step in and run his life.

"Is that what Shauna told you she think?" Mouse said. "That I oughta take the job at Busch?"

"I aint been talkin to Shauna. Jackie told me."

"Jackie?! You people got nothin better to do than gossip 'bout my life?"

"Your life? If you makin babies, you makin my grandbabies. We aint even talkin 'bout your life. Anyway, whatchyou up on your hind legs about?"

"I'm a grown man, ma."

"Then act like it. I aint comin down on you. I gotta be thankful for this, cause it don't look like Jackie gonna give me any grandchildren, so if you serious 'bout this girl, then I'm gonna be serious, too. And I'm gonna try and help you."

Mouse took his mother's cup from her and drank a mouthful of tea. "I don't even know what to do, ma. I know I gotta think about the baby, but I don't want my baby thinkin Anheuser-Busch is somethin to be proud of."

"Do you love Shauna?"

Mouse stared at the table. There was no other word for how he felt about Shauna, though it seemed more complex, more mixed-up than he'd ever dreamed love would be. "Yeah."

"Well, then, that baby got a lot to be proud of already. You know, I wish you'd've found a nice girl from a good family like Jackie did with Marvin, but if you love Shauna and she pregnant, then God gonna smile on you, and if God's smilin on you, I caint help but do the same. But you gotta do your part, Mouse. If you wanna bring a baby up right, you gotta have a little money. You gotta be responsible, and havin a good job is a prideful thing. Aint nothin shameful 'bout Busch."

"Ma, I been responsible. I always been responsible."

"Alright, Mouse. I jus want what's right for you, what's proper."

"You know, Shauna got a house out in Rock Hill. We probably gonna live out there."

"That's good. That's real good." Mrs. Watkins took her cup back and sipped tea, evaluating this idea. "It's nice for a child to have a little room to play in, you know, like you and Jackie did."

"I know."

"Whatever happen, we here for you, Mouse. Jackie, too. I know you and her don't always see eye to eye, but you two a lot more alike than different, whether you believe it or not."

"Maybe." Mouse stood up. "I gotta go now."

Mrs. Watkins got up from the table and and hugged Mouse. "Gonna be nice to have a baby in the family again. You gonna be surprised what it do for your outlook."

She took her teacup to the kitchen sink. "You bring Shauna over for dinner," Mrs. Watkins said. "I wanna know this girl real good, if she gonna be my grandbaby's mama."

"Alright."

"She gonna be the first white girl in the family, so we gotta make sure she know how to cook and sew and take care of things."

"I'm pretty sure white people know what to do with babies, too, ma."

Mouse took out his mother's trash, and then came back and grabbed up his plastic bin of Bad Apples memorabilia. His mother walked him to the door and gave him another hug.

"You think Sable a good name for a girl?" she said.

"Better for a girl than a boy."

"Sable for a girl. Cambrion for a boy: it's pretty, but still manly. Think about it."

Mouse drove across the Poplar Street Bridge from East St. Louis and tried not to look at the Arch gleaming over downtown. The Arch was the country's largest national monument, a towering upside-down curve: a frown. The Jefferson National Expansion Memorial had been built to celebrate the infinitely expanding frontier, because happiness for Americans was always just beyond the next conquest. As Mouse crossed the river, he wondered what dreams might come when America had nothing left to conquer but itself.

Highway 40 to the Kingshighway exit. About a mile from the highway, he entered Central West End, with the whole expanse of Forest Park stretching away to his left and Barnes-Jewish Plaza looming up on his right. He turned into the cobblestoned streets of Cathedral Square on Laclede Avenue and parked at a meter.

The sidewalk in front of Barnes was bustling, even at this late hour, with men and women wearing surgical scrubs beneath heavy overcoats, delivery men wheeling handcarts loaded with boxes, a haggard old woman leaning on a cane, smoking a cigarette. Mouse went in and scanned the atrium, but Shauna was nowhere to be seen. He dialed her cell number from the Information Desk, and she told him that she was upstairs and had to cover the last few minutes of someone else's shift. He took a seat next to a fake potted palm near the escalators and watched people ride up and down while he waited.

Mouse didn't know what to think any more. Everything was all mixed up together—Shauna, Gateway, his mother, the Busch job, suburban Rock Hill. The baby. His baby. He wished he could see the pattern in these things and make sense of it, but as soon as he almost understood the meaning of one thing, it was consumed by something else. The revolutions of the escalators and their *whirr-shush-clunk-clack* as they slid flat into the floor put him into a trance.

whirr-shush-clunk-clack
whirr-shush-clunk-clack

At eleven o'clock, Shauna emerged from the elevators near the gift shop. She wore light blue hospital scrubs and a heavy black peacoat over them, but she could have been dressed in a ball gown the way she sashayed down the corridor. Since she'd learned she was pregnant, she had walked with a lighter step and spoken with a laugh constantly burbling beneath her words. She wasn't showing and hadn't had morning sickness yet: for the moment she was a glowing Earth Mother, still lithe and nimble. Mouse walked across the lobby to meet her and she threw her arms around his neck and kissed him.

"Hey handsome! How'd it go with Gateway?"

"Whatchyou tell my sister?"

"Lots of things," Shauna said.

"You told her you was pregnant?"

"That was one of the things."

"Why you tell her that?"

"I didn't know it was a secret."

Mouse broke their embrace. "But my sister? Maybe I wanna tell her myself. Maybe I wanna tell my own mother myself, before we start shoutin to the whole world. Jackie told my moms, and then she sprang it on me. Why you go and tell her behind my back?"

"It wasn't behind your back. I didn't even mean to tell her, actually. It came up while we were talking about something else."

The prospect of his girlfriend and his sister gossiping together annoyed Mouse, because it seemed one more way for Jackie's disapproval to find him, through a back door. "Why you talkin to my sister, anyway?"

"I can't talk to your sister? She's gonna be our baby's aunt, and I'm not allowed to call her on the phone?"

"I thought we was in this together. I thought we was makin decisions how to have a family *together*."

"We are, but like I said, I didn't mean to tell her, it just came up. What difference does it make? There was something I needed to talk to her about, and in the course of convincing her to help me, I had to spill the beans."

Mouse put his hands on his hips. "Whatchyou need my sister's help for?" He became conscious of people looking at them. "Whatever. We late." He turned abruptly and strode toward the exit.

"Hey," Shauna said. She caught up with him and grabbed his arm. "Hey! Look at me. What's goin' on?"

"You know how I feel 'bout my sister."

"You love her, right?"

"That aint what I mean. I don't want her all up in my life. She aint never been someone to trust."

"I understand, but you need to trust me. I didn't do anything wrong. You need to not get mad at me for something till you ask me about it. You're just wrong about this."

"You don't know how Jackie is."

"Maybe you don't either."

Shauna fastened the buttons of her coat, and they walked to her car. She held Mouse's hand and swung his arm back and forth the way a child would, tugging at him and smiling coyly. With her red hair flouncing and flowing against her black coat, her smile crinkling the corners of her eyes, her cheeks tight with cold and the rolling snow-draped meadows of Forest Park over her shoulder, framing her in winter white, she looked like a fairy-tale princess. Mouse wanted to believe in her.

Shauna took the driver's seat and started the car. They jostled over the knobbly cobblestones through Central West End's patrician estates and gated drives. Each mansion was more massive and ostentatious than the last, and at every street corner, eight-armed brass streetlamps, like chandeliers hanging from steel posts, threw golden light on the opulence around them. This was old, old St. Louis money.

"The reason I was talking to Jackie," Shauna said, "was to invite her and Marvin to your retirement party tonight."

"What?! That aint how you put it, is it?"

"What?"

"Retirement party?"

"Sure."

"Shauna, that aint the kinda joke my sister tend to like. Besides, whyn't you tell me you invited them? I thought it was Zack and Chloe."

"I wanted to surprise you."

"I aint really in the mood for surprises like this, you know."

"Fine, but let me tell you what happened, so you can see how dumb you're being and get over it. I wanted Jackie and Marvin to come tonight—"

"But why?"

"Would you let me talk? When I invited them, Jackie started asking all these questions, and I felt like I couldn't answer any one of them without giving the big picture, the whys and wherefores of everything that's been happening, so I invited her over for coffee."

"Jackie came to your house for coffee?"

They turned left onto Lindell, the heart of the old money district. One side of the street held high-end shops, art galleries and gourmet restaurants; the other held ever more lavish mansions set back from the street, separated from each other by beveled brick walls and tall hedges. The whole neighborhood was gated off from the ones around it: the streets leading north and east from Central West End had been blockaded with concrete posts and iron rails stuck into the middle of the road, so that cars could not travel from the squalid, impoverished North St. Louis neighborhoods to the blueblood boutiques within the gates.

"Your sister and I had a heart-to-heart, and Mouse. . . it was like—" Shauna put her hand to her heart and sighed. "It was like she was my real sister. She stayed the whole afternoon! And we just talked and talked, and you'd think, on the face of it, that we'd have nothing in common, but we actually have quite a lot. She's very strong, your sister, very brainy and together."

"But what'd you say to her?"

"I told her the truth, that's all. Your sister's totally behind us. She's behind having the baby, and she thinks it's a great idea for you to move in with me, and she thinks you could make a living teaching drums. You could set your own hours, spend a lot of time with the baby."

"You messin with me."

"She thinks the two of you are in the same boat."

"Me and my sister in the same boat?"

"You're both musicians. Neither one of you could make a good living just playing your instruments, but you both have these great people in your lives—" Shauna pointed at herself. "—these great people who love you, and now you're both gonna be music teachers, and she thinks you're gonna make a great dad, too." Mouse couldn't believe his ears. "Did you know she's wanted children for years, but Marvin doesn't, and it's causing huge problems for them?"

"Yeah, I know."

"So we talked it all out, and that's why she's okay with your retirement from Busch, and she's going to be there tonight. I don't know if Marvin will or not. She said it's probably too late for him to come out. But I think she and I are going to be great friends. I mean, a sister-in-law should be a great friend."

"Sister-in-law?"

"Why not?" Shauna said. "We are having a baby together."

"I guess," Mouse said, still unable to comprehend this news about Jackie, who had never said an approving word about Mouse to his face. "Where we goin' anyway?"

"Brandt's."

"The jazz club?"

"That's the one. You know it's my all-time favorite place, right? They serve this chicken breast wrapped in prosciutto."

They left the mansions of Central West behind and took Kingshighway to Delmar, which was a wide, pockmarked, down-and-out street, anchored by liquor stores, check cashing centers and secondhand shops. Most of the streetside commercial buildings were boarded up, and there was a feeling of desolation even in the businesses that were still open. As they approached University City, a few straggling restaurants and curiosity shops appeared, desperately clinging to the fringes of the University Loop for survival; and as they entered the Loop, the bright lights and busy sidewalks announced Washington University's prosperity and hipness. The university district had no idea that poverty was just a block away to the east.

"Brandt's caint be your favorite place," Mouse said.

"Why not?"

"It's the most bourgeois club since the invention of jazz. It's all like bland, smooth-jazz wallpaper. I caint have a bourgeois girlfriend—that's the last straw."

"Bourgeois fiancee, you mean."

"Fiancee?" Mouse said. "Who said that?"

"I just proposed to you."

"What?"

"Yeah, just now. And you said yes."

"I did?"

"I said, why shouldn't Jackie be my sister-in-law. And you said, 'I guess.' That doesn't mean 'yes' where you're from? I guess?"

They stopped at the pedestrian crossing signal in front of the Tivoli Theater. Shauna turned to face Mouse. She wore a mischievous look that was infectious, and Mouse felt a goofy grin surfacing on his lips, like a diver floating up slowly to avoid the bends. Shauna bounced in her seat and grabbed Mouse's arm.

"I guess?" she said.

Mouse couldn't have stopped himself if he'd wanted to. "I guess," he said.

Shauna giggled like a little girl. She locked the hand brake, grabbed Mouse around the neck and kissed him. "I guess," she said. She kissed him again, and they kept kissing until the light turned green and the cars behind them honked. By the time

Shauna disengaged herself and settled back into the driver's seat, the light had turned red again and the honking blared around them. She pulled Mouse toward her and they kissed some more, until Shauna stamped her feet against the floor, clapped her hands and shouted, "I guess I guess I guess I guess I guess!"

Mouse was flummoxed. "You all right?"

The car behind them honked again, and she rolled down her window and yelled, "My man just said 'I guess!'" The car kept honking, and Shauna honked, too, and the two cars honked each other all the way up the Loop.

They parked at a pay lot and promenaded down the St. Louis Walk of Fame, stepping on the burnished bronze stars imbedded in the sidewalk. The Walk was an imitation of the Hollywood Walk of Fame, only much shorter, since Missouri could muster only a quarter-mile of celebrities worth remembering. Mouse tripped over the Chuck Berry star, but Shauna caught him and helped him keep his balance.

Holiday lights were still up in the shopfronts, winking at the klatches of Wash U students hustling from theaters and record shops to late-night cafes. Shauna draped herself across Mouse as they wended through the crowds, leaning into him. Every few feet, under the plastic mistletoe hanging from streetlamps, she would stop, give him a lavish kiss on the mouth and whisper, "I guess."

"You crazy, woman, you know that?"

"I guess."

Keeping Time

Music vibrated through the windows of Brandt's: a small combo loping through syncopated riffles, a trumpet noodling around the melody of a Miles Davis tune. Mouse opened the door and they stepped into a dark lounge, where red lava lamps at each table jellyfished up and down, and red leather loveseats lined the walls. The stage was a spacious platform in front of the plate glass windows; frosted spotlights shone down on the musicians from racks up above, and footlights beamed through gels, bathing the stage in warm ruby and russet colors.

The cafe was almost empty. A waiter leaned lazily against the bar, talking to the bartender, who inspecting a dirty glass. Chloe was sitting by herself at a table near the stage.

"I was starting to wonder about you two," Chloe said. She stood up and hugged them both. "I guess I should say you three." She rubbed Shauna's belly.

"Is Jackie here yet?" Shauna asked.

"She went into the kitchen—she's talking the chef into making paella. They stop serving food here at eleven, which was like three minutes ago, so we'll see what happens."

Mouse was surprised to see Zack on stage, sitting behind an electric keyboard, wearing pitch-black Raybans. "Zack never told me he was in a band."

"He isn't," said Chloe. "It's a pickup group. Every Wednesday they have an open stage here, and people just sit in."

Though there was nothing remarkable about this information on the surface, Mouse could not quite make sense of it. In addition to Zack, he saw Ricky Hart stationed behind a drum kit: he had never heard of a professional drummer with real chops lugging his own kit to an open mike night, and he'd never known a club to invest in a set of community drums, but there they were. In front of the drums, an overweight guy with short, tight dreadlocks was channeling a 1950s hepcat groove through his stand-up bass, and this, too, struck Mouse as odd. A stand-up bass was not a portable instrument that could be whipped out whenever the mood struck you. Horns were one thing, but to get an electric keyboard, drums and a stand-up bass to a club took a certain amount of trouble—and the combo sounded tight, not like a pickup group at all. It wasn't out of the question for such a solid rhythm section to appear spontaneously at an open stage—lots of jazz players liked to sit in, anytime, anywhere, and if there was a standing free night at a particular club, the players might know each other well and play well together. For that matter, great musicians could coax good sounds out of a tune even when they didn't know each other. Still, something didn't add up here: this group was too tight, somehow, and they almost seemed rehearsed.

Mouse might have believed that Shauna had called in the group to play in his honor, to celebrate his last day at Busch. But Ricky himself had told Mouse that he didn't play out any more. And Mouse didn't believe that Shauna had invited Zack to Brandt's this evening for drinks, and Brandt's just happened to have an open mike night tonight, and Zack just happened to bring along his keyboard. And he didn't believe that Ricky just happened to lug his drums down so he could sit in, completely unaware that Zack and Mouse were going to be there. Mouse wondered if Shauna had conspired with everyone to set something up. But then, why not just say that she had gotten a band together for his retirement party? Something strange was going on.

They sat down at Chloe's table and ordered drinks. Mouse watched Ricky swinging the groove in an unvarying two-bar pattern, riding the hi-hat just above the beat and playing lots of rim clicks. He glanced through the shadows of the club, at the few people slumping into loveseats along the walls. Brandt's was dead, typical for an open mike night in the middle of the week. Mouse wondered if Jackie would wheel a giant cake out of the kitchen in his honor.

Mouse's beer came, a frosty Oatmeal Stout from the Schlafly Brewery. He toasted his unemployment silently to himself and drank. Now this here's a damn beer I could get behind, he thought.

Jackie walked up from the back of the lounge and took a bow. "You will be pleased to know," she said, "that the chef is making food for the whole table—his personal specialties—owing to his great respect for the august occasion which brings us all here tonight." She motioned toward the bar. The waiter rushed over with a loaded tray: a bottle of champagne in an ice bucket, with champagne flutes.

Chloe signaled to Zack on stage, and Zack held up his hand and curled his fingers into a fist, to kill the tune. The song train-wrecked to a halt with some ragged tooting and cymbal crashes, and the bass player played "Pop Goes the Weasel."

The waiter poured the champagne, and then at another signal from Zack, the band launched into "Auld Lang Syne." Jackie raised her glass in a toast over the music.

"This gathering is in honor of my brother Joseph Watkins," she said, "who has been one of the key players in the success of Anheuser-Busch in the last twenty-five years and two months. In the first twenty-five years of that time, he caused thousands of dancers to become thirsty and consume Anheuser-Busch products. In the last two months, he helped replenish some of the supply, completing a cycle known in beer parlance as the circle of life. His retirement is richly deserved." At another signal, the band segued into "For He's a Jolly Good Fellow," and Shauna, Chloe and Jackie serenaded Mouse.

When they had finished the song, Zack and Ricky came off the stage to the table, and the remaining combo staggered into an oddball rendition of "To Know Him Is To Love Him." Mouse couldn't take it all in, especially Jackie's toast. He was amazed at how playful she seemed tonight, how happy and relaxed. He'd seen her act the role of Congenial Socialite many times in many different settings, but rarely had he witnessed such a natural performance at such an unlikely and disreputable occasion as the celebration of unemployment. Particularly his own unemployment.

"Now that that's out of the way," Jackie continued merrily. "We have something even better to celebrate. Something worth celebrating! No offense, Mouse. So let's forget all that nonsense so Shauna can tell us about the baby!"

Of course. Jackie was practically floating on her enthusiasm for Mouse's baby, as if she'd just learned that she herself was pregnant. She wasn't here for his "retirement" at all, but at least she was in a good mood.

"So we have to think of a good name for the baby," Jackie went on, "and when's the baby due? And when would you like your baby shower to be?" She couldn't stop saying the word baby. It occurred to Mouse that what he and his sister had needed all along was not more understanding, but more family members. He was sure that if Jackie had become pregnant, he would have remained on the outside of her graces looking in, but as it was, Jackie had no choice but to project her own maternal feelings onto Shauna, and therefore onto him. "And did I mention I'm available to babysit?"

Chloe jumped out of her seat and elbowed in front of Jackie. "For your information, I'm the best babysitter in St. Louis," she said.

"No fighting," said Shauna. "As of right now, I'm declaring you two Official Aunties, and don't be surprised if I take you up on those offers. I'll remember."

"But I'm an auntie anyway!" Jackie exclaimed.

"Then meet your new sister Chloe."

Jackie cozied up to Shauna, touching her arm and leaning into her when she laughed, and Mouse was astounded that they had developed such rapport so quickly. Jackie's exuberance made Mouse believe that his sister felt a genuine affection for Shauna, in addition to her vicarious enjoyment of Shauna's pregnancy.

He remembered that the same instantaneous rapport had developed between Chloe and Shauna. It had taken barely a week after they'd met at Thanksgiving to become bosom buddies. Chloe loved Shauna. Now Jackie loved Shauna, too. Everyone loved Shauna! She never appeared the least bit abrasive, abrupt or difficult in their company. In fact, Shauna seemed engaging and sweet any time she and Mouse were out with anyone else—it was only when they were alone that she turned unpredictable and contrary. Could it be that I'm the one who's abrasive, abrupt and difficult, and Shauna has only been reacting to me? he thought. Am I the one who's always contrary?

The chef sent out a feast of appetizers on a silver platter, steamed mussels, peeled shrimp, cajun crab cakes, smoked duck quesadillas, and a wooden board with fruits, cheeses, bread and preserves. The spread was so extravagant that Jackie's charm alone clearly had not persuaded the kitchen to stay open, and Mouse wondered if the story about talking the chef into serving late had also been a ruse. Something about this party still didn't quite add up.

The band finished riffing on "To Know Him Is To Love Him" and the bass player wandered over to their table. "Hey Mouse," Ricky said. "I wanna introduce Leroy here." The bass player shook Mouse's hand. "Leroy new in town. He been playin on a cruise ship out of Miami the last few years and he wanna hook up with some people, maybe play out some."

"I caint help much there. I aint in the jazz scene. But you got a real nice feel."

"Thanks," said Leroy. "Ricky says you're the funkiest drummer in St. Louis."

"They aint a whole lotta funky drummers around here no more."

"Aint no call for modesty, man," Ricky said. "This here's *your* party."

Another bottle of champagne arrived as if by magic, and Mouse poured Leroy a glass. Shauna, Chloe and Jackie were discovering endless variations on the theme of babies, and Leroy settled in and raised his glass in a silent toast to Mouse. They polished off the appetizers, and the waiter brought out half a dozen entrees, and everyone sampled a little from each dish. Mouse ate most of Shauna's favorite, the chicken breast wrapped in prosciutto, and he had a vision of himself as a bourgeois husband eating bourgeois chicken in a bourgeois suburb, and he suddenly felt old. He realized he would have to grow his afro back to its full, immense, bushy proportions, to make his declaration of purpose to the Rock Hill PTA. He imagined his baby in the maternity ward with an afro twice the size of its body.

A trumpet player and saxophonist on stage were dueting around "Somewhere Over the Rainbow," and Mouse listened to them trading riffs and trying out different harmonies. It was a long way from the Funk. Mouse had always found jazz too cerebral. He liked the old gut-bucket barrelhouse blues and big band swing, but cool jazz and be-bop seemed trapped in the head. Nobody could dance to bop, and no matter how complex the structure of the music, no matter how technical the writing or clever the improvising, it still meant nothing to Mouse if no one could dance to it.

"I think I'll sit in again," Zack said. "It's time for a weepy old chestnut."

Zack sauntered to the stage and slid behind his keyboard, as if he were sitting down in his favorite armchair at home. He led the players through "Moonlight in Vermont," and Mouse was surprised at how solid he was. Not every pianist who could play Ravel could also find his way around a jazz standard, trading improvisations with horn players. Mouse watched the way Chloe looked up from her conversation to cast a loving eye on Zack as he played.

As Mouse's party finished its third bottle of champagne, Leroy excused himself to rejoin the combo. Zack called for Ricky to go back up, to give them a beat.

"You wanna play awhile?" Ricky asked Mouse.

"Naw, that stuff's too fancy for my blood."

"Nothin fancy about it. All you gotta do is play something funky and they'll follow. You know how horn players are— they aint got many ideas of their own, and Zack can boogie down a little if you show him the way."

"I dunno," Mouse said. He didn't feel he had the energy to play with solid players right now, even at an open mike—or whatever this was.

"Well, somebody gotta give these cats a beat," said Ricky. "Cause they soundin terrible." He pushed his chair away from the table and paused to give Mouse a chance to stop him.

"You should play," Chloe told Mouse. "I'd love to hear you."

Jackie chimed in. "You've played this kind of music plenty of times before, Mouse. I've heard you."

"Not really."

"No trick to playin jazz, man, you know that," Ricky said. "Lay off the backbeat a little. Hit some accents. Hell, you can play *all* accents if you want. Once you get the groove goin', you can make these cats funky as you wanna be, and Leroy'll get dirty some too. Jus play time, yo."

Everyone awaited his decision a little too anxiously, Mouse thought. The craving, encouraging hope in Shauna's eyes made it plain that, jokes about his retirement and chatter about baby showers aside, this was why she had brought him here tonight, to manufacture an opportunity for him to play out, and she had apparently conspired with Ricky and Zack to do it, to assemble a halfway decent band. Mouse felt that if he got up there on stage—the first time in years he would be playing as anything but a Bad Apple—it would be entering a different musical world altogether. As bad as he felt about his playing just then, he didn't think that would be such a bad idea: Gateway had a new identity, so maybe it was time Mouse had one, too. Jazz cat? As usual, Shauna's timing was perfect. He pushed his chair back.

He remembered Chloe in her piano shop, playing the weird ditties about birds she had composed for her father; he recalled Ricky's students, gangly kids trying to pound out steady time in a drafty gym that smelled of old socks; and he thought of Jackie, playing music of unbelievable complexity that took a lifetime to learn for an audience of eight in her parlor. Jackie was staring at him impatiently. His torment over the Bad Apples must have seemed like a joke to her, since she had dedicated her whole life to a music that only the elite of elite players got to perform in public and practically no one listened to any more. If she hadn't lucked into money, Mouse felt sure she would still be living in a cheap student apartment near Wash U, scraping by giving lessons, dedicated to music in complete anonymity because she loved it more than anything. In that moment, he felt that he did not love music as much as Jackie did, or even as much as Ricky and Chloe and Zack did. He had sacrificed his life to a band, to an identity, but perhaps not to the music after all.

Fortune and fame had always been essential to his musical dreams. His world-beating success had always been the happy ending of his story, the "happily ever after" that made all the hardscrabble times playing two-bit dives make sense. But what if his dreams of glory had led him only to an open mike night at Brandt's? Would that be a failure?

He squeezed Shauna's hand, and she smiled at him and clapped silently. Shauna understood him better than he understood himself, he thought. She had said that she would love him if he never played drums again, but Mouse felt sure that he would never love himself in that case. He wanted to do something special for her, in return for all the things she was doing for him. He suddenly wanted to do *everything* special for her—it was a feeling he had never had in quite that way before, and making music all at once seemed a responsibility he owed not only to himself but to Shauna, and to his unborn child, as well. He could not articulate this notion fully in his mind, but something about it struck a chord in his soul. He owed it to his child to create something beautiful, not to be famous or successful in any traditional sense. What would a child care about a face on a billboard or a name in lights? A child wanted love and beauty, and fun. That's what music was supposed to be.

He looked around Brandt's, at the empty tables, at the lazy hipsters half-sprawled across the sofas at the back of the lounge, and he realized that those people weren't his audience. No one in any club would ever be his audience again. His audience would feel its father's music through the pulse of its mother's heart. He felt a new pulse in his own heart, in his own mind, and he clapped Ricky on the back and went up to the stage with this new pulse beating in his veins, a new beat that he wanted to find in the drums.

He picked up Ricky's sticks and sat behind the kit. Zack nodded encouragement from the keyboard. Leroy leaned over the ride cymbal and played a few fat slides on his bass to welcome him.

The last time Mouse had sat in at a jazz session was six or seven years before, in a church basement in Alton, a familiar place with familiar players playing familiar songs—not like this. His stomach fluttered, and he tried to remember the clever jazz players he had heard over the years. He thought of his grandmother's records, which had introduced him to the drums, the records he'd mimed when he was young and still hungry to discover his own limits: Chick Webb and Gene Krupa and especially Sonny Payne. He heard the jumbled jazz syntax he'd learned incompletely from drummers on the road, when he'd gone exploring the blues clubs from Tuscaloosa to Atlanta to Chicago, the rhythms he'd heard in the chugging, clanging, grinding, huffing freight trains passing near his mother's house in Brooklyn. He looked at the snare drum and felt the sticks in his hands, and it seemed as if he'd never played drums before.

The horn players gathered in a knot around him, and Zack introduced Mouse all around. "Call it," the trumpet player said. "New guy calls the tune."

Mouse tried to think of a standard that everyone might know, but his memories of those jazz records and blues clubs from once-upon-a-time were wistful. He could not specifically think of any songs anyone had ever played. He tried to recall a jazzy funk number, but even here he drew a blank, and with this ad hoc combo hovering around him, waiting for him, his mind was terribly, completely blank, frozen in stagefright like he'd never had before.

His thoughts raced instinctively back to Gateway for help. He thought of his trip through the Illinois countryside tonight, and his mind came to rest on a familiar symbol, the silver Arch shining high above the city, sleek and pure. Unlike the river it towered above, the Arch offered movement in more than one direction at once: it was a cosmic portal that opened onto different worlds, depending on which way you stepped through it. Just as the physical form of the arch achieved stability by balancing the tension between its two legs, the metaphysical form achieved stability by balancing the tensions between the old and the new, the soulful and the spiritual, what came before and what could only be imagined, what came next. Through the Arch, you could see the best hopes you could dream for yourself and the worst aspects of your life at once; and a single figure rose up suddenly before Mouse, and a song with it, at once a requiem and a blessing, a response to the call of the Arch.

"Y'all know Ray Charles' version of 'America the Beautiful?'"

"I know 'America the Beautiful,'" the trumpet player said.

"Well, Ray did it as a slow blues. And I mean slow. I'll count it off. You wanna take it first, Zack?"

"Sure. A-flat all right for everybody?"

Mouse counted off slowly, and Zack played the hymn alone to start, in a shimmering, mournful organ voice. Leroy came in underneath him, and Mouse played the backbeat cross-stick on the rim of his snare and added quarter notes on the hi-hat, giving them a little air with his left foot to push more tension into the song. The horns all played the melody together once through, and then each player took a turn, playing grim, soulful improvisations, accenting one another with runs or counter melodies. Mouse found that he was more familiar with this vibe than he had given himself credit for, like a student of Latin arriving in modern-day Rome and reading the signs fluently. He heard Ray Charles' voice singing the verses in his head, but in this combo's hands, the slow tempo made the song sound like a dirge, with none of the complexity of Charles' delivery. By the end of the third time through, they were playing a funeral for Brandt's open mike night, and Mouse decided to turn it around, the way a Dixieland band would shift from lament to laughter on the way back from the cemetery.

At the end of the saxophonist's final phrase, he snapped a quick roll on the snare and then triple-timed into a Purdie Shuffle, laying into the backbeat on the kick drum and playing sixteenths on the crash. Leroy took it immediately, walking into the rhythm, then the trumpet player slithered around the melody like mercury squiggling through water. Zack rocked forward in his chair and threw Mouse a big grin, and "America the Beautiful" turned into a jump blues.

Mouse looked out at his retirement party. Shauna was shimmying in her seat. Jackie and Chloe were swaying and clapping together, and Ricky was tapping time against the table. Mouse let his focus go soft and lost himself in the groove, gliding in front of the beat instead of sitting back in the pocket.

He couldn't remember the last time he'd enjoyed playing so much, where the give and take between players was free and relaxed and not something he had to manage. To play a standard tune with musicians who cared about the performance for its own sake, for no other reason than the song's own expression, was like taking a long, deep breath.

The future with Shauna would be as much an improvisation as the song Mouse was playing. With her, Mouse would have to stop telling life what he was going to make it and start asking what it wanted to be, a phrase Shauna often used. His life now seemed different from anything he'd ever imagined, smaller in its proportions but grander in its meaning. He had a home to live in with the mother of his child, a child who would marvel at the world they created. New people were around him, ready to become his friends—perhaps even his sister included—and he had time to figure out what to do about work. He wondered if the job at Schlafly would be as terrible as the job at Busch. He wondered if St. Louis Parks and Rec would hire him to teach drum clinics. He wondered if he knew how to change a diaper.

Leroy finished his solo and Zack came back in. Mouse heard a yell from one of the tables.

"Give the drummer some!" It was Ricky.

Zack put one hand to his ear and leaned forward. "What's that?"

"Give the drummer some!" Ricky yelled again.

Zack turned to the horn players. "Should we give the drummer some?"

"Yeah!"

"Should we give the drummer some?"

"Let's give the drummer some," Leroy said.

"Give the drummer some?"

"Yeah!"

"All right, Mouse," Zack said. "You got it!"

Everyone fell out and gave Mouse the solo. He stayed locked on the beat, unsure where to go. He saw Shauna, watching him intently, and he thought about the pulse of his unborn child. He wondered if the baby squirming inside Shauna even had a heart yet. It humbled him to think of the new life they were creating, a new heart out of old, bad blood. He felt his own heart pumping, and he gave himself up to the rhythm of his breathing, to the moment, to the music, to a wild solo over the foundation he'd laid down, and let the pulse of new life come pounding through his drums.